BEN CRAIB

Love Is The Answer

Dear Libby

Thanks so much for having
me - I had a blast -
and all the best with
future writing!

Ben Craib

tusk

TUSK
An imprint of QuoScript
71-75 Shelton Road, London WC2H 9JQ, United Kingdom

www.quoscript.co.uk

This paperback edition 2021

A CIP catalogue record for this book is available from the British Library

Typeset in Sabon LT std

ISBN: 978-1-8382672-1-6 (paperback edition)
ISBN: 978-1-8382930-1-7 (electronic edition)

For Mum

*These violent delights have violent ends, and in their triumph die, like fire and powder, which as they kiss, consume. Friar 2.6 **Romeo and Juliet***

Before

"I just think . . . it's never going to happen."

I scrape the drops of hot chocolate and bits of froth from the bottom of my cup. Mum's made an effort to dress cute with a denim jacket over the hospital gown.

"Why is it so easy for everyone else and not me? It's like, there's being single and being in a relationship, this long rope bridge between them, running across this giant ravine, and they're all like, walking across, singing and whistling, la-de-da-de-da and I'm like, there is no bridge, just a massive, ten-mile drop onto razor-sharp rocks and I'm standing here, with my binoculars, watching them make out and be couply and I've had enough!"

"It's only a matter of time," she says.

"I'm sick of it!"

Mum smiles and winces at the same time. She reaches into her handbag, removes her debit card and places it on the bill.

"Maybe this is a way of distracting yourself from what is going on with me," she says, holding out her hand. I take it and slide my fingers in between hers.

"I've always been like this. Like I'm never gonna

get close to anyone. That I'm always going to have a label on me, like Scarlett has the plague, don't touch!"

I laugh. She laughs.

"I'm *serious* though."

"You know what I do when I feel like there's no hope?"

"What?"

"I go to the chapel."

I scowl.

"It's not because I've turned religious. It's on the top floor. It's got the best view of the whole of London."

I spoon the remaining froth into my mouth. It tastes burnt.

"Seeing the lay of the land always makes me feel better."

"Thanks, Mum."

"Just have some fun."

The last time I "had fun" was at a party with a random called Gavin who kissed like a Labrador at dinner time.

"I've done that," I say. "I hate it."

The waitress arrives and makes a theatrical show of shoving the card machine in our faces so we can see she's entered the correct amount. The machine beeps, she rips off the receipt, hands it to my Mum and she's gone. We walk, arm in arm, through the corridor and back to her ward.

"I shouldn't be talking about myself," I say. "I'm being totally selfish." We wash our hands with antibacterial gunk while we wait to be buzzed in.

"I'm sorry."

"I will be here for you, to listen to you, to support

you, till my very last breath. Even if my legs and arms are chopped off."

"Like the knight in Monty Python and the Holy Grail. Who carries on fighting even though he's basically dead and can't move," I say.

We laugh. I walk her through the ward and help her into bed. I hate the screens, the wires, the drip-connector in her arm, the ridiculous amount of pills in a cup by her bed. I watch her put her headphones on and open the Classic FM app. She says the music keeps her sane in here.

"I love you so much," I say.

"I love you too. And Scarlett? When you know, you'll know. . . ."

"Thanks, Mum. See you tomorrow."

"Sure."

I squeeze back my tears and walk out of the ward.

One year later

1

The front door slams shut.

"Fuck!"

I slam my hand over my mouth, hope Dad didn't hear me, and my last memory of Mum disappears.

Soon he'll pop his head round the door and pretend he's greeting me when he's actually checking my revision status. At least I'll *look* good, cross-legged on my bed, *The Making of Modern Britain* revision book open in front of me. It's not like I haven't been *trying* to revise. He won't know my notes don't make sense – the ones that aren't illegible because of my rubbish handwriting, that is. I've sat here an hour and haven't read more than four lines.

A boy in tracksuit bottoms walks past on the opposite side of the road. Stubbly face, shaved mousey hair growing out. He's deep in thought with a cute little frown. I feel a sharp pull towards him, like he's shot me through the chest with a harpoon and is reeling me through the window. Our entire lives play out together in a millisecond.

But now he's gone and I'll never see him again.

"Helloooo," says Dad as the stairs creak. He arrives at my doorway in his work mac, straining to smile. I jump off the bed and hug him.

"What's this for?" he says.

We walk down to the kitchen. I've left it a tip. Dirty plates, cutlery, a used pan, colander, and chopping board are strewn across the counter. My half-finished hot chocolate sits in its own pool of milk.

"I'm sorry," I say.

"It's fine," he says, insincerely.

It doesn't matter that I spent Sunday afternoon mopping the bathroom floor and putting away the washing. I want to shout *I'm a slob. Mum wasn't and I am, I can't do anything about it!*

Instead I wash up and microwave him a chilli while he pecks away at his phone.

"This is just what I need after two days of drinking beer and talking tax," he says.

It's his standard spiel, making accountancy sound like rock and roll. It's meant to be ironic. Kind of.

I think about the boy who walked past my window. What was he worrying about? Did he realise some random girl was lusting after him? Deep down, could he *feel* I was there?

"Scarlett," says Dad. "I wasn't entirely straight with you."

I freeze. The mole on his head is cancer. He needs chemo. Husbands who lose wives can't go on.

"I haven't been straight with you for a while."

He speaks with a smile, as if he's amused, as if the sun is shining. How can you smile when you announce your own death?

"I played hooky for half the talks. Because I've been seeing someone," he says.

He looks at me as if he wants me to congratulate him.

"Your old dad's still got it!" he says.

The muscles in my back spasm.

"Scarlett?"

I force myself to concentrate on hanging the frying pan back on its hook.

"Have you finished your dinner?" I say.

He nods.

"Was it nice?"

"Yes."

I think he told me the only news that could make me feel worse than him being ill.

"I think we need to stop eating microwave meals," I say. "They're not healthy."

"You're right," he says.

I put his plate in the sink and squeeze on too much washing up liquid. I can feel his eyes bore into my back as I clean it.

"Congratulations," I say.

"Thank you," he says.

"I've got to go to Elliot's to revise."

"Scarlett . . ."

I'm already in the hall, pulling on my Converses.

"There's something else-"

"Can it wait?"

He carries on but I'm out the door. I slam it shut and hear the painting of a witch that I did when I was seven slip off its nail and crash to the floor.

2

I sit on the front garden wall and do my laces. It's still light but we're barely a week out of April and there's an annoying chill in the air and I'm only in my Incredible Hulk t-shirt and a pair of shorts. I pat my pockets. No keys or wallet. I should have thought this through. Goose bumps erupt down my arms and legs. But there's no way I'm going back inside. Five minutes to my left is the smoggy busyness of the Holloway Road, which I definitely don't want so I walk up the street towards Elliot's. I picture his spacious attic room and his housekeeper Maria appearing with toasted hot cross buns and ice cream.

I call him, walking as fast as I can.

"Yo," says Elliot.

"I'm coming round."

"Hoooold on a second."

He owns a mechanical keyboard for gaming and when he hits a key you hear a loud clack. Right now it sounds like a machine gun.

"See you in a minute, okay?"

"I said hold on a second!"

Clack-clack-clack-clack-clack-clack.

"Yeees!" says Elliot.

Clack-clack-clack-clack-clack-clack.

"Put the porn away," I say.

"This is stupendous."

"Your camp voice is stupendous."

Elliot is one of those boys who everyone thinks is gay because he has shoulder-length hair, likes flowery shirts and wears mascara. But he's straight as hell and I should know because he spends his life telling me how every female within five metres is making him horny and how hard that is for him to deal with.

"I just bought us priority tickets to Comic Con!" he says.

"Great!" I say. "Actually, what are you doing? Comic Con is in the middle of study leave! We've had this conversation!"

"Screw study leave," he says.

Elliot goes for people he can never have. Like Aya – the super-manicured Japanese girl in his art class who is so reserved I don't think she's ever said more than two words to anyone in college. Totally hot, totally untouchable.

"You know my dad has turned into the You-Must-Study-Nazi," I say.

"Even people in fascist states need days off," he says.

Me and Elliot love moaning about how single we are. That's what I want to do right now, moan about how single I am. I want to kick back on his battered leather sofa and moan until the entire universe has shrunk down to the two of us.

"Not in my fascist state. I'm in a "If-You-Don't-Make-Your-Leeds-Offer-You-Will-Be-Decapitated-And-Your-Head-Stuck-On-A-Spike-Outside-The-House scenario," I say.

I'm at the top of my street. Across the road is Paradise Park. It's just a crappy square of grass but you can get into his garden via a broken bit of the fence.

"C'mon, Scarlett . . ."

"You should have asked me," I say. "I could have checked. Worked on him."

"It's *Comic Con*. We get to laugh at the washed-up bitter actors who used to be hot in Power Rangers and perv over the people in costumes. Plus spend hundreds of pounds we don't have on merch."

"I know, I know, I know. I'm coming in the back way," I say.

"No, you're not," he says. "And you can't come to my house, either."

"Elliot . . ."

"It's my dad's birthday. We're about to go out."

"So?"

"So it means it's my dad's birthday and we're about to go out."

"Five minutes."

"No."

"Can't I just stay in your room?"

"Why would you want to do that?"

I used to spend long summer days in the playground here, hanging out with whichever local kids decided to show up. That turned into me and Elliot sneaking in after dark to drink vodka on the swings.

"My dad just told me he has a new girlfriend," I say.

"Oh."

"And it's really messing with my mind."

A gust of wind blows into the phone mic, hurting my ear.

"It hasn't even been a year!" My voice cracks.

"That must really suck."

"I just need to be somewhere else right now."

His mum calls his name from another part of the house.

"Plus, I'm wearing my pyjamas, I don't have my keys and I'm freezing," I say.

His mum shouts again.

"Not tonight, okay? Any other night, yes. We're going to some stupidly expensive restaurant and there's no way my parents would be cool with you being here. I can meet you before college tomorrow if you want to talk about it."

The café is closed. There's nowhere to shelter from this wind unless I lie in a bush, which isn't going to happen.

"I need you . . ." I say. But he's hung up already.

3

A few minutes later I'm outside *Food and Wine*. Cenk (pronounced *Jenk* – he told me I was his friend because I'm the only one who says his name right) sits behind the counter. He stands there with his aquiline nose and designer stubble, watching football on his phone. Doesn't matter if it's seven-thirty a.m. or eleven-thirty p.m., he's always here. I think he sleeps behind the desk. He's also sold me alcohol since I was sixteen. That's really useful when you're one of the last ones in your year to turn eighteen and everyone else you know is legal.

I walk up to the counter, fold my arms and lean towards him.

"Hey," I say.

"Can I help you, love?" he says in his half-Turkish half-cockney accent.

He must get away sometimes because he's ripped, with a broad chest and big thick arms and that doesn't come from shifting tins of tomato soup.

"What's the score?" I say.

"Two-nil, Besiktas."

I can't pretend I care.

"Will you loan me a bottle of Smirnoff and I pay you tomorrow?"

"We don't do accounts."

"You know I'll be back," I say. "I always come back." I tilt my head to the side like some ditsy bimbo.

"Tomorrow. I promise."

I touch his hand. I kind of wish I did fancy him.

He puffs his cheeks, blowing out.

"This is bad," he says.

"Eight-thirty on the dot."

"This is really bad," he says.

He reaches behind the counter and gives me a litre bottle. I was only after the half-one but I'm not going to complain.

I'm almost at Paradise Park when a maroon Range Rover – Elliot's car – turns into the road. With painful inevitability, Elliot's dad sees me and brakes. His lips move and I think he swears. Elliot sits behind him in the middle back seat, gawping. Then the car speeds off back past *Food And Wine* and right on to Tufnell Park Road.

I sit down on the bench opposite the playground and panic. What if Elliot's parents call my dad? What if this results in some horrific punishment? What if Cenk thinks I was pimping myself out, offering him sexual favours in return for free alcohol?

I message Elliot.

What just happened? Is everything okay?

I anticipate his reply. "Run for your life, the Stazi are coming," or "Ditch the vodka and get home before your dad appears with a machine gun."

The message says delivered. I stare at the screen waiting for the three dots to appear, but there's nothing.

I pick up the vodka and rip off the plastic seal,

screw open the cap and take a swig. My oesophagus burns. I'll drink just enough to catch the right buzz, pour the rest away and then go home to Dad, apologise for storming out, congratulate him again, make everything okay.

But someone's near me. Nike trainers. Tracksuit bottoms. The frown, the mousey hair, those huge eyes. He's older than I thought, about twenty. It's definitely him. The guy I saw through the window.

"I hope you don't mind me saying – that is a massive bottle of vodka," he says.

4

"Yes it is," I say.

"Tough day at work?"

This is really weird.

"Tough day revising."

I've given away how young I am. Too young for him, probably. I blush. Then I blush harder because I'm blushing.

"The less said the better," he says, nodding at the vodka.

"Yeah," I say.

His eyes sparkle. My whole body tingles.

"Fuck revision," he says. "Drinking alcohol will do more for your life than education ever will."

I laugh. Some words bubble up inside me, my body turns to slush.

"You want some?" I say.

"I thought you'd never ask."

I shove the bottle towards him. He takes it and sits down, splaying his legs like he's the King of the Park.

"You are way too young and way too hot to be drinking tramp-levels of vodka on your own."

He holds up his hands and shouts, "If there are any tramps in the park, then I apologise!"

I stand up, hugging myself, bobbing up and down

on the balls of my feet as he unscrews the cap and takes a swig – it's a big one, like he's drinking water – and when he's done he makes a loud noise which is half-disgust, half-satisfaction. I giggle. He holds the bottle up. He's drunk a third of it.

"I did not mean for that to happen."

"It's okay."

"I'm not a tramp. Sorry tramps!"

"It's okay!"

"The worst thing is," he says, "I hate vodka!" And now we're both in stitches, me holding my stomach and him bending double, so far over his face practically touches the grass.

As he sits back up and frowns his lovely frown, he notices my goose-pimpled arms. He takes off his coat and offers it.

"It's not gonna bite," he says, looking solemn and sad and seriously cute.

I put it on. An hour ago he walked past my window and now I'm wearing his coat.

"How can you forget you hate vodka?" I say.

"Ten years ago, I drank a whole bottle and carpet-bombed an entire Tube carriage with puke."

I wince.

"After that I couldn't even look at a bottle without feeling like I wanted to vomit."

"I guess time did a good job of healing the horror," I say.

"Time did a good job of healing the horror," he says, nodding. "Or maybe *you've* healed the horror by making me face my demons right here, right now."

My cheeks are as red as an electric cooking hob turned up on full.

"I saw you earlier," I say.

"You did?"

"I mean – I saw you out my window."

"Okay."

"I couldn't concentrate. I was revising."

"As long as you weren't spying for the feds."

His brown eyes look black in the hazy twilight.

"I bet it was Maths," he says.

"What?"

"That drove you to the booze."

"Yeah. I mean no. I hate Maths. I dropped Maths the moment I could. It was other stuff, actually."

"Like what?"

"I got some bad news," I say. "Someone let me down." I take another swig, closing my eyes as my wind-pipe burns. "Someone wasn't there when I needed them."

"Me too!"

"Seriously?"

"Someone let me down too!"

"High five!" My skin slaps onto his.

"So, what happened to you?" I say, sitting back down and swinging my knees up on to the bench. I don't think he heard me because he's staring at my t-shirt.

"The Incredible Hulk," he says.

"Yeah. I'm a major Hulk fan."

I hand him the vodka. He takes another swig, in spite of what he just told me.

"What's wrong with Spiderman?" he says.

"The Hulk is so much better than Spiderman."

"The Hulk is big and green and ugly. Spiderman shoots webs."

He makes a gun barrel with his index and middle finger.

"Pee-ow! Pee-ow! Pee-ow!"

"You know nothing about comics, do you? I bet you've never read a comic all the way through."

"No. I haven't."

I laugh.

He frowns. I can smell boy-aroma in his coat.

"I'm deficient in my comic-education. I'm comically challenged."

I laugh again. He looks me straight in the eye and the ground spins.

"I'm Scarlett," I say.

"Hayden." I hold out my hand. He shakes it.

"What are you doing?" he says.

"What?"

"Looking at me."

"I'm not doing anything."

"Yes, you are."

My whole body tingles and I think I might pass out.

"You're freaky," he says.

To the left of his ear I catch sight of a tall skinny man with a beige, bald head. I stand up, yanking Hayden with me. I pull his hood up and lead us into the undergrowth behind the bench.

"I have to go. Take my number."

I'm still holding his hand.

He takes his phone from his pocket, brings up the dialling screen and hands it to me. I type in my number, checking it manically for typos.

"My dad," I say moving my face close to his. "He's behind that hedge. He's the one who let me down." He leans his lips towards mine. I turn away, place the bottle on the ground, remove his coat and shove it into his hand.

"Keep it," I say, before jogging on to the path. A minute later, as I turn the corner past the tennis court, I bash my head into my dad's chest. He cries out.

"It's okay! It's me."

I grab his arm and lead him back to the exit.

"You shocked me," he says.

"I needed some air," I say.

I watch Hayden leave through the small gate on the opposite side, coat on, hood up, clutching the bottle, looking like any other London street guy.

"Where's the booze?" says Dad.

"What booze?" I say.

"You haven't drunk a whole bottle, have you?"

"I haven't drunk any!" I screech.

Now he pulls me forward like I'm a reluctant toddler and doesn't let go until we're home.

5

Dad turns making me coffee into a guilt trip. He stirs the cafetière with exaggerated seriousness. He waits for it to brew with his arms folded, eyes on the floor. He eyeballs me as he plunges it. "You need this," he says as he places the mug front of me.

"Got any milk?" I say.

He shakes his head.

"More shopping I forgot to do," I say, rolling my eyes.

"I just want you to pick up the basics when we run out. It's a life skill."

His fingers are curled up tightly. It's like we're at the funeral of someone I murdered.

"I'm sorry!" I shout and stand up abruptly, knocking my chair backwards on to the floor. Dad looks at it as if I'd shattered a priceless vase.

"I spoke to Elliot's father," he says in his small, I-never-get-worked-up voice. "He said you were 'roaming the streets'." He glances at his spirit cupboard and I know he wants a drink himself, but he can't exactly do it while bollocking me for doing the same thing.

"Sadie said it would take years to move on. For both of us," I say.

"You're quoting Sadie now?"

I hated Sadie. Her forehead would crease up as she listened, making a show of her "empathy" while the more I tried to tell her how I felt, the more inferior and uninvolved I actually felt. She suggested that keeping on going to college every day, writing my UCAS application and attending campus open days was the best way forward. Then, by the time I did go to university the worst would be over and it would be like a "reward," I'd be happy that I'd done it, I'd be proud. Having a purpose would get me through. I didn't need her to tell me that. I didn't want to sit alone at home all day in an empty, mum-less house; but she spoke to me like I was a five-year-old who had to learn how to cross the road. At the end of the six sessions, college was ready to make an "emergency exception" and offer me another six. I had to fill out a form giving them my feedback. I filled out positive answers just so I wouldn't have to go back.

"I'm sure Sadie would also say this isn't the time for immature strops."

He takes out a packet of jammy dodgers from the cupboard, removes one and takes a bite, spilling crumbs on to the worktop.

"Mum told me, 'Don't spend your life wedded to a ghost.'"

"Am I not allowed to find this difficult?"

"You can find it difficult *without* drama . . ."

"But . . ."

"The only difference between an A and a C is discipline . . ."

"Why are you so obsessed . . ."

"Because I'm your dad and there's no way you're going to mess up the next two months on my watch."

"That's all you see when you look at me. A report card. I've been revising all afternoon. I'm going to Leeds. It's happening."

Dad swipes the crumbs off the tabletop.

"And even if I *had* drunk something, it wouldn't affect anything."

Dad decides he doesn't like the crumbs on the floor so he grabs the dustpan and brush from the cupboard under the sink and sweeps them up.

"Nice try, but you're grounded for the entirety of your A Levels," he says, smiling as he stands up.

"Seriously?" I say.

"Seriously."

"I'm about to leave school. Grounding is for fourteen-year-olds. No one gets grounded at my age."

"In *two months* you leave school. And technically you're not eighteen, so Dad rules rule," he says smugly, emptying the crumbs into the bin. "It's not for very long. It'll be over in no time."

I'm not going to give him the satisfaction of doing anything that could be further interpreted as drunk or dramatic. I'm not going to moan about the injustice of a mid-July birthday meaning you're always considered immature. I carefully pick up my chair and place it back under the table. The truth is, he *wants* me out. Get me to university, get me out of his hair, so he can shack up with her, redecorate my room, and write me out of his will.

"As you wish," I say and head upstairs to my room.

6

It's the morning, I'm idly doodling, and I end up writing 'Hayden' in red felt tip on my wrist. Part of me feels embarrassed I did it and the other part just has to glance at his name and I see his face, feel the clamminess of his hand, hear his laugh and I tingle all over again.

Those red letters have kept me sane during my English test paper and cushioned me from all the college noise pollution – the relentless banter, tinny phone music, the screeching and laughing that normally drive me nuts.

My Coke thunks out of the common-room machine, snapping me out of my daydream as I press the ice-cold can to my cheek. My phone vibrates in my pocket and in my haste to get to it I drop it on the floor. It's not *him*, it's Dad, reminding me to go straight home from college. I ignore him and join Elliot and Bad Ben at the far table. It's not too busy – some Ethiopian girls doing their homework and a couple of Greek boys playing cards sharing an AirPod. I sit with my wrists held upwards so the red letters are visible. I want my friends to notice the writing and ask me about it.

However, they are both more interested in what Bad Ben is drawing in his sketch book: a cartoon girl with over-sized blue eyes, pouting lips and hands tugging at the lining of tiny denim shorts. She has two huge breasts and a little heart-shaped jewel in her belly button.

"He's doing porn now," says Elliot.

"This isn't porn," says Bad Ben.

"What is it then?"

"Do you see nipples? It is not porn."

"Why's she taking off her shorts, then?" I say.

"She's not taking them off, she's being playful."

I snort.

"The only reason you're gonna do an animation degree is so you can animate porn and spend the rest of your life wanking to your own drawings," says Elliot.

Bad Ben grips his pencil as if he's about to plunge it into Elliot's neck.

"My art exam is gonna be, like, two days of still life. This is my way of unwinding during a stressful period."

When me and Elliot saw Bad Ben, with his leather trench coat and greasy ponytail, in the common-room in the first week of Year 12, we felt an instant attraction. When it turned out that he'd been drawing and selling his own comics since he was thirteen, he had to be part of our gang. But there are two Bens in our year. One is skinny and blonde and boring – so we called him Good Ben. Bad Ben has long greasy black hair, tubby pasty face and dark rings under his eyes: there was no other name for him.

"But does she *have* to have the biggest breasts known to man?" I say.

"It's just a sketch!" says Bad Ben.

"You can set up a Patreon," says Elliot. "Five pounds a month for three new dirty drawings."

"Elliot, the expert in how to make money from masturbation," says Bad Ben.

What am I thinking? When they're in this mood there's no way I can talk to them about last night. They'll just take the piss and say I'm stupid and naive, which I am. I turn my wrists over.

As if on cue Aya walks in. Elliot visibly tenses as she scans the room like a deer checking for wolves before sitting down as far away from any human being as she can. She looks like she's in a photoshoot for the Japanese Addams family, wearing a black armless dress, black boots and black knee-length socks. I'm conscious of the bags under my eyes, my GAP hoodie with frayed cuffs and my half-mousey-roots, half-peroxide hair. Compared to her I feel like an old kitchen: no matter how much you scrub and clean, the dirt will always be ingrained.

"What is up with you?" says Elliot.

"Nothing,"

I stand up, bashing my knee on the table. I force myself not to limp as I walk out of the room.

7

I do what I normally do when I feel lost: follow Mum's advice and seek out a view. Luckily, my college is next to Parliament Hill – the tallest hill in London. You can see it all: Canary Wharf, St Paul's Cathedral, the Shard, the City of London and all the office blocks, council estates, building sites, cranes and church spires in between. That's where I am right now, on my favourite bench, watching the little orange Overground train run along the bottom of the hill towards Hackney.

Before she died it was like everything was where it should be. Then a giant hand came down from the clouds, picked up my life and shook it like a snow-shaker and now I feel like I'm walking on the ceiling when everyone else is walking on the ground. I think that's why I work so hard to cook and clean for Dad, and why he expects it of me. We want everything to feel like it's back the right way up.

A deep voice says, "Don't move or you die."

I shriek and leap off the bench, but it's just Elliot, holding a white paper bag.

"I thought you could do with something sweet," he says. I didn't have any breakfast today and I snatch the bag from him. Inside are two crumbling chocolate muffins.

"One each, okay?" he says.

I take one and shove the bag back. He sits down next to me and we eat in silence.

"So are you going to tell me how much you're pissed with me for getting you in trouble?" he says, wiping his mouth. "When it was actually my dad's fault and nothing to do with me?"

"You could have replied."

"It was my dad's birthday, phones were banned."

"What about when you got home?"

"I was tired."

"Oh my God!"

Elliot licks his fingers and rubs a chocolate stain off his thigh. He's infuriatingly stubborn sometimes.

"So, tell me about this girlfriend," he says.

"They've just been on a dirty weekend."

"What?"

Some boys from the private school on the other side of the Heath jog past, their teacher barking at them to go faster.

"I kind of stormed out. And then I didn't have any money so I . . . flirted with Cenk to get vodka on tick and sat in Paradise Park and drank it," I say.

"You what?"

"See what happens when you ignore me?"

I've eaten the muffin too quickly. I've got heartburn.

"And I'm totally grounded, by the way."

"Well my dad said he wouldn't be a responsible adult if he saw you marching down the street two weeks before study-leave, half-naked, clutching vodka and looking like a wild woman, and didn't say anything."

"Half-naked?"

"My theory is that you looked like one of his daddy-girl fantasies and he couldn't handle it."

I laugh. Elliot's dad is a perma-tanned venture capitalist who travels the world on first-class flights and who forgets to browse porn in Incognito Mode.

"Can we just leave that thought there and never ever return to it, please?" I pick a crumb from my lap and place it in my mouth. "Anyway, I wasn't naked, I was in my pyjamas . . ."

"Who's Hayden?"

He's looking at my wrist. I bury my hands between my legs.

"Just some guy," I say.

Elliot does this annoying confused expression where he curls up the right side of his mouth and lifts up his left eyebrow at the same time.

"Hayden is a guy in Paradise Park who asked for some vodka. We almost got off with each other. Then my dad came and I left."

"Is Hayden homeless?"

"No! I thought something "happened" between us. And before you take the piss out of me just know that, on reflection, he was probably just after vodka or sex, and yes, I wrote his name on my wrist this morning but I'm going to wash it off, okay, I don't know what came over me and it's over, and it's never to be spoken about ever again."

"You thought something "happened" between you?"

"End of story!" I snap.

I look around to see if anyone heard me. There's a new mum with a pram on the next bench, but she's wearing a massive pair of noise-cancelling head-phones. My cheeks redden anyway.

"Okay, so I was a bit wild. When Dad told me, it was like my mum died all over again, okay?"

I met Elliot browsing comics in Forbidden Planet when we were both fifteen. Turned out he was at an all-boys school in Hampstead and I was at an all-girls school in Hampstead, we both lived five minutes from each other and were both obsessed with Marvel – not just the movies, but collecting the old-school printed comics, on which we both spend a lot of money. He was a boy who didn't get on with other boys and I was a girl who didn't get on with other girls. He likes girls and I like boys. It's like we were glorious weirdos and we'd just met our glorious weird separated-at-birth sibling. We both took the decision to leave our single-sex schools and come to this wear-what-you-like-be-who-you-like college because we didn't want to be terminally single. Maybe the problem wasn't our schools. Maybe it was us.

"I hate meals with my parents. They do something to me. It's like we go to these ridiculous restaurants with these poncy waiters who treat us like royalty and we eat this food that's Michelin starred, and we sit there with nothing to say and I feel like I'm dying, literally dying, for the whole meal. So, sorry I wasn't feeling up to emotional support at the end of last night," he says.

We watch the schoolboys run round the athletics track at the bottom of the hill, and some of the weight we are carrying falls away. I can't put it into words or give you a reason why, but things start to make sense again. This is what Mum was talking about.

"And the solution to all this isn't running off with dodgy men in parks and writing their name on your body in felt tip pen."

"You agree with your dad, don't you?" I say, placing my head on his shoulder.

"Oh, shit," he says. "You need to get un-grounded so we can go to Comic-Con."

"Uh-huh."

"Sal Buscema is going to be there. He's eighty-five. This might be the last time we can see him live." Sal Buscema is a Marvel comic artist. I have a signed print in my room that he drew in nineteen-eighty, of a giant, snarling, thick-bodied Hulk running-head-on.

"Serious? He can sign my poster!"

"He's already signed your poster."

"It's got to be worth more with two signatures, right?"

Me and Elliot always preferred the old-school sixties and seventies Hulk, when Sal Buscema was the artist.

"Three weeks' time, Scarlett."

"Study leave. I'll still be grounded."

"It's just a day."

I let his enthusiasm seep into me. He's right, I do need to have more fun. Maybe it's a good thing Dad came, before things got out of hand.

"Elliot?" I say. "If we're still single when we're thirty, will you marry me?"

Elliot frowns.

"Um . . . okay," he says.

I sit up. "Pinky promise?"

"Sure," he says with more conviction. We join our pinkies. Then I kiss him on the cheek and rest my head back on his shoulder. His breathing becomes deeper. Then his arm lurches up and he looks at his watch.

"History test paper. Ten minutes." And now he's up and ambling down the hill and I have to run to catch up with him.

12 days later

8

One of the things that always – without exception – makes me happy is hot chocolate. Now the kitchen floor is mopped and the mugs are lined up on the shelf with their handles all pointing towards the door. I've emptied the food waste bin, sorted the recycling and put the boxes out for the collection tomorrow. The milk is warming up in the pan.

As I reach into the cupboard for the tin of Cadbury's, a rush of hissing steam makes me jump. I leap across the kitchen and switch off the hob as my pan boils over and milk floods the cooker. I pick up a tea towel, mop up the mess and stuff the tea towel into the washing machine. I pour the remaining milk into my cup and miss, flooding the worktop. Milk drips down the cabinet and on to the floor. I snatch back the tea-towel and wipe the counter edge, but because it's already wet it won't absorb the liquid. I run upstairs, grab a hand-towel, soak up the milk with that, scrub the floor, shove both towels into the washing machine and slam the door shut.

Why, when I've made the kitchen look so beautiful, do I have to come this close to immediately trashing it?

I dump four heaped teaspoons of chocolate powder into what little warm milk is left and stir. It's much,

much too sweet – just how I like it. I think about curling up in bed.

The front door slams. Dad pushes past me into the kitchen and dumps his laptop bag on the table. He unzips it, rips out his laptop, wakes it from sleep and starts work on a spreadsheet. He hasn't even bothered to take off his coat.

"Is there any food?" he says, without looking up. I roll my eyes and open the freezer. I pull out a stir-fry, remove the packaging and pierce the plastic film. It's an unappealing jumble of broccoli florets, split peas and chicken pieces, all covered with some kind of radioactive powder.

I open the microwave, choose the five-minute cycle and switch it on. I pick up the outer packaging to read the words DO NOT MICROWAVE.

"GRGARGH!" I shout.

"Can you give me a moment please?" says Dad, polite-but-furious. I see him like Bad Ben would draw him: angry-vibrations firing from his forehead, shattering my body into pieces. If I was a superhero, I'd put up a psychic force-field to stop him. But I'm not, so I just feel awful. I open the microwave. The food is still frozen. It hasn't exploded.

"It's all good," I say.

Dad double clicks a spread sheet cell and adjusts the formula.

I don't know what I can do to make things okay. Since my vodka-guzzling-storming-out-episode I've had almost two weeks of busting my ass to keep this place nice. I cleaned the bathroom. I picked up his dry cleaning without him asking. I even spent two hours scrubbing ancient blackened bits of fat and food from the inside of the oven. Even Mum never did that.

But he's too busy with Microsoft Excel and his spreadsheet the size of a double-decker bus. Line upon line of tables, numbers, graphs, all interconnected and colour coordinated. He's like the Michelangelo of Microsoft and his Excel file is the Sistine Chapel. A skinny, balding, hairy-handed man whose real super-power is number crunching. He works for a national supermarket chain but acts like we should put his work in a museum.

I get out the wok and stir-fry his dinner. I place it in front of him and he pushes it away and leans closer to his screen. I dream of smashing the wok over his head, but don't do it. Instead, I put the wok into the sink and go upstairs. It's ten-thirty by the time I'm in bed.

I didn't tell Dad, but the day-after-the-vodka I got a D. I've told myself it's a one-off. That's what the comments at the bottom of the paper said. *Not up to your usual standard. I'm sure this is just a blip.* I've re-read *The Making of Modern Britain.* I even did a practice exam by myself in the library after school, choosing at random an old question on Tony Blair and foreign policy. I've done everything I can not to mess up. Nevertheless I lie there obsessing about missing my ABB offer, Elliot swanning off to Leeds without me and Dad punishing me by kicking me out on to the streets.

I must have fallen asleep, because I'm woken by my phone vibrating. It's 12.30 a.m. and the light from the screen hurts my eyes. I don't recognise the number. I press the red cancel button and pull the duvet over me.

I'm just drifting off when it buzzes again, bob-bling along the bedside table with each vibration. I catch it before it falls and press the red cancel button again.

If it's important, they'll leave a voicemail.

No voicemail notification.

Maybe it's a serial killer? What if it's someone out-side my bedroom wanting to listen to my breathing before they burst in through the door and stab me through the heart with a knife?

The phone vibrates in my hand.

I answer.

"Hello?"

"Scarlett!" says the voice.

"Yes?"

"I've woken you up."

"Um . . . yeah."

Footsteps on the pavement.

"It's you," I say.

"Last time I looked I was me, yes," he says. "Hold on, which 'you' are you thinking about?"

"Hayden."

"Thank God for that. You could have got me con-fused with your other boyfriend."

"I don't have another boyfriend."

"That's good to know."

I giggle. My tiredness disappears.

"If *I'd* just got woken up, I'd tell me, in no uncer-tain terms, to hang up the phone and die a long, slow, painful death."

I laugh.

"Well . . ."

"I won't mind."

"No."

"That's what I'd do."

"I don't want to."

Why am I so happy?

"What are you up to?" he says.

"Sleeping."

"Oh, yeah. Hold on a second! You would not be speaking to me if you were sleeping."

"You woke me up," I say.

"We've already established that."

A car engine roars and fades.

"So, how you doing?" he says.

"Shit."

"Serious?"

"Yeah, shit."

"That's not good!"

"I know."

"I meant to call you earlier. Like days and days ago. It's just . . . things got mental. But yeah, I'm calling you now."

A bus door hisses open.

"Do you want to come to a party?" he says.

"What?"

"Do you want to come to a party?"

"What, like *now?*"

"Yeah."

"I've got exams."

"Oh yeah."

"Do you wanna just chat?"

"Paradise Park."

"You what?"

"The sign says Paradise Park."

"What are you doing in Paradise Park?"

I get out of bed, walk to my window, open it, and strain my neck to look up the hill.

"Want to come to a party?"

I think he's drunk.

"If you don't want to come then you don't have to."

"It's Wednesday!"

"Technically, Thursday."

"You need to pick your moments better."

"Okay. You're right. See you later," he says.

"Wait!"

"What?"

"Cross the road."

"Where are you?"

"Walk down Hamilton road."

"Hamilton Road?"

"Cross to the other side and go down the first street you see."

"Cross to the other side and go down the first street?"

"I'm looking out my bedroom window."

"This is like the Crystal Maze," he says.

"Left side of the road."

His footsteps quicken, and his breath becomes shallow. "Is this a police sting?"

"Why do you keep thinking I'm the police?"

"Scarlett!" he shouts. "Scarlett!"

I see him. Marching down the middle of the road, phone pressed to his ear.

"Stop! Hayden!"

He stands opposite my house, bending over his knees to catch his breath. He wears a black jacket with his hood up. His stubble has grown into a small spiky beard and his hair is newly cropped. He looks up and smiles.

"Do you want to come to a party?"

I shove my finger across my lips and waggle my phone.

"Oh, yeah. Daddy." He takes off his rucksack, opens it, and produces a litre bottle of vodka.

"Payback time!"

A car turns into the road and accelerates down the hill. Hayden scrambles to pick up his bag, runs out of the way, trips and slams into a parked van next my house. I laugh and cringe.

"Where is this stupid party?"

"My house."

"Where's your house?"

"Down the road. I'll get us an Uber."

"Study leave started today."

"I'll get you an Uber home. You can leave when you want."

"No way . . ."

"Do you have an exam tomorrow?"

I shake my head.

"When's the first one?"

"Next week."

"Hold on: study leave means you don't even have to be at school at 9 a.m. You can sleep in! Sorted!"

He taps and swipes at his phone before returning it to his ear.

My stomach twists in a knot.

"Muhammed is three minutes away in a green Volvo," he says.

In this moment I know that if he gets in that car without me I will never see him again.

"You bastard!" I say. "Give me ten minutes."

9

What am I doing? I'm giddy with the insanity of it. My hands shake as I cast around for a hairband and sort through the pile of clothes on my floor for something clean and not completely boring.

I change into a baggy black t-shirt with a roaring tiger on the front, my favourite green hoodie and a short black puffa skirt that'll go with my Converses. I can barely apply my mascara because my fingers keep shooting off in erratic directions, and it's only by holding my right arm still with my left that I manage to get the cat-eye correct. I smudge a bit too much glitter on my temples.

No, actually, you know what? I *am* hot.

Why don't I realise this more often?

He kicks around, scraping his boot on the pavement, swinging his arms. He whistles something jaunty which echoes down the street.

My bedroom door groans, but there's no Dad-breathing, no coughing, no feet on the floorboards. I place my soles on the very edge of each stair to avoid the creaks. I slip on my trainers and open the front door, cringing at its piercing click.

There's the Volvo, Hayden leaning into the driver's window and talking in a low voice. He turns, revealing Mohammed, who has a long, greying beard. They both eye me approvingly: I've made the right decision. Hayden opens the back door, gets in next to me and slams it with a bang. I look up at the top window, anticipating my dad's light switching on or his shadowy face pressed against the glass. But there's nothing.

"So, where are we going?" I say, trying to sound calm but coming across as a bit hysterical.

"Elephant and Castle."

"You didn't tell me we were going to Elephant and Castle!" I blurt.

Hayden blinks, like someone's just chucked a bucket of cold water over him. I grip the door handle, poised to open it.

"Elephant and Castle is *South London*," I say.

"Any time you want, I'll get you an Uber back," he says, quietly.

"South London isn't Africa," says Muhammed. "There are no tigers in South London. Plenty of people have made it to South London and lived to tell the tale." Then he laughs. Hayden laughs. I laugh. Why am I laughing?

"Sorry." I say. "Let's do this."

Heart Radio is on low. It doesn't matter what country they're from or what religion they follow, taxi drivers listen to the same radio stations. Right now it's Sandcastles, by Beyoncé. The song is about a relationship breaking up, but it reminds me of Mum. When she was diagnosed she said, "I have no intention dying. I'm going to see you grow up." I believed her. Three months later she was dead.

We turn on to the Holloway Road, past the old Odeon cinema, past a queue at a late-night pub. An old man in a turban smokes a shisha outside a cafe. One young guy stuffs a kebab into his mouth while his friend laughs. Then we swing to the right and we're driving down the Caledonian Road. My hands are by my side and Hayden's are by his and I feel the temptation to reach out and link our fingers together. As if sensing this, he meets my eyes.

It's like someone's plugged me into the mains and thousands of volts surge through my body.

"I used to live up this way," he says.

"No way! Where?"

He nods out the window, just as we stop at the crossing by the tall beige walls and giant blue door of Pentonville prison.

"In there."

The driver laughs uncomfortably and shakes his head. Then Hayden laughs, dirtily. Then me.

"Only joking. The road behind. Jeez!"

Then the driver laughs again, more relaxed, and I laugh, too. Hayden shakes his head.

"You guys. Ye of little faith."

And then we're past the Overground station, under the blue railway bridge with THE CALLY emblazoned in large white letters, across the canal and cutting through the side-streets into Bloomsbury: Central London proper.

Hayden bites his upper lip. He needs a shave. He looks pensively at his knees. I want to tickle him under his chin and say, "Why are you sad?"

He turns to me and says, "Tonight is going to be immense."

10

We can hear the manic chatter and *thud, thud, thud* of the music from half-way down the street. Hayden's house is at the end, one of the few that haven't been converted into flats, four floors of shabby yellow brick. We step over recycling boxes over-stuffed with the wrong sorts of rubbish to a peeling, battered front door. A bright yellow smiley face is painted next to the door handle.

"What's that?" I say, but he doesn't reply and sticks his key in the lock. It won't turn. He swears and kicks the door as hard as he can. It swings open, revealing two guys clutching beer cans. They hug him like he's their long-lost brother.

"Everybody, this is Scarlett," he says, but their eyes are on him and he's off inside meeting and greeting like the Prime Minister. Kisses on both cheeks for a six-foot woman with dreadlocks, a private joke with a skinny black man in a vest, winks, handshakes and high-fives for everyone else. I bump, squeeze and apologise my way through, trying to avoid elbows in my guts and face.

Hayden stops by a ratty-faced guy. He places both hands on his shoulder and whispers something in his ear. The ratty guy winces, turns to me and says, "You gorrany pills?" in a thick Spanish accent.

I shake my head.

"You're very beautiful," he continues, covering me in beery breath.

I step forward but he moves to block me. I change direction but he does the same, like a toddler playing a stupid game. Then Hayden's strong hands lift him up and place him beyond me. Hayden grabs my arm and leads me into the kitchen.

"I see you've met Alejandro, my pervy flatmate."

He sits me down at the table opposite two snogging girls with Mohawks.

"These two are also pervy," he says. Without looking away the taller one flips him the V sign. He produces the bottle of vodka from his rucksack and dumps it in front of me, grabs a plastic glass from a pile on the side and hands it to me.

"I always repay my debts."

"You're like a celebrity."

"I wish," he says. "Wait here."

"Where are you going?"

"I'll be right back."

The couple snog. Others rummage through cupboards, fixing drinks and talking amongst themselves. The black and white chequered Lino on the floor is peeling. The lettering on the cooker dials has long worn off. Directly behind me, a door with a cracked window leads into the garden.

I pour myself some vodka. Then some more. The girls snog. I do everything I can not to take out my phone. I take out my phone. It's 1.45 a.m. I watch the door like a faithful dog. No Hayden. 1.55 a.m. The two girls come up for air.

"Hi, I'm Scarlett," I say. But they either don't hear me or choose to ignore me and then they leave, hand in hand. More vodka. Two French boys chase each other into the room.

"Who founded Gryffindor?!" screams the tall one in the baseball cap.

"What?"

"Who founded Gryffindor?!"

The other, small and hawk-nosed, looks like his eyes are about to burst.

"Godric?" I say.

"I told you!" says Baseball Cap.

"She's lying!" says Bursting Eyes.

"I had a major Harry Potter phase," I say. "I don't like to admit it."

Bursting Eyes wipes the sweat off his glistening forehead.

"Have you seen Hayden?" I say.

"Who?" says Baseball Cap. The end of his front tooth is black.

"So you're the only people in the whole party who don't know who Hayden is?"

I step into the garden. I can't believe the neighbours aren't complaining. Maybe what's happening is normal round here.

2.15 a.m.

He's gone.

He's left me.

He called me because he was drunk and didn't even know what he was doing.

I've no idea how I'm going to get home.

I'm going to find him and tell him I'm leaving.

The living-room is dark, full of people dancing to techno that sounds like steel girders clashing together. None of them is Hayden. I fight my way up the stairs to the second-floor landing. It's empty and quiet. Somewhere a toilet flushes and a tap turns on. Low and urgent voices come from behind a door to my left. I try the one opposite: it opens into a messy box-bedroom stinking of hairspray. It's like the wardrobe has vomited: there are bras and t-shirts strewn on the bed and jeans, dresses and knickers all over the floor. I leave the light off, open the window and sit on the bed. Outside a car pulls up and three girls get out and bang on the front door.

I take out my phone to write a message to Elliot.

Am at party in Elephant and Castle. I need to escape. Help!

"Who the hell's in my room?'

The light switches on.

I stuff my phone in my pocket. A girl, my height, but chunkier, with thick black mascara and an electric blue dress and broken fairy wings, comes in and sits next to me.

"Sorry," I say.

I stand up to go, but she blocks me.

"Who do you know here?" she says.

"Hayden. He invited me. Kind of a last-minute thing."

"*Ooooooh*." She's Australian. She eyes my vodka. "May I?"

I hand her the bottle. Something about her makes me blurt out what's happened: that I thought we were

48

coming on a date and he said he'd be back in one second and that I don't do well in crowds. She's wearing thick foundation which I now notice is there to cover up her acne.

"Sorry," I say. "I totally just dumped on you."

She puts her arms around me and pulls me to her bosom, which is huge. It's a little awkward.

"It's my birthday today!"

"Happy birthday!"

She twirls round and does a curtsy.

"I'm not having anyone being unhappy on my birthday. What's your name?"

"Scarlett."

"Harper!"

She takes my hand and leads me out to the landing.

"You have to understand some things about Hayden, that when he's here, in this birthday party context, he's going to be busy. So sometimes he gets a bit distracted, you know what I'm saying?"

Harper knocks on the door where the voices are coming from.

"Open the door, you twat!" she screams. She turns back to me. "If he gives you any shit, let me know okay?"

"Okay."

"Hayden! Open up!"

The door swings open and a tiny waif-like girl with a pixie cut walks out without speaking. Hayden stands in front of us looking sheepish.

"Don't you ever leave her on her own out there ever again," says Harper and shoves me inside and slams the door.

11

"I think I want to go home."

Two Technics decks and a mixer sit on a desk at the end of the room, next to an old iMac and scuffed leather chair.

"Are you some famous DJ?"

"Why do you keep thinking I'm famous?"

"Why does it annoy you that I do?"

"I'm sorry," he says. "Things got crazy."

"Can you call me an Uber?"

On the opposite wall is a tapestry of club night posters and DJ names laid out in thick all caps typefaces against fluorescent backgrounds with names like *Revelations*, *Together* and *Love Saves the Day*.

"You are a famous DJ!" I say.

"I'm a legend in my own bedroom."

There's a cork-board of clubbing photos. Hayden with his arms up. Hayden smiling with sweat glistening on his forehead. Hayden hugging someone clutching a bottle of water. He moves away from me and sits on the bed. I sit down next to him.

"I shouldn't have come," I say.

"What happened?"

"Everyone's *wasted*."

On the bedside table is a clear plastic bag stuffed

with large yellow pills. He looks at the pills then looks at me, picks up the bag, pours a couple out on to his hand and hands me one.

"What is it?"

"UPS."

The top is a perfect moulded replica of the delivery company logo, a golden shield with UPS written in large lower-case letters across the top.

"I don't do drugs," I say.

"I don't do drugs," he mimics. My cheeks are scalding hot.

"I sell, all right? I'm not famous."

"Oh, I just . . ."

"That girl who was here – Cristina, my flatmate – owes me. Trying to get money from her is like squeezing blood from a stone. There's a bunch of pill-head students down there who are going to scoff every single last one of those."

I should be shocked but I'm not. It all starts to make sense. He hadn't forgotten me. He was doing his business. I take a big swig of vodka.

"Are you a student?"

"Used to be."

"What did you study?"

"Accountancy."

I snort. Then he laughs. I laugh.

"You've never been raving?" he says.

I shake my head. The duvet is charcoal grey with black polka dots.

"I think I wanted to hang out with you. I just . . . I don't know what I expected. I didn't know it would be like this."

"You didn't expect me to be a scummy dealer?"

Our eyes meet. The room, the decks, the flyers and the photos fade away. Whatever happened last time is happening again. His jagged, thin-lipped smile and serious eyes. His baby face and half-beard. He's not exactly a poster boy for a men's health magazine but there's something about him I can't put my finger on.

"I didn't think this through, did I?" he says.

His knee touches my thighs.

"Neither did I," I say. "I mean, you could be anyone."

"Sorry," he says taking my hand. "I'm sorry."

"*Hayden, you in there?*"

He looks at the door and then looks at me. He waits.

"Hayden! You in there?"

He puts his finger on his lips.

Bang! Bang! Bang!

He hikes his feet onto the bed and curls up behind my back as if he's trying to hide behind me.

"*I've got money, you wanker!*"

He puts his hands around my waist.

The person outside heads down the stairs.

He returns his hands to his lap.

"Sorry. Don't know why I did that. So, yeah, I met you the other day in the park and we . . . yeah . . . so I thought . . . if you want . . . this is a mess, isn't it? I'll get you an Uber. Shit, it's three . . . it's all got a bit messy, hasn't it?"

"My life is a bit messy."

He kisses me. His hands rest on my cheeks and my fingers round his neck. Our tongues meet. My body tingles.

"That was nice," I say.

"Yeah," he says.

And then we're kissing again, falling on to the bed, our arms and legs pressed against our backs. His hands slip inside my hoodie, under my t-shirt, snapping my bra-strap, inside the waist of my jeans . . .

"Don't!" I say.

"Sorry."

"I mean, I like it, but don't."

Our lips are back together, slower, more careful, smaller kisses this time, but who are we kidding, I'm hungry, he's hungry, he's back on the bed, our hands rubbing, squeezing, pulling at our clothes, mine inside his t-shirt, pressing against the outline of his ribs, the taught skin around his hips. Every nerve on every inch of my skin is burning as I pull him upwards and strad-dle his lap.

I take off his t-shirt and he takes off mine, and then my bra.

"Um . . . how did this happen?" I say.

"It's a mystery," he says.

"Do you have a condom?"

"I thought you said, 'don't'."

"I'm confused."

"Me too."

He opens a draw on his desk and rummages around.

"In a word, no."

He turns to me.

"You're so hot I think I might go insane."

I'm sick of being good, I'm sick of trying to do the right thing, I want him more than anything, and I have since the moment I saw him.

I pull him towards me, back down on to the bed, my jeans are off. His trousers too.

This is it.

Bang! Bang! Bang!

"Hayden. You're needed! NOW!"

He rolls away and falls on to the floor, scrambling up like a cat to the door. He opens it a fraction, showing his nakedness.

"One minute."

"Jesus man, I can't unsee that!" I recognise the voice – it's Baseball Cap. He does know who Hayden is.

Hayden slams the door shut and manically we scramble into our clothes. I swig some vodka. The door opens and the party bursts into Hayden's room.

12

Hayden holds court. He's got the same spiel for all of them:

These are what pills used to be like.

Only have them in quarters.

No PMA. I never sell pills with PMA. Only MDMA. Only the best.

Really clean, no comedown.

I'm a pill guy. I don't even sell powder. I do one thing and do it well. Stick to what you're good at.

Single drop is the new double drop.

I've got a hundred for myself private. Seriously. No one's touching them.

He carefully counts out pills on to a small tray on his bed while they hover by his desk and sit on his floorboards like kids waiting for their mum to pay for a Kinder Egg. Baseball Cap has unplugged Hayden's decks and taken them downstairs, leaving a space rapidly filling up with beer cans and plastic glasses. Even though it's a couple of hours until sunrise he doesn't seem drunk or high, while I feel more and more pissed because all I do is sip vodka and smile and nod.

He's best mates with everyone. There's always a discount. A pile of fives, tens and twenties grows up around the beer on his desk. I'm doing all I can not to throw up. I wonder if I can make it out of the door, across the landing and get my head over the bathroom toilet in time.

It's 4 a.m. In five hours I should be sitting at the kitchen table, revising English.

Maybe I should tell Hayden to order the Uber.

Maybe I should take one of the pills.

I want to kiss him again.

"Scarlett!" says Hayden. Was I asleep? "Come with me."

The living room is thick with weed smoke. The little ratty Spanish guy and Harper kiss on an armchair. She practically crushes him, her right fairy wing now snapped off, his right arm outstretched, clutching a beer.

"Flatmates," says Hayden, rolling his eyes, before yanking me through the crowd. He stands behind the decks and taps a button. A base note plays so loud, so abrasively, I almost fall over. I push myself on to the window ledge behind. I'm out of vodka. And then the beat kicks in, *boom, boom, boom* and the whole hot, heaving room moves and whoops and whistles. I stand up to dance but my stomach says no. I have to get an Uber. But I can't interrupt him. I want to smash through the window and out into the cool night air and run. There's a piano riff, chunky and euphoric. I want to dance but my body has officially quit. My stomach erupts. I fall towards the decks, sending them crashing over, then black.

13

The sunlight hurts my eyes. My muscles feel red raw.

"Easy now."

Hayden cups my cheeks with his hands and kisses me on the forehead. He helps me out of the car and I stand, disorientated, on the pavement.

"Just in time for revision," he says.

"Where am I?"

"Home. At least I hope you are. If I got the wrong address then you're screwed."

"Oh my God." But then I see my front door a little further along.

I hug him.

"What happened?"

"Nothing a bit of bleach and a mop can't sort."

His pupils are big and black and he's chewing gum.

"I puked, didn't I?"

"It happens."

I can smell the bitterness on my breath.

"Sleep," he says.

Don't leave me here, I want to say.

He kisses me long and slow and all I can think about is if he can taste the puke. He turns and gets back into the Uber. I watch it drive up to the top of the road and turn left by Paradise Park.

Somewhere, a crow caws. Outside my door my hands shake, my keys jangle, my heart beats. I run up the stairs into the bathroom, lean over the toilet basin and retch and retch until there's no liquid left and then I retch some more. I stagger into bed, fully clothed, and pull the covers up to my neck. Dad walks in without knocking, bleary-eyed and bad-tempered.

"I just threw up," I say.

"I heard."

"I think I'm sick."

"Oh dear," he says, smiling, and my whole body convulses with his anger.

"I think it was that lunch at Dixie Chicken."

"Exam today?"

"Next week!"

"Of course. Maybe you should go to the doctor?"

"I just need to rest."

"Okay."

He rubs his forehead.

"I can still revise from bed."

"You never do things the easy way, do you?" he says. He pulls his dressing gown more tightly closed. I want to punch him.

"I told you that place was filthy," he says, before walking downstairs.

I should be happy that I've got away with it. But someone's drilling inside my head and all I want is the duvet to swallow me up so I never ever have to get out of bed.

9 days later

14

It's Friday and I've just spent two and a half hours debating the statement *To what extent was Labour Party policy directly responsible for the growth of trade union militancy in the years 1964 to 1970?* I scribbled every stupid thought and every random quote I could. My final line was *Why do we always have to blame people for stuff? Why is it always a result of some failed politician? Maybe people are just people. Trade unions are militant. Maybe we should just accept people for who they are. But we won't, because people are idiots.* I probably shouldn't have done that, but it was written from the heart and maybe the examiner will take pity on me.

Unfortunately, my exam finished at home time. Next to my college is an all-boys school and across the road is an all-girls one. This means two thousand eleven-to-eighteen-year-olds have just erupted on to the street. It's the first boiling hot day of the summer, the pavement is buzzing, and not in a good way.

Aya slips past me, pretty as porcelain in a short white dress and black PVC sandals. Two Ethiopian boys eye her up and she doesn't seem to notice. I hate her. An Arab boy swears at his shaven-headed, white mate who gets him in a headlock and punches his ears.

I find myself next to the policeman who's always outside our school and who is meant to make us feel safe. I feel just like he looks: sweaty, fat, and excluded from the party.

I check my phone. They say that playing it cool always works, so I decided not call Hayden. I lasted eight whole days, until yesterday. *How r u? Thanks for helping me get home.* No reply. I called. Straight to voicemail. I didn't leave a message. I wasn't going to humiliate myself further.

I still keep checking my phone, though.

I shriek as someone grabs my waist but it's just Elliot. He takes my hand – he's got into the habit recently – and we walk. He's full-on androgynous today, tight trousers, hair down to his shoulders, flowery top. He tells me about an Instagram confession account that everyone's following where someone said that when they see him stare at Aya it's rapey. He had to spend the whole day telling people he doesn't fancy her.

"Is that why you're holding my hand?" I say. "So they believe you?"

"No," he says, and lets go.

Our bus stop is insanely crowded so we decide to walk to the next one, joining a stream of other students, some spilling on to the Heath, some snaking up the road towards the giant houses and leafy streets of Hampstead Garden Suburb.

"So, have you ungrounded yourself yet?" he says for the millionth time.

I shake my head. I want to tell him about the party, but his lips are pursed and I'm scared of how he'll react. We pass the tennis courts, where a grey-haired man with a pot-belly serves the ball with a grunt.

"I've got my costume!" he says, brightly. "We're going as the Incredible Hulk."

I stop so abruptly a girl in a green uniform bumps into me.

"I speak the truth."

"What do you mean, *we're* going as the Incredible Hulk?"

He leans towards me. There's a few pink spots on his normally smooth chin.

"My dad knows someone who does costumes for the movies. We do an hour in make-up. In a TV studio. I'm gonna have a bodysuit! We'll be like Hulk husband and wife."

"The Hulk's a loner, Elliot. A sad, misunderstood loner who everyone tries to trap and kill."

"I thought you'd be up for it."

"Hulk husband and wife is totally against the spirit of the comic."

"Forget I ever said husband and wife! We're gonna look movie quality! We're gonna get photographed! We could get internet famous for this!"

Elliot's bottom lip wobbles and I'm reminded of a four-year-old who's told he can't play with his favourite toy.

"This can be your early birthday present as well!" he says, recovering his poise.

I sigh.

"I've been a good girl for three whole weeks," I say, "There's a small chance he might be open to negotiation."

"I think you'd look hot in green body-paint," he says.

"Since when do you care how hot I look?"

"You don't know how lucky we are to get a retired guy that used to work in the movies, and my dad had to pay a *premium*," he says.

We reach the bus stop just as our bus pulls in. He stops me from getting on and looks me in the eyes.

"I just want you to be happy."

My irritation disappears.

"I'm sorry I'm so crabby," I say.

"You are so getting ungrounded and I'm making sure of it."

I'm calm when we reach my front door. I anticipate me and Elliot drinking tea and talking crap in the garden for hours.

But the door is unlocked, and when I open it there are bodies behind the lacquered glass of the kitchen door. Elliot bristles like a cat poised for action.

The door opens, revealing my dad wearing jeans.

"Hi David," says Elliot.

For some reason my dad introduced himself to Elliot as David. So Elliot always calls him David, and it always makes me cringe. Now they shake hands. Elliot strides down the gangway past the oven and sits himself at the table between the other person and the large indoor tree-plant-thing.

"Hi!" she says, in an American drawl. She wears a floral dress down to her knees. She's tiny. Her arms are impossibly skinny and golden-tanned. A mass of copper brown ringlets frame a slender face and long sharp nose. She holds a floral tea-mug that me and Mum chose for Father's Day when I was seven. On the table is a box from Gail's bakery containing a triple-layered strawberry cake.

"I thought you deserved a treat," says Dad. He flicks the kettle on.

"Grande Earl Grey please," says Elliot, cheekily, as if he's ordering at Starbucks.

"Jennifer – Scarlett and Elliot," says Dad.

"How did it go, guys?" says Jennifer. "It's the business end of college, huh?"

"I guess," I say, my cheeks burning.

"I prefer to call it squeaky-bum time," says Elliot. Dad and Jennifer laugh politely.

"I'm sure it went well," says Dad. There's pride in his voice but it's not in my work.

"Well done!" says Jennifer. Her teeth are insanely white and make me not want to open my mouth ever again.

Dad begins with an exam-interrogation. *Have you answered the question before? Did you check your spelling? Could you remember your quotes? What did you write?* I give him the positive version. *I wrote a lot. I checked my spelling. I had lots to say.* Then Jennifer asks about university, which is my cue to recite my well-rehearsed story about me and Elliot getting Leeds interviews on the same day and my weird group evaluation where it was obvious I'd never actually done much History of Art compared to the geeky posh girls that surrounded me. In spite of this, I still got my offer.

"You must have come across as a bright spark," says Jennifer, making me blush.

"I don't really know why I chose it," I say. "They made it sound good on the website. Kind of."

Luckily, Elliot steps in and tells us all about how amazing Leeds is and he doesn't even mind that it rains all the time because he loves being inside when it's pouring. It reminds me that in a few months everything's going to change; I feel sick. Jennifer tells us she studied ballet at the Central School in Covent Garden and that she teaches dance, which explains her rake-straight posture and freakish skinniness.

My dad holds his mug, legs splayed, stroking the wispy strands on his balding head like he's the accountant version of Brad Pitt. Jennifer's grin bores into the side of my face.

"So can Scarlett come to Comic Con with me tomorrow?" says Elliot out of nowhere.

"Scarlett is grounded," says Dad, blinking.

"I've already booked," says Elliot. "Plus, my dad is paying for costumes."

"Right . . ." says Dad, clearly trying to work out what Comic Con is.

"It's a celebration for comic fans," says Elliot, "where nerds like me and Scarlett come together to worship our heroes and pretend we live in a fantasy world. Just for a day."

"But technically you're in the middle of the most important exam period of your entire education to date," says Dad, now scratching his chin.

Last year we saw two sci-fi stars have a literal fist fight at a Q and A and the dwarf from Austin Powers behind an autograph table with no queue looking like he's going to kill himself. We did enjoy perving over all the cos-play, though.

"Scarlett," says Elliot, putting his hand on my shoulder, "has been working too hard. She can get back to it on Sunday. Sometimes a bit of time off *improves* performance."

"I said you were grounded until the end of the year. If Comic Con was early July it would be okay."

"Early July I'm going to be in Hawaii with my parents," says Elliot. "This is my chance to give Scarlett a special birthday present as I won't be around for her actual birthday. And it's one hundred percent sober, I promise."

Elliot winks as he says *one hundred percent sober*. It's an audacious move – anyone else might get punched. But my Dad laughs, awkwardly.

"We just want to blow off some steam, dress up and be idiots for the day," says Elliot. "We all finish our exams on the same day. We'll save our drinking for then. Scout's honour."

Jennifer's eyes are fixated on Dad. I can feel her willing him to let me go. I have no idea why.

"Okay," says Dad. "One day."

"Amazing!" says Elliot. "Can she come round tonight too? Back by 10 p.m., I promise. Sober."

Dad looks at Jennifer.

"Oh – okay! Yes, you can!" says Dad magnanimously, as if he's Father Christmas who's just appeared down my chimney. He looks at me as if expecting a hug. I don't oblige.

15

Elliot's housekeeper Maria is small and stocky, like a miniature tank, and she shunts his door open with her arse, arms full, carrying an eighteen-inch pizza on a tray. Although it tilts precariously as she strides across the room she manages not to drop it. As usual she's unsmiling, her face lined and severe. I feel bad because I don't even know which country she's from, or anything about her other than she makes cheesy bespoke pizzas from scratch.

She puts the pizza on Elliot's coffee table, checks if we want anything else and leaves. It's obvious that we're way too old not to be fixing our own food. I wonder if she has a starving grandkid back home. Maybe she sends him her wages. Maybe she's imagining a revolution: Elliot, Bad Ben and I are rounded up and hanged.

"Scarlett, eat!" says Bad Ben, holding a slice dangerously close to Elliot's giant Spiderman cushion.

Elliot sits on the edge of the sofa playing his guitar, messing around, strumming a tune, attempting to sing. He only knows three chords and his singing voice is whiney.

"Put the guitar down," says Bad Ben, mouth full. "Or I will be forced to shoot you."

"Never," says Elliot, and strums louder. I realise his bedroom is a shrine to how gloriously weird he is – his Avengers bedspread – his make-up table like some Victorian lady's – a hundred rare comics in boxes in the corner – plus a framed picture of his thirteen-year-old self with ninety-year-old Stan Lee, the guy who invented all the Marvel superheroes, a grinning, dumb younger him, teeth in braces. At once I'm so overwhelmed with love that I want to put slobbery kisses all over his forehead. Elliot catches my eye, twangs a string and swears. He puts the guitar down and eyes the food.

"No, but seriously, Jennifer was kind of hot," he says.

"Yuck," says Bad Ben.

"I mean dance teachers *are* hot. It's a pre-requisite for the job."

"Your dad's dating a MILF," says Bad Ben, mouth full.

"You love MILFs," says Elliot.

"Actually I do love MILFS. Can I come to your house?" says Bad Ben, looking at me.

"No!" I say.

"It's a good job your mum is rough, that's all I'm saying," says Elliot.

"You're implying I love MILFS so much I would shag my own mum, thanks for that, Elliot."

"I kind of found her repulsive," I say, and reach for the vodka.

Elliot struggles to pick up a slice, long strings of cheese extending up from the pizza and sticking to his hand.

"So how long has your dad been banging her?" says Bad Ben.

"I don't want to think of my dad banging anyone," I say.

"But she's so thin. And American. And tanned." says Elliot.

"She's American?" says Bad Ben.

"Her teeth are scarily white," I say.

"They bleach them," says Elliot.

"You can bleach teeth?" says Bad Ben.

"Guys, don't you think there's something wrong about this?" I say.

All I can hear is the sound of the cheese slopping around Bad Ben's mouth.

"Wrong that your dad's getting some and we're not?" Elliot.

"Yeah! No! I don't know. Isn't he on some horrific mid-life crisis rebound? Don't you think it's kind of soon?" I say.

"I think he's totally in some mid-life crisis rebound and it's disrespectful to do it right in front of your nose," says Elliot, monotonously. I wonder if he's saying it to make me shut up.

"He was poncing around the kitchen like he's a middle-aged Justin Bieber!" I say.

A piece of cheese flies from my mouth into Bad Ben's Coke, which makes him laugh and then I laugh again and a bigger piece of cheese comes out, after which I bury my face in my hands.

"You're such a slob, Scarlett," says Elliot.

"I am not a slob!" I shout.

Both boys look towards the floor.

"Sorry to raise my voice but I am not slob," I say.

Elliot sits down next to me on the sofa.

"It's like . . . did he even *love* my mum?" I say.

Bad Ben and Elliot share the briefest look, and my stomach twists.

"I know it's really shitty but your dad is moving on. And maybe you need to move on, too," says Elliot.

"Fuck off."

Now I'm full of feelings and I've no idea what they are or what they mean. I don't even feel like I'm in the room any more. Hayden's face flashes in front of my eyes. He is sitting in his room, placing a bag of pills into Baseball Cap's hand. I'm not sure it even happened. Maybe Hayden was an alien and the Uber was a spaceship and his house in Elephant and Castle was another planet.

"Is that what you guys think, that I need to move on?"

Elliot shrugs and purses his lips.

"And you two are experts in grief?"

"I'm an expert in pizza. Maybe we should concentrate on that," says Bad Ben. We eat in silence; the whole room is thick with anger.

"Anyway, I've got some news. I think I've met my soulmate."

Again, that flicker of a look between Bad Ben and Elliot.

"Have you ever had that thing where you *just know*?"

Elliot opens his mouth but nothing comes out.

"I guess not . . ."

"Actually, I have" says Elliot.

"I'm not talking about that stupid Japanese tart."

"Harsh," says Bad Ben, reaching for more pizza.

Elliot stands and picks up his guitar.

"I think I've met someone who *gets* me. Like I've always known them. I didn't even think it was possible . . ."

I have their full attention. So I let it all out. The struggling to get to sleep, the late-night phone call, the party, the Harry Potter weirdos, the self-absorbed gay girls, the amazing kiss, the catastrophic sex, the giant yellow pills, the relentless music, the much-too-much vodka, the throwing up, the passing out and the waking up outside my house. The more I speak, the more the atmosphere turns sour. It feels like I'm confessing to molesting children or murdering one of my parents.

"So you slept with him?" says Bad Ben, witheringly.

"For thirty seconds," I say. "Not the way I *imagined* . . ."

Bad Ben puffs his cheeks and blows.

"But I don't care, I don't mind . . . because it was him."

"And you think he's your soul mate?" says Elliot.

"Yes."

You could fry an egg on my cheeks.

"I find this interpretation . . . interesting," says Elliot.

"What do you mean?"

Elliot puts down his guitar and walks across to the room to his comics. He studiously browses through the top box, as if looking for something, before giving up and turning to me.

"With all due respect you don't know this guy from Adam. He could be anyone. He could have raped you. He could have murdered you. He could *still* do that. It's the year of our lord two thousand

and nineteen. I didn't think women got into cars with dodgy men anymore."

"He's not dodgy. Well, the selling drugs is, but the rest isn't."

"Isn't a soul mate supposed to be *romantic*?" says Elliot.

"Yes!" I say. "It was romantic!"

Elliot scoffs, grabs the guitar again, sits back down on the sofa and strums it. I hate him, so superior and cool, like he's my second father. He lives in a luxury cocoon. What does he know about life?

"He shagged you and then never called you. That sounds like the most un-romantic night I could imagine," he says.

"I guess we don't choose love, love chooses us," I say, staring at my feet.

"He's an asshole but love chose me so that makes it okay?" says Elliot.

"Maybe there's a reason," I say, but it sounds pathetic. I fold my arms tight and look at the floor.

"You should have done a pill," says Bad Ben.

"What?" says Elliot.

"If you're gonna have a messed-up night out you might as well go the whole hog," says Bad Ben.

"You're teetotal, since when have you encouraged people to take drugs?" says Elliot.

"Just saying, if I was Scarlett . . ."

I rip off a slice of pizza. I'm so hyper-aware of spilling something and being labelled a slob again I eat it in slow motion.

"At least he took her home," says Bad Ben.

"I feel . . . like I'm an electrical cable." I make

a chopping motion with my hand. "Severed in the middle. When I'm with him . . ." I bring my hands together. "The circuit is complete."

Elliot snorts.

"Mr Perfect a.k.a. Mr Soul Mate hasn't even called you. Case closed."

"I'm going home," I say.

"I thought we were going to watch a movie," says Bad Ben, as if that was the most distressing thing about this whole argument.

Elliot follows me downstairs and we pause on a giant mat that has *Welcome. Beware of wife. Kids are shady. Husband is cool* embroidered into it.

"At least you're not grounded anymore," he says brightly.

He takes my hand.

"Thanks," I say grudgingly.

"Sorry if I was harsh." He rubs the flap of skin between my thumb and my index finger.

"I'm sorry if I was harsh about Aya."

"You coming tomorrow?"

"Of course," I say.

"We're gonna have such an amazing time, all this other stuff is going to just fade into the background."

"His and Hers Hulk."

He smiles. He needs to reapply his mascara. There are little stubble flecks on his chin.

"It was terrible what happened to you with your mum. That shouldn't happen to anyone. I just . . . I want to see the old Scarlett back. The happy Scarlett," he says.

"Me too," I say.

Now he puts his hands on my shoulders making me take a step closer. I wonder if I should kiss him, if it will make me forget.

"Go back upstairs before Bad Ben finishes the pizza," I say.

I peck him on the cheek.

"Screw pizza," he says. "I'm not hungry."

He watches me from his door as I walk down the road.

16

It's a relief to feel the cool air in the empty street. The sky is turquoise and the streetlights have just switched on. The cars crossing the junction ahead appear half in this world, half in another. I consider buying vodka, climbing over the fence and sitting in the dark park to drink it. Maybe I'll meet another boy and begin a romance where everything goes smoothly.

I spot a figure with close-cropped hair similar to Hayden's, his back to me, smartphone gripped in his right hand. He jogs across the road and into Food and Wine. I run across after him, forcing a double-decker bus to brake. The driver shouts at me from his cab but I hover outside the shop and pretend I'm interested in the big boxes of knobbly potatoes and giant tomatoes. Through the window I glimpse a pair of charcoal tracksuit bottoms and bright white trainers and my heart leaps out of my chest.

I duck inside. Cenk is behind the till, back to me, his phone propped up on the counter playing some ridiculous Turkish soap opera with histrionic voices and melodramatic music. I sneak forward, eyes on the scuffed lino floor, until I reach the fridge full of milk that lines the back of the shop. The door to the office is closed.

I'm the only one in the shop.

"Can I help?"

Cenk has crept up behind me.

"Um . . . no?".

"You want milk?"

His eyes pin me to the fridge.

"You owe me something," he says. I follow him back to the counter. "I thought you never come back."

"Sorry," I say.

"We had deal."

"I was a dick," I say. "I forgot."

The price of a large vodka bottle appears on the till screen and I wince.

"It's not nice for a girl to swear."

His biceps bulge out of his t-shirt. I tap my card on the card machine.

"Why are you upset?" he says.

His eyes look beyond me. I turn. Hayden stands in the doorway.

I know that this moment – only this moment – is my chance to find out if everything I feel is my imagination or if it is true.

Hayden turns and leaves.

The card machine waits to connect.

I feel like I'm going to explode.

The printer whirrs and I snatch the receipt from Cenk's hand and run outside.

Hayden stands under the bus shelter. He looks at the map and traces a bus route with his finger. I walk towards him. Our eyes lock. A bus stops and its doors open. Children talk, heels clip-clop, a baby cries, someone laughs. The doors hiss closed.

"You're doing it again," he says.

"What?"

"You just look at me and you do it."

I'm a balloon. The slightest gust of wind could blow me miles.

"I was thinking about you," he says. "I thought you didn't want to see me again."

My mouth hangs open. It's the last thing I expected him to say.

"Can we talk about this somewhere that's not *here*?" I say.

We end up in the Starbucks by Archway Station. He buys me a hot chocolate with cream, marshmallows and full fat milk while I find a table in an empty corner downstairs. When he arrives with the drinks I see he's chosen a double espresso for himself. It reminds me of the Eastern European builders I see smoking outside cafés with their cigarettes.

"I thought *you* didn't want to see *me* again," I say.

"I thought *you* didn't want to see *me* again," he says.

He downs his espresso in one.

"This is stupid because I thought you hated me."

"I thought you hated *me*."

In spite of myself I laugh.

Then he laughs.

"This is stupid," I say.

"I know."

"I don't hate you."

"I don't hate you."

Then I remember like a knife in my gut.

I cup my mug in my hands and lean towards him.

"You didn't call me."

"You didn't call me."

"Yes, I did."

"What?"

"I did!"

He pulls out his phone, opens the Phone app, and looks down the list of missed calls.

"Oh," he says. "You did."

"Why didn't you . . . ?"

He shakes his head, closing the conversation. I want to know what he's been doing the last week and a half.

"So, I guess you know Food and Wine's dirty little secret," he says.

Cenk looming over me by the milk fridge. Hayden disappearing and then reappearing.

"No, what?"

Hayden leans forward.

"They're dealers," he stage-whispers.

"No!"

"Shhhhh!"

In the far corner an Indian lady is hunched over some printed-out sheets of A4 and on the sofa nearest to us sit two Asian girls in bright purple school uniforms.

"Feds are everywhere," says Hayden.

Cenk's dad deals pills out of Food and Wine. That's why I met Hayden in Paradise Park. That's why he was near my house on the day of the party. He was picking up. He schlepps across London each time.

"I'm surprised. But not surprised," I say, blushing.

"I only met Cenk recently – I used to pick up from his uncle – it's all connected – they have access to a whole load of product, they do everything, yay, pebs, I swear even Viagra – but they like me, they know I'm just a party-enabler, I'm not one of these big business killer gang types – I just want my mates to have a good time. They got some direct channels to the labs in Holland. I used to pick up from this estate in Haringey. It's a proper fortress there, CCTV in every room. But now they send me to the shop. Cenk's a part of it."

He leans in closer, speaking right into my ear.

"They do good product at good prices. That's why I still come up here, even though I moved down south. I don't want to order from some anonymous weirdo on the dark web," he says.

"Yay and Pebs?"

"Crack and smack."

Hayden's phone rings. He reaches into his pocket and produces a cheap feature phone, not the iPhone he had before. A burner phone. He answers it, turns his face away from me and completes the conversation in a low, unintelligible voice. He hangs up and smiles.

He's a dealer. I knew this already, but maybe a bit of me hoped it wasn't true.

"So, what now?" I say.

He opens his mouth as if to say one thing and stops. He leans in close.

"After you left, that party didn't finish for two more days. I kept trying to get people to leave and they wouldn't. Hardest Comedown Ever. Today is the first day I've actually left the house. I could barely talk for a week." He points to his phone. "This was on Do Not Disturb. I just sat there in the dark staring at the wall."

I should be angry but instead I laugh.

Then he laughs.

Him sitting, staring at the wall is the funniest thing and we've got the giggles again like the first day we met at the park.

"I must have sold two grands' worth and ended up

with five hundred quid. If I ever get it in my head to have a party in my house again you have my permission to shoot me."

He examines his empty espresso cup, contemplating the remaining orangey froth.

"How did you go from accountancy . . . to this?" I say.

"Long story. A side hustle that got out of hand. Anyway, going out tonight to do it all again!"

"What?"

"Recovered just in time!"

"*Why?*"

He leans back on his chair and folds his arms.

"Mikey Miles."

"Who's Mikey Miles?"

"Come and find out."

"I don't get it. Why are you doing it again if you just spent a week in the dark?"

"I said: because it's Mikey Miles. And this is just one night, not a three-day bender."

"Who's Mikey Miles?"

"Why don't you come and find out!"

Hayden reaches into his pocket, produces a creased flyer and hands it to me. It's black, apart from PARADISE emblazoned across the top, and MIKEY MILES underneath, in neon yellow capital letters. On the back is an East London postcode.

I'm interrupted by a green-aproned man with a large afro telling us it's closing time. The two girls in the purple uniforms stand up and the taller of the two gives Hayden the eye as she passes our table before walking up the stairs. She must be all of fourteen, but I feel jealous.

"It's all right, you 'don't do drugs', it's not your style," says Hayden.

The Indian lady keeps looking up at us as she puts her sheets of A4 into a plastic folder. The University of London crest is on the top of each one.

"This is why I thought you didn't like me," he says. He leans forward again, so close his lips are almost touching mine. "You think I'm dealer scum. Like everyone in the party were scum. A lot of them were, by the way, but that's not the point. You threw up on the decks. I'm a DJ and you threw up on the decks. That says it all."

"Is that what you really think?"

"Yes."

How stupid are we?

I was at home being paranoid about him and he was at home being paranoid about me.

"I was scared. Because I like you and that's scary, so I drank too much."

"I like you and it's scary too," he says.

An instant tsunami of feeling. I want him so much I could eat him whole like a snake.

I *knew* there was more to him than appears. Elliot's such a judgmental asshole.

"I'm sorry I didn't reply. I honestly missed it. Completely. I'm a dick."

"That's what I said to Cenk!"

"You what?"

"Doesn't matter."

Our fingers interlink. Our mouths come together and our breath is heavy, he stands up, I stand up and then we falls backwards onto the sofa, him on his back, me on top, kissing, pawing and groping.

Five minutes later Afro Guy tells us that Starbucks is closed.

We recover, apologise and brush down our clothes. I check my face on my phone. It's bright pink. At least I'm not blushing.

"So . . ." says Hayden.

"Let's go see Mikey Miles," I say.

17

Shall I tell dad I'm staying the night with Elliot? He might think I'm too wasted to make it home or that me and Elliot have got together and I want neither of those thoughts to enter his head. I stuff my phone into my pocket and finger the small plastic bag containing one and a half UPS pills. I can still taste the acrid bitterness of the first one in the back of my throat. "Half will be all you need," said Hayden. "The rest . . . emergency." He's sandwiched between me and Alejandro in the middle of an Uber back seat. I look up at him and he winks. I slip my fingers into his hands and rest my head on his shoulder. I'll deal with dad later.

I am filled by the spirit of *fuck it* and I love it.

We're somewhere near the City of London. Our car turns a corner round a glass skyscraper and swings on to a dual carriageway. It's 11.30 p.m. and the office doors are locked, the foyers are empty, sandwich bars shut and a bunch of men in suits drinking outside a pub are the only sign of the working day.

For the past three hours I've followed Hayden around London. I waited at Camden station while he disappeared into a pub, sat in a small square in Kennington while he climbed the stairs to someone's flat and lay on his bed while a stream of people came to buy their drugs as his crappy phone buzzed away on his desk. Some wore smart office wear. Some were cruddy with stained jeans and bad skin. They were mostly young, with a few a bit too close to Dad's age for comfort. Hayden is sober and on top of his game. He smiles politely, shakes hands, asks about their pets or where they went on holiday. He carefully counts out change. He could be working in some up-market coffee shop.

Cristina with the pixie cut sits in the front seat, her shoulderless red dress looking like it's draped on a twig. On her bony back is a sprawling tattoo of a giant Cobra springing out of a crack in the ground, mouth open, fangs bared. It's unusual. I catch her eyes in the rear-view mirror. She smiles and I smile back. I know I've made the right decision.

The Uber drops us in a narrow street with a bare brick wall on one side and faceless concrete buildings ranged along the other. Up ahead, a line of people queue outside a set of battered double doors. Cristina lights a cigarette while Hayden grunts and stretches. Alejandro places his hand on my shoulder and speaks in my ear, standing a little too close.

"All the clubs in London are closing. But these guys, they're bringing raving back!" he says.

He looks at me as if he expects me to know what he's talking about. The awkwardness is broken by someone calling my name from further down the street. I turn and see it's Harper, clutching a half-full pint glass and striding towards me in high heels. She puts the beer on the pavement and pulls me tight. "I'm so glad you could come," she says. My nose creases at her sharp perfume.

I turn to see a man with a shaved head and greying beard checking people's names on an iPad, behind him a chunky security guard.

"How much is this going to cost?" I say, remembering my meagre bank balance.

"It's okay," says Cristina and before I can reply she walks up to Bearded Guy and he kisses her on the cheeks. He swipes and taps on his iPad before lifting the rope.

"It's great when you've got friends in high places," says Harper, stuffing her heels into a bag before putting on a pair of trainers and pouring her beer into the gutter. Hayden man-hugs Bearded Guy like they're old friends. He turns to me and beckons me in.

I follow him down a narrow stairwell to a cramped landing where a bored girl with a shaved head sits at the cloakroom window. The racks of jackets and jumpers press into her back and her forehead glistens with sweat. We hand over our coats while people push past us in both directions. I grip Hayden's waist in case I'm knocked over and follow his bright white trainers along the concrete floor.

We enter the main room and the bass is so loud the floor shakes. It's so dim I can barely make out anyone's face. At the far side the DJ stands over his decks on a stage flanked by two pillars of speakers. It's not what I expected a club to be like, more of an empty cellar that's got taken over for the night. To our left is a home-made plywood bar. To our right large neon letters that spell out the word PARADISE. We head to those and sit down on a row of wooden crates serving as benches. It's half empty. Some stand to the side, drinking beer and talking; the rest dance in small pockets, in plenty of space.

Hayden turns to me and mimes drinking a drink.

A random memory from drug education in Year 7 enters my mind.

"I thought you weren't supposed to drink on pills."

Hayden rolls his eyes and heads off to the bar.

A snare drum rattles faster and faster. The beat stops, followed by a whooshing, rushing sound. A couple of the dancers clap their hands. There's a moment of silence and then a massive, hard, chunky rhythm and the claps turn to cheers.

Hayden returns with two vodka shots.

"How are you feeling?" he says, handing me one.

"I think it was a dud."

"I don't do duds," he says and downs his shot.

I decide Hayden is wrong. I feel nothing, not even the vodka. It's too loud and too disgusting. I bet there's rats here. I'm tired. The club's filling up and I'm claustrophobic. I'm in the middle of my fucking exams! Hayden's sitting there like he's relaxing on a park bench in the sun. Some bloke with a shaved head shouts in his ear. Hayden's all smiles and then he presses something into the guy's hand and the guy presses a note into Hayden's. I don't want to watch him deal drugs all night. I don't want to be the arm-candy of a drug dealer. I shouldn't have done the pill and I don't care if I got in for free: I should just go home.

I excuse myself to go to the toilet. People are yelling into each other's ears, laughing and baring their teeth. One girl elbows me in the stomach, winding me. I turn to confront her but she's dancing with her eyes closed. Some people film the DJ on their phones, but all he's doing is tweaking knobs. He looks pleased with himself, but no matter what knobs he twiddles, I can't hear any difference to the sound. Who is this guy and why would anyone want to film him? I want to take a gun and shoot them all.

I find an empty cubicle and lock the door. I sit down and close my eyes and listen to the running taps, mindless banter and doors slamming. Thirty minutes ago I was certain I wanted to be here and now feel completely the opposite. What is wrong with me?

Then it happens. So fast and so unexpected I have to hold on to the wall to steady myself. It's like I've come down with an instant vomit bug but instead of wanting to puke sick, it's happiness. There's so much of it, my stomach heaves and *whoosh*, up into my heart, lungs and into my brain. My eyes roll up inside my skull and I blink over and over to push them down.

This is what he was talking about.

I have to tell him.

I have to find Hayden.

I force myself back through the crowd but it's hard to focus and when I do I'm overwhelmed by the *rightness* of this moment. It's so *right* that we're here. I want to apologise to everyone for hating them. I want to stop everyone and tell them that it wasn't them, it was me. I keep giving strangers the thumbs up. They give me the thumbs up too! It's all right! They don't hate me!

I follow the PARADISE. That is how I will find him. I *am* paradise. That's why they call the night PARADISE. I get it now!

There are the benches. Some guy wearing thick glasses sits where Hayden was. I circle the whole club, sticking to the edges. I bob my head to the rhythm, snaking round like a one-woman conga. The walls are covered in sweat. How did it get so busy? But I'm back to the guy with the glasses and he smiles at me. He likes me. Then, just to the right – Hayden! He was sitting next to him all along! I was right the first time! His eyes are closed and his head is nodding to the rhythm.

I sit on his lap.

"I'm sorry I took so long," I say.

His kisses shoot electric shocks from my mouth to my feet. He squeezes my back, sending pleasure through my spine, out of my head and all the way to the moon.

"All the way to the moon," I say. Hayden frowns. How can I explain?

And then this baseline. *Bom, bom-bom-bom, Bom, bom-bom-bom:* it's funky. It's too funky, it's relentless. An American man speaks, monotonously.

Music brings us together.

It is the answer.

Music brings us together.

It is the answer.

And then the beat comes back and I scream and pump the air with my fist and dance-jump around.

No more talking. I yank Hayden up and pull him towards the stage.

We're surrounded by a thousand people but it's only me and him. Every beat, every whoosh, every thump, every boom, every bleep, every word *is* us.

When we dance the shock waves thunder into space and give birth to whole galaxies. Solar systems and planets and new Earths with new civilisations come into being, full of people like us. I shout in his ear.

"I get it now."

"This is what pills used to be like," he says.

"Shall I do the other half?" I say.

"That's my girl," he says.

18

We sit in a circle around a cracked flowerpot full of cigarette butts. I watch the burnt tobacco embers explode like mini-fireworks while Alejandro rakes the orange stubs rhythmically with a stick. For Hayden, Alejandro and Harper it's an ashtray, but for me it's like we're involved in a crazy ritual, worshiping the God of Cigarettes, calling them to come down from the sky and . . . I don't know . . . save us from lung cancer?

I'm knocked out of my reverie by Harper talking at a thousand miles an hour.

"Seriously. I'm trying to say to him that I didn't realise that you could only apply for a year. I would have done two if I could. The money would have been in my account a year ago before I came so can't we just, like, pretend it's a year ago? He says that I need three hundred quid to re-apply. And they might not let me, they're cracking down. I don't have three hundred quid I can pull out of my ass, just like that."

We're in the cramped back yard, flanked by high rise offices, sitting underneath an old outdoor heater which is switched on despite it being the end of May. High above us, the sky lightens to a dirty blue.

"I love how like a few hours ago everyone was working their ass off stressing in all these office blocks caring about pointless bollocks and now we're here having the time of our lives," I say.

"Isn't she sweet?" says Harper. Her cigarette cherry dances around like the tip of a magic wand. Maybe *she's* the God of Cigarettes, come down to earth, morphed into human form.

"This girl has her priorities straight," says Hayden. He watches his cigarette closely, like it contains a secret message.

"But seriously," says Harper. "I'm like, going to my boss, you don't have a better consultant than me. You don't have anyone else who gets on the phone and finds you the miserable wankers desperate for cash and gets them to work in these nasty buildings wiping the desks, mopping the floors, emptying the baskets for under the minimum wage and pretend like you're doing them a favour at the same time."

She gestures to the building behind us.

"If you see a cleaner up there, then I probably got them the job. Do you know how soul-destroying that is? Giving people the worst jobs in the world while pretending that you're doing them a favour? And I'm the only one in the whole office who hits those targets over and over so you better sponsor me as Fast Track Executive Director to stay in this country so I can continue taking the piss in London and raving with these guys and hot girls like Scarlett."

"Me?" I say.

"My visa can't run out. We've only just met!" says Harper.

I love her. I'm so blessed to have met her.

"I don't ever want to get a job," I say.

Hayden holds up his hand towards me. I high-five it and rest my head on his shoulder.

"And you know what," continues Harper, "If I was Executive Director, I'd triple their wages. I'd put the cleaners on the same level as the nurses. I'm serious. I'd start a revolution."

Cristina slides in next to Harper, crossing her spindly legs, left hand pulling her dress down so we can't see her pants, right reaching up, fingers interlocked with some guy standing behind her. I follow his fingers, past his chunky watch and up his hairy arm to his t-shirt, which is covered in fluorescent yellow kitchen tables repeated in a pattern.

Who thought kitchen tables would make such a cool t-shirt?

I recognise the curly close-cropped hair. He's the hyperactive, knob-twiddling DJ from a few hours ago. We all shift up so he can squeeze in next to Cristina and as he sits down she rests her head on his shoulder. My head is on Hayden's shoulder. We're like mirror-image head-on-shoulder girls.

"You're a really good DJ," I say.

"Thanks," he says.

"The music you were playing was making me dance, well done."

"Thank you," he says.

"Isn't she sweet?" says Harper.

"What's your name?" I say.

He and Cristina share a look.

"Mikey Miles."

"Oh, yeah, of course you are, that's so cool!"

"See what I mean?" says Harper. "I have to stay in this country so I can hang out with this cuteness."

I don't think Mikey Miles heard, because he's snogging Cristina. Alejandro's eyes have rolled into the back of his head and he's murmuring incoherent nonsense.

"Is he okay?" I say.

"He always does this," says Hayden.

"I'm worried about him."

"Alejandro's like a homing pigeon. No matter how far away he goes he always comes back in the end."

"You been DJing for long?" I say to Mikey Miles.

His head is big and Cristina's is small, it's kind of weird.

"I've got to go," says Mikey Miles.

"But we've only just met!" I say.

"Back-to-back with Toth," says Hayden.

"What's back-to-back?" I say.

"It's when they take it in turns to play the tunes," says Cristina.

"Till close," says Mikey Miles.

"Who's Toth?"

"Anders Toth."

"Sounds like a vampire," I say.

"I'm gonna tell him you said that."

"Hey, guys, what if this flower pot is like an altar and if we say the magic words, and chant *Visa, Visa, Visa* then the God of Cigarettes is gonna give Harper a visa and she won't have to go back to Australia?"

"Errrrr . . ." says Hayden.

I hold out my hands and chant: "*Visa, Visa, Visa.*"

"You're such a weirdo,' says Harper, taking my hands and joining in: "*Visa, Visa, Visa.*" And then Hayden's doing it too, and holy crap, even Cristina and Mikey Miles are doing it and then random people from inside the club are doing it, there's like, twenty of us chanting *Visa* over and over, half the people have no idea why, and I'm going to remember this forever, this night, in the backyard of Paradise and I got like, twenty random people chanting *Visa* at the top of their voices.

And then we're back on the dance floor just as I'm coming up off the second half-pill. As they play back-to-back I think it's funny to make Hayden stand back-to-back with me. I don't think he agrees. On pills he's more quiet than he normally is and I'm louder. Or maybe we're in some strange symbiotic relationship where when one of us is loud when the other is quiet and vice versa. Anders Toth actually could be a vampire because his skin is really pale and when he smiles his teeth look extra-pointy.

I look up and there's Mikey Miles. To my left, there's Mikey Miles. To my right, there's Mikey Miles. Some guy with a striped t-shirt reaches out and hands me a cardboard Mikey Miles mask. I put it on my face and now *I'm* Mikey Miles. There must be thirty or forty people. We're all Mikey Miles!

Hayden sticks two fingers in his mouth and blows a piercing whistle, sweat dripping off his forehead. How does he do that? A hard, relentless beat electro-shocks our body, the rolling baseline urges us forward, making us work. My hands are in front of my face: up, down, left, right, up down, left, right. The beat disappears and Mikey Miles claps his hands. I think he's waving to us. And then he turns a knob and a blissful, tranquil chord lifts our hands into the air before the beat slams back in and we're careering down a mountain at a million miles an hour.

I look up. Hayden's smiling. There's Harper sling-ing her limbs as hard as she can. On the stage is Cris-tina, arms pumping, clutching a bottle of water. We're all here, we're all sharing *this*, and nothing can take it away from us. Every difference we have, every country we're from, our ages, our politics, our baggage, none of that matters any more. None of it ever mattered. I realise this now. I have to bottle this moment. I can't ever forget it.

I'm about to share this revelation with Hayden when someone turns on the lights. Whose idea was that? People are chanting for one more song. Mikey Miles and Anders Toth punch the air. A bouncer tells me to leave. Hayden appears with water bottles. We stand in the queue to the cloakroom, his arms around my tummy, locked together. The shaven-headed girl is still there but the clothes racks are nearly empty. I'm trying to focus on my phone but my pupils are too dilated. I ask Bearded Guy to read the screen. He tells me it says:

Dad – 15 Missed Calls.

The sky is bright blue. The doorman laughs and says, "Naughty girl."

"No I'm not!" I say, but Hayden drags me into an Uber.

"What's the time?"

"6.30 a.m."

"How did it get to be 6.30 a.m.?"

"Creeps up on you," says Hayden.

"I should be at Comic Con in three hours. And my dad thinks I'm dead."

Hayden shrugs his shoulders. Harper blows kisses from the pavement.

"Where's she going?"

"After party," says Hayden.

"What's after party?"

"Not today."

"I want to go. Promise you'll take me another time?" I say.

Hayden hands me some gum.

"Why would I want this?"

"You're gurning so hard you're going to chew your mouth off."

I touch the side of my cheek. My jaw muscles are solid and my teeth push against each other as hard as they can.

"I didn't notice!" I say.

I chew the gum and there's a minty explosion. It's wonderful.

The Uber beeps its horn at a group of clubbers walking down the middle of the alley. Alejandro is with them, singing something.

"Alejandro, you have to find your way home," I shout, but the car window is closed and he can't hear me.

"I've completely screwed up my life," I say.

The Uber swings back on to the main road and I blink as the sun shines in my eyes.

"But it was worth it," I say.

"It's always worth it," says Hayden.

"Yeah," I say, "It's always worth it."

19

I listen to the dial tone and brace myself. I'm the Incredible Hulk about to confront Tyrannus, a baddie who can drain your life force with his mind. That's what Dad does to me. It's not what he says, it's what he doesn't say: it's the heavy muscle ache I get when he glances at the toast crumbs I've spilt on the floor or the stomach-twisting sensation I feel when he wonders if we have any curries in the freezer and I've forgotten to buy them.

Plus, Tyrannus also drinks a magic elixir to keep him young. Well, there's Dad with his skinny dance-teacher-bit-on-the-side acting like he's drunk on it.

My dad is so blatantly Tyrannus.

I picture my tree-trunk arms smashing him round the face. BADOOM!

Just when it's about to go to voicemail he picks up.

"Scarlett?"

His voice cracks and so does my heart.

"Are you okay?" he says.

"I'm fine."

He exhales loudly, stifling a sob.

I don't ever think I've seen him cry. Not even at Mum's funeral. I don't think that's a good thing.

"I'm sorry," I repeat, my voice trembling.

"Are you coming home?" he says. It sounds like he's
doing the washing up. Or someone near him is.

"Later."

"Later, when?"

"Tonight."

"Now."

He says it like an order.

"I'm coming home later!"

"No, you're not, you're . . ."

I hang up and slam my phone on to Hayden's bedside table. One moment I want to hug him forever and
the next I never want to see him again.

BADOOM!

Well, as BADOOM as hanging up a phone gets.

I pick it back up and call Elliot, who doesn't answer.
I'm relieved.

Hayden appears, topless in tracksuit bottoms, holding two beers. His abs ripple as he hands me one. It's
ice cold, straight from the fridge, and the frozen, bitter-
sweet taste immediately takes the edge off the hollow,
wasted feeling that's been growing since the last UPS
began to wear off. It's midday and I've been awake for
twenty-eight hours. Half of me is ready to collapse and
the other is so wired I could do it all again.

Hayden's is a single bed, and as he slides in next to
me we can't help but be sandwiched together, skin on
skin, from head to toe. I bite his shoulder, lick his ear,
press my face into his hair and inhale. He rubs his
nose against mine and I shudder as I fall through his
golden-brown irises into some kind of vortex where
everything is weightless and time stands still. He kisses
my lips, my neck, then my whole body, slowly and
carefully, as if he doesn't want to miss an inch. There's

no one in the house now. No drug-crazed students are going to ruin this moment.

An hour later I'm watching his sleeping head rise and fall on my chest. I list all the human bodies that have ever been close to me. Big, soft cuddles from Mum. Brittle, tense cuddles from Dad. Elliot and his slightly pathetic hand-holding thumb-rubbing thing. This is a million times better than all of that combined.

I wish Elliot could see us now, so he could know how wrong he is. So he can realise what a judgemental prick he is. As if hearing my harsh thoughts, Hayden stirs. I stroke his hair and I pull him tighter towards me and wrap my legs round his. It's like we're two puzzle pieces and we've finally been put together.

We wake up late afternoon, wash and shower and now I lace up my Converses as Hayden stands over his iMac working with a music creation program which I don't understand at all. The bottom of the screen contains a row of ten digital faders like the ones on his decks. The rest of it is full of random green and orange rectangles like the ship's computer on *Star Trek: The Next Generation*. He taps the spacebar. A bass drum plays, *thump, thump, thump, thump*. He pauses it, plays with the mouse for a while and does it again. The bass drum becomes slower and deeper and he nods his head.

"I'll . . . see you later," I say.

He grunts. I'll miss his scrunched-up duvet at the end of the bed. His iPhone and his burner phone on the bedside table. His jeans on the floor, the pile of bank notes, proceeds of last night's dealings, spilling out of his pocket. I'll miss all the *himness*.

"See you later," I say. A snare kicks in, *ticka-takcka-ticka-tacka*.

I step forward and kiss him on the cheek.

"Bye!" I say.

He doesn't look up. I walk downstairs and open the door.

What was that about? Is that it? Have we gone from one hundred percent to zero in five seconds?

The floorboards creak. I turn and he pulls me tight, pushing me up against the wall, kissing and groping me and for a second I think we're going to do it again, right there with the front door open and the whole street watching. He places his hands on my cheeks and presses his forehead to mine.

"I feel like making music again."

My cheeks flush.

"Last night. You reminded me why I do what I do. Why I need to make music. Why never stopping dancing is the most important thing."

This isn't jokey Hayden. This is intense Hayden. I like intense Hayden. My smile is so wide my cheeks are going to rip apart. He sticks his head out the door, as if he's about to announce it to the whole street.

"It's all about the music," he says.

"It's all about the music," I say.

"And making the people dance."

When I reach the end of his road my phone pings. It's him!

You are an angel.

I don't even think about it. I just write the three words and hit send.

I love you.

Is this a bit soon?
Is this a bit crazy?
The three dots appear, then disappear.
Have I done something completely stupid?
I love you too.
I squeal out loud, right there in the street.
I know why he spent a week in his room in the dark
on a comedown.
He didn't have any love in his life.
Anyone can deal with anything when you have love.
I get this now.

20

Dad and Jennifer sit across the kitchen table like two cops at the police station. I'm distracted by the unusual smell of a home-made curry. Unless my dad has discovered a way to download cookery skills straight into his brain like in the Matrix, it must have been made by Jennifer. I think it's Thai, because the sauce is green and there's a packet of supermarket lemongrass on the kitchen counter, next to what looks like freshly unpacked shopping: organic porridge, spirulina powder, a basil plant, together with a pestle and mortar. Jennifer's wearing jeans and a camisole, exposing her slender shoulders.

I was all set to be sorry but now I'm here I'm not sorry at all.

"I stopped him from calling the police," says Jennifer.

Dad's wearing a t-shirt that reads: *I'm an accountant. To save time let's assume I'm always right.* For once he's not cheerful, his face like one of those Ancient Greek tragic-face masks. My intestines knot themselves so tight I don't think I'll ever be able to undo them.

"Um . . . thanks?" I say.

"He was out of his mind but I told him that you were okay," says Jennifer.

"How did you know?" I blurt. "I could have been murdered."

"Were you okay?"

"Obviously. Yes."

It's 8 p.m. I need to sleep. For a thousand years if possible.

"What your dad wanted to know was where you were. It's okay to be angry, we just wanted you to make a call." Jennifer's eyes are bright green. They cast a spell on me, as if she's saying, "I understand you better than you understand yourself."

She must have stayed the night, I realise.

"Where were you?" says Dad.

My face is hot. I have officially lost patience with my cheeks going red. I wonder if they've invented a drug to stop it happening.

"You weren't at Elliot's, because I called his dad."

"I know what it looks like and I know what you think but I was fine, nothing bad happened and I'm not going to mess up my exams."

Dad looks at me with such disrespect I want to shove the table so hard it chops him in half.

There's no way I can ever explain to him what I have experienced this weekend.

"I'm seventeen years old."

"I was right to ground you. I got conned. Even Elliott got conned. You conned us all!"

"I didn't know I was going to . . ."

"I *knew* this was going to happen."

Jennifer throws him a sideways glance and he looks down at his lap.

"Your father might be open to your going and

103

staying somewhere else. He just wants your communication to be clear."

Hi Dad, I'd like to go out and do industrial strength pills.

"I was safe," I say. I believe it.

"From now on, you're under curfew – you're not out past seven," says Dad.

"He's like this because he's scared," says Jennifer.

"This is an interrogation," I say. "It's Good Cop. Bad Cop."

Dad exhales. He stands up and stirs the curry absent-mindedly.

"The thing that bothers me most is the lie," he says.

"Jesus!" I shout. "One thing! One thing I've done wrong!"

I'm sick of being the good daughter who's there with those shitty meals when he comes home. I'm sick of hanging out with Elliot and Bad Ben and no one else. I'm sick of my shit life.

"I have a boyfriend . . . you've never met him . . . I was with him," I say.

Have a boyfriend. Did I actually say those words?

"Since when do you have a boyfriend!" says Dad, his voice shrill and squeaky. The sound is so odd that I laugh and Jennifer laughs too.

"Someone from college?"

"No. He's a musician. And don't act so surprised, it had to happen sooner or later."

"Why didn't you mention him before?"

"Why didn't you mention Jennifer before?"

"Having a private life is healthy," says Jennifer.

Why the hell is she sitting there talking to me like

she's my actual mother? Who is she to play the family counsellor when it's only the second time I've met her?

"Having a boyfriend is a big thing . . ." says Dad.

I'm blown away that he actually believes I would want to talk to him about my love life.

"So is Jennifer living with us now?" I say.

Dad scratches his head.

"She *is*?" I say.

"Not yet. But very soon. I said she could stay with us while she looks for a new place. She's been given unexpected notice on her flat."

My mouth hangs open.

"I was hoping he would have told you," says Jennifer.

"I tried to . . . that night you . . . But you were already out of the door."

"You've had weeks . . ."

"I know."

We've reached an impasse. For what feels like minutes there's only the rhythmic bubbling of the pot.

"I know that me coming to live here is a big change," says Jennifer. "And I think that we all could have handled this better. I would have rather come . . . after your exams . . . when you were at university. Or after I'd had some time to get to know you. I wouldn't be here if I wasn't in a tight spot. But I thought we could use the opportunity to make some positive changes for all of us."

She thinks she's Oprah Winfrey.

"The first thing I did was tell your father that a seventeen-year-old girl shouldn't be cooking and cleaning like a slave. And that you both shouldn't be eating all that unnourishing food."

I fold my arms. My shoulders hurt.

"I thought we could try doing some activities together. All of us. Get to know each other. Like yoga."

I catch Dad's eye. He knows that I clock the ridiculousness of that statement. "Cut down the unnourishing food. Try some yoga," I repeat.

Dad suppresses a laugh. For a second I almost feel close to him.

"Aren't you going to say something?" says Jennifer.

The kitchen is spotless. Someone's scrubbed the skirting boards. The coffee drips on the front of the washing machine have gone. Someone's even cleaned the grease from the dials on the front of the cooker. It's like Jennifer's arrived and taken over my jobs. So why do I resent her so much?

"It's okay, I guess."

If I agree I might be able to get out of here and go to bed.

"You're still curfewed," says Dad. "You live in this house, you play by my rules. When you move out, you can do what you like."

When you move out . . .

Dad pushes up his spectacles.

"We're almost at the finish line . . . you're almost free."

Finish line. Free. He wants me gone. Scarlett out. Jennifer in.

"I'm doing my best, Dad."

"Glad to hear it."

What if my best isn't good enough? What if studies aren't as important as everyone says? What if life is about experiencing connection with another human being, not pieces of paper with grades on them?

Jennifer stands up and turns off the heat on the hob. She takes three bowls out of the cupboard and ladles some curry into each.

"You're so like your mum, sometimes I wonder if there's any of me in you," says Dad.

I'm not like my mum. I'm *Scarlett*. I just want to be *Scarlett*.

Jennifer places a bowl in front of me. The watery green liquid is full of wrinkly beige things. I think they're tofu. I finish half of it and stand up.

"I'd like to meet him," says Dad, attempting some kind of reconciliation.

I'm so disgusted I don't reply.

3 weeks later

21

My hand and wrist ache. I've spent two and a half hours writing so hard my fingers are twisted with cramp. At the end it didn't even feel like me writing anymore, it was like some spirit flowed into the top of my head and down through my arm and *made* me write. Was it a guardian angel or a life-sucking devil? I have no idea. But I did it. I guess that's something. It's over. I'm free.

Now I want to celebrate, but I have no friends. I haven't spoken to Elliot or Bad Ben since not-turning-up-to-Comic-Con. I have to give them credit for their ability to avoid me. It's easy to ignore my messages. But here, at college? We all sat the same English exam. As I queued for the hall, they were nowhere to be seen. Once I got inside, there they were. Bad Ben in the front row, Elliot at the far right by the wall. The moment the exam was over they disappeared. They must have run home, literally. It's like I've got the plague.

Some people are going to the Heath to smoke. Some to the off licence. Some to Costa. I don't want to be with any of them, so it's just me and the policeman. Up close he's younger than I realised, with brown hair and blotchy cheeks. He seems weighed down by his radio, handcuffs, baton, taser and whatever else he's got strapped on, like he's wearing a rubbish version of Batman's utility belt.

"I've just finished my last exam," I say to him.

"Congratulations."

"Do you want to go for a drink?"

"I don't think so."

Why did I say that? How desperate am I?

I asked at the office and they told me Elliot was in. I've been loitering in the corridors and hanging around his locker like some moping dog. Yesterday I saw Bad Ben in the distance, walking towards the Heath clutching a big bag of KFC. I shouted his name but he was too far ahead. I picture him and Elliot hiding in a bush, praying I don't spot them, while I drift along the footpaths like some jilted lover. I've messaged Elliott ten times. I can see he's read them all, but hasn't replied. Elliot and Bad Ben have just finished Art. They should be here! I *need* to talk to Elliot! I *need* to restore some balance! He's my best friend!

My phone vibrates. It's Hayden. *He* messages me from the moment he wakes up to the moment we go to sleep. Even when he went clubbing last week without me; even when he was coming down. I lived it with him via WhatsApp and sad-cat GIFS. At least I don't have to worry about him.

I know the difference between Sainsbury's and Cadbury's.

Today, he's talking about premium chocolate.
What?
Sainsbury's Taste the Difference tastes of coconut.
You're kidding me.
The other tastes of tree bark.

How do you know what tree bark tastes like?
Do you think I would make a good wine taster?
No.
There's this coffee shop near me that adds chilli flakes to chocolate.
No!
Have you tried it?
No.
They add garlic to chocolate as well. We need to stop chocolate being destroyed. WE NEED TO SAVE CHOCOLATE!

I never knew falling in love would mean spending hours and hours writing stupid messages. It's an unexpected surprise and definitely very cool. In fact, it keeps me going. I write:

I just had a revelation. You and me. We're both weirdos. We don't fit in anywhere apart from with each other . . .

He doesn't reply instantly. The three dots appear, reappear, appear, reappear.

How dare you call me a weirdo.

I've upset him. I've destroyed it.

Only joking, of course we are.

Thank God.

Except can I call myself a misfit now I've found someone I fit with?

The policeman catches my eye. He knows I'm chatting with a drug dealer. Hayden is right to be obsessed with the feds.

So by the way, it's officially holiday time!
Woo hoo! Congratulations!

Fourteen years of school, over. It feels like such an anti-climax.

Come over right now and I promise I'll change that. ☺

A couple of times a week I went out to "revise" in Starbucks Archway but actually to meet Hayden. We made out in the same corner we sat in when we first realised we liked each other. We were good: we even resisted the temptation to lock ourselves in the toilet.

I've got something to do.

Come over!

I have to sort something first.

What do you have to do that's more important than coming over?

It feels so good when he tells me to come over.

I'll pay for an Uber. We can listen to my new mix.

I can come tomorrow. I just need to sort this one thing. Also my dad wants to take me for dinner.

I need to see you!

I need to see you too.

Miss you.

Tears well up. I force the feelings down.

Miss you, too.

While I've been messaging, home-time has begun. A bunch of Somali boys talk loudly in Arabic. Three girls from the year below, one Vietnamese, one bleach blonde, the other curly brunette, sit on the wall behind the policeman, like some kind of manufactured pop band. A young Bengali girl in a headscarf. A tall white guy with a shaved head. An Afro-Caribbean boy with a comb sticking out of his Afro. Then Aya, wearing a pleated beige skirt with the letter G patterned all over it, a black long-sleeved top and several lots of pearls round her neck. There're too many people. I can't move. But then I spot it – a glimpse of a leather coat, a shoulder squeezing through the crowd. I push myself forward, reach out and grab his arm.

"Hey."

"Hey,' says Bad Ben, turning around. "Damn," he says as he sees me.

"Finally!"

He looks at the pavement, disappointed.

"Where's Elliot?"

Bad Ben puffs out his cheeks and blows through them.

"You guys owe me an explanation!"

I fold my arms and stand there.

"Okay! Not here though."

He sets off and I follow him.

22

We walk towards the Heath in silence. I want to put my hands on his chubby cheeks and shout, "Spit it out, you fat bastard." Why did me and Elliot let him join our gang?

"Have you done any more porn pictures recently?" I say.

"I don't draw porn!"

He's stooped-over, as if he's following a secret trail of marks on the ground. Since exams started he's grown a bum-fluff goatee which I think he thinks is manly but makes him look younger. Today he's holding his shiny black portfolio case and although it's very warm he's still wearing his black leather trench coat. The overall effect is *I'm on my way to shoot up a school*.

"I decided to turn her into a comic," he says.

"Seriously?"

"I wanted something to do over the summer. Plus, there's loads of comic book meet-ups."

"Comic Con."

"Not that commercial crap. I'm talking meet-ups with people who draw their own comics. Not super-hero bollocks. Sorry, I know you like super-hero bollocks."

"I don't think about the bollocks on super-heroes."

"Bollocks on super-heroes would be massive."

I frown.

"Anyway," he says. "You should come to one. The level of storytelling is . . . superior."

Now we're climbing Parliament Hill. A man jogs across the grassland with his kite trailing behind him, hoping to get it off the ground. As we pass him it gets tangled on a tree branch.

"I realised that if I'm going to be an animator, I'm going to be making art for other people, so I wanted to do something for myself. And yes, my style is sexy and I like drawing girls with cleavage, but it's not porn, it's me."

"And what's she going to do in this comic?"

"I'm thinking of basing it on my life."

"And how much experience do you have with girls? Apart from me?"

He doesn't respond and we climb the rest of Parliament Hill in silence. I lead him to the bench where Elliot and I made a pact to marry if we got to thirty and we were still single.

"My mum was good at painting," I say. "Really good. But she stopped. I never understood why."

"She had you."

"What's that supposed to mean?"

"I don't know. You get busy when you have a kid?"

"She was a housewife. She did nothing. Apart from clean."

The Overground train trundles along behind the athletics track. Just beyond a giant crane lifts an enormous concrete pre-fab block.

"It's really nice here," says Bad Ben.

"Congratulations. You've been here two years and you've only just realised."

"Scarlett, stop biting my head off."

"I'm not!"

Bad Ben runs his hands through his hair and ties it into a ponytail.

"So . . ." he says.

"I've sent him loads of grovelling apology texts. I've humiliated myself."

"He says what you did was 'unforgivable'."

"Unforgivable?"

"After he told you about the costume. He went out of his way to cheer you up. He totally manipulated his dad into paying all this money. He got you ungrounded. He's been so worried about you."

"Worried?"

"It was a dick move, Scarlett."

I pull out my phone, find the message and shove it into Bad Ben's hand.

I feel awful about what happened. I have to explain. I need to make this up to you. I'm sorry.

"*Unforgivable means it doesn't matter what you say, it's still unforgivable.*"

"And do you agree?"

"We don't really get what's going on in your head right now."

"You sided with him?"

I cross my arms, then re-cross them, then scratch at my wrists.

"We want the old Scarlett back."

"When are you going to realise the old Scarlett is dead! When your fucking mum dies it changes you forever!"

Bad Ben squirms in his seat.

"Stop biting my head off, please."

"I'm just saying HOW I FEEL!"

I scream the last words at the top of my voice.

The concrete block inches its way between two thick steel girders. I remember when that building site was a decaying nineteenth century hospital building infested with rats and pigeons. It was a write-off, but people still protested because they didn't want an ugly skyscraper to replace it.

"I think . . . I think I don't like comics anymore. I don't *want* to dress up as a super-hero, I don't *want* to go to comic conventions. Comics are like, *dead* to me."

"Why didn't you tell him that?"

"Because I didn't realise it until this second!"

My words hang in the air.

"The Hulk never wins. No matter how many bad guys he destroys, the government will always want to put him in prison. He's never going to be able to tame the monster within. They just keep the story going on and on forever so they can make more money. There's never a happy ending."

Some weird gust of wind carries a shout from the building site all the way over to us. Or maybe I imagined it.

"Can't he just talk to me for five minutes?"

"No."

"I have a reason, you know, I didn't purposely blank him."

"Yeah?"

"I was with Hayden."

"The drug dealer guy?"

"He's not just a drug dealer guy."

I turn towards Bad Ben and lift my feet onto the bench.

"So, you gonna be a druggie now?"

"This isn't about drugs!"

"He's a dealer, so dealers must be druggies."

"Have you ever taken a pill? Have you ever been raving?"

Bad Ben says nothing. He knows that I know he doesn't have a clue.

"It's like, this whole *world* has opened up – in my darkest hour – which I never knew existed."

"You've lost me, Scarlett."

Beyond Bad Ben, a sycamore tree stands alone on the hillside, thick branches unfolding into a graceful mesh of twigs and leaves. It's so strong and ancient and beautiful . . . and *sad*.

I realise I'm never going to sit on this bench ever again.

"Elliot likes you, Scarlett."

"I know."

"He *likes* you."

"Yeah."

"*Likes*."

"He likes Aya."

"He used to."

"He *likes* Aya. For ever. Everyone knows it."

"He was going to ask you out at Comic Con."

"What?"

"He was going to tell you he was in love with you."

"No!"

"It was the shaming account. It confirmed it. He realised that he was creating this whole fantasy about Aya in his head. That he goes for the unobtainable."

"Hello? I told him that like a million times."

"He said that what he fantasised about in his head. He already had. With you."

I close my eyes.

"He's still doing it. He's decided he likes me the moment I become unavailable."

"He didn't know you were with Druggie Guy when he decided this."

"But he knew I'd met someone–"

"He decided this before Druggie Guy. Comic Con was supposed to be the big romantic day you got together."

My fists and shoulders tense. Bad Ben stands up.

"I think I'm going to take a vow of chastity. Human relationships confuse the hell out of me," he says.

"I just need a best friend right now."

Bad Ben watches me for a while. Then he reaches into his art folder and takes out a piece of paper.

"I drew this."

It's a picture of Elliot, me and Bad Ben inside Elliot's bedroom. Elliot is strumming a guitar and Bad Ben has made him look like a pop star with his hair drooping over his face and his lips pouting as if he's singing a song. Bad Ben lies on the sofa, stuffing an entire pizza into his mouth. I'm sitting cross-legged on the carpet swigging from a bottle of vodka, my eyes crossed and spinning. We're all drawn Bad-Ben-sexy-style, with giant eyes. Elliot and Bad Ben have muscles and my breasts are three times their real size.

I hand it back to him, but he doesn't take it.

"It's yours."

"Really?"

"I did one for all of us."

"Thanks."

I look at it more closely.

"It's nothing like us . . . but it totally captures our essence."

Bad Ben smiles. He's really pleased.

"We're never going to hang out like this ever again, are we?" I say. "It's over, isn't it?"

"I hope not. I mean. I think I was secretly hoping to bump into you today. So I could give it to you."

"Because you knew it was your last chance."

After we say goodbye I watch him disappear down the hill and into the trees and I use every last ounce of energy I have not to cry.

23

"If they called a restaurant *Mi Casa*, they'd want it to feel like home, right? Then why does it look so unwelcoming?"

A queue ten people long has spilled out on to the street. Outside the restaurant diners sit round tiny metal tables on which wine coolers fight for space with small plates of tapas, wine glasses and ashtrays. Everyone talks loud and loose and even though it's Wednesday it feels like the weekend. Dad and Jennifer sit on stools at the bar, Jennifer's backless dress exposing her bony shoulders. My phone is clamped to my ear.

"Oh my God she's dressed for Prom and I'm wearing jeans."

"Don't they do those nice little bowls of chorizo?"

"I don't care. I can't go in. I wonder if this is the night she actually moves in?"

Elliot feels like dying when he goes to restaurants with his parents. I get what he means now.

"See if they do those little bowls of chorizo."

"This is supposed to do the most *Spanish* Spanish food in London. This is supposed to be a reward. Why do I feel like it's an attack?"

"You'll change your mind when you start eating."

"I don't want to eat! I want to be with you."

"Even I would blow me out for chorizo."

"Why am I so ungrateful, Hayden? Why can't I just accept this gift? Why does it feel like he's going through the motions?"

"Beware of Greeks bearing gifts."

I expect Dad to turn and look at me but he doesn't. He's deep in conversation with her. What do they talk about? Next to him is a guy in a pink shirt and next to Jennifer is an old woman in a flowery dress. They haven't even saved me a seat!

I walk up the road and into a small square.

"The price of the restaurant is in inverse proportion to how much he cares. He's compensating."

"I don't understand what that means, but it doesn't sound good."

"Plus, Jennifer's a health fascist who wants to turn me all yoga-vegetariany. How can someone pretend to be so nice but actually they want to control and dominate your free will by making you eat tofu curry?"

"We eat Wotsits for breakfast at my house."

Two homeless guys are playing table tennis, their dirty backpacks next to them on the ground.

"My life is like living in a washing machine on spin cycle," I say.

"So, come and live with me."

"Yeah, right."

"There's something wrong when you're not with me."

"I know."

"I just sit on my bed fantasising about you."

"Hayden!"

"It's true!"

Now a police helicopter hovers above me.

"It's too noisy here."

"Come and live with me. We'll have a summer of love. I'll look after you. You're free now. Even your dad agrees with that."

"Serious?"

"Serious."

"What would I tell him?"

"Whatever you want."

He is serious. Oh my God.

"This is nuts. I should go. He's trying to be generous. Or something."

"You know what's really nuts? Every second I spend when I'm not in your presence."

I buy a quarter bottle of vodka and take the Tube home. I auto-direct my Dad's number to voicemail. I grab his posh business luggage from his wardrobe. I connect my phone to my crappy Bluetooth speaker and play Hayden's latest mix at full volume.

He tells me *I'm* the reason he's mixing again.

At least someone sees the value in me.

If the last month has taught me anything, it's *trust yourself.* Even if Elliot, Bad Ben, Jennifer and Dad disagree.

I pack my underwear, jeans, t-shirts, a raincoat, just the basics.

What will I do for money?

What will I do *full stop?*

What will happen when I'm meant to go to Leeds?

I have to trust. Trust that love is the answer.

A Latin house track plays. Wooden blocks counter the rhythm with their *ticka-tacka-ticka-tacka* and a sped-up Spanish woman sings: *Tengo todo el amor que necesito.*

I have all the love I need.

The next beat mixes in, more aggressive, a big bass drum going *boom boom boom*.

I take a massive swig of the vodka.

I love this music and I love him.

I want to dance with the one person who makes life make sense.

Is that a good definition of love?

Tingles run down my spine and fizziness fills my body.

Love makes life feel like it makes sense.

The rat-a-tat snare builds and builds and then the beat drops and I punch my hand in the air and scream.

24

Dear Dad,

I know you will be freaking out right now and I'm sorry I did a no-show again.

I'm not going to go all silent like last time and Jennifer won't have to stop you calling the police.

When I'm with you for some reason I can't express what I really think so I'm writing it down instead.

I've gone to live with my boyfriend.

I know that me moving out was supposed to happen in October. I guess it's good for all of us it's happened earlier. I know that the responsibility of having me to yourself was something you never wanted and I hope that this will be a relief now that you and Jennifer will have the time and space you need to be happy.

I know I won't cook for you anymore but Jennifer is a much better cook and is much healthier so that's a good thing too.

The thing is, I'm changing. What I thought I wanted isn't what I wanted. Life is opening new doors and showing me new things.

I always thought of our family as the solar system. Mum was the sun and me and you were planets that revolve around her. She loved being the sun, and making sure we lived in a beautiful, safe, clean, loving space. That's what she needed to do. Just like you need to do your job and tell everyone how great an accountant you are. And I need to . . . I dunno, I'm working that one out.

I'm a fake sham sun and you and I both know it.

I will be fine. I am happy.

When Mum died I thought I was cursed.

Now I feel like the luckiest person in the world.

That's why I'm moving out.

We're aliens to each other, that's just the truth, it's a bloody sad truth but there we go.

But I wish you the best, I really do.

May all your spreadsheet columns add up correctly.

May you share many great tofu curries with your hot girlfriend.

You can cancel my allowance if you want.

Hayden will look after me while I find my feet.

I'll find a way.

Don't worry.

I love you.

Scarlett

2 months later

25

I hurry down the alley, over crushed cans and polystyrene kebab containers and past the shuttered bingo hall, its wall plastered with mouldy posters of quiz nights and cheesy comedians, all long since passed. It stinks of piss. Two tatty figures sit opposite each other in the fire exit alcove. One, a young girl covered in acne, looks up and tenses like a startled cat. Her hooded companion grabs their rucksack and shoves it on top of whatever they're doing. The end of a pipe pokes out from underneath. I look away and hurry past.

The alley widens into a street and now I'm walking next to a multi-storey car park, its walls covered in garish bulbous graffiti, most long since defaced by amateur artists and their shitty little tags.

Finally, I see it: *Ink Positive,* in ornate red 3D letters. Pallid neon light shines through frosted glass windows. I press the bell and there's an uncomfortable twenty seconds before I'm buzzed in.

The place is immaculate. The bright yellow walls are hung with framed prints of Hindu Gods, geometric patterns, Harry Potter coats of arms, Gothic cartoons, tiger faces and more. Two large black leather chairs with matching footrests are at one side and opposite to what look like two massage tables. A small mixed-heritage man in a striped t-shirt reclines on the nearest chair, his feet perched on the footrest.

"Hi. I'm Scarlett?"

He sighs.

"Cristina said I would be coming?"

"Who?" he says, frowning.

"Cristina – she said that you would . . ."

"What are you talking about?"

My cheeks heat up.

"Only joking," he says and springs off the chair and shakes my hand. "Just playing with ya."

He scoops a piece of printed paper from the tray of a large black laser printer on the desk. It must be the stencil. I shiver with nerves.

"Any friend of Cristina is a friend of mine. I even open on a Monday when we're normally closed and wait for random people she knows, even when it looks like they're no-shows."

I glance up at the clock on the wall. 3 p.m. I should have been there at two.

"Sorry. I woke up late. Thank you. Sorry."

"I remember when I used to go to bed at four every morning," he says.

I smile weakly.

"Eat-sleep-rave-repeat . . ." I say, by way of explanation. He nods.

We actually went out raving three days ago, and last night we just binge-watched The Flash until 4 a.m., then when we woke up we just binge-watched more. There's steam coming off my cheeks, I'm sure of it. I don't know why I wanted him to think I went out last night. Maybe I was trying to impress him. He turns and types the price into the card machine. I punch in my pin, the machine beeps, he hands me the receipt, nods towards the leather chair and I sit down.

First he places the stencil on the inside of my left forearm, moving it around until I tell him it's where I want it. He puts on a pair of disposable gloves and even though there's no hair on the skin just there he shaves it anyway. Then he washes with soapy water and dries it, applies a deodorant, then grabs my wrist and rests it face-up on the side table. He is very calm and steady, resting the stencil on my forearm, pushing into its centre with two fingers before smoothing it out to either side with rhythmic movements. When he's satisfied it's adhered to the skin he carefully peels back the paper.

"Are you ready?" he says.

We both look at the tattoo gun, all polished stainless steel, ugly nobs, thick screws and intimidating bulbous modules. There's no escaping that it looks like a torture device.

"It won't take long," he says, winking.

I sit back in the chair, my left arm out at a right angle. The gun switches on. It's like a dentist's drill, but higher pitched and whinier. I gasp as the first sharp pricks pierce my skin. I close my eyes and remember why I'm here.

26

It was dark when I arrived in Hayden's road. My legs felt like balloons, my breath was shallow and the hand that wasn't pulling my suitcase was shaking so much it was slapping my thigh. I was about half-way down when I passed a lady in a hijab returning home with her two young boys. I slowed and watched as she opened the door and they took off their shoes before running up the stairs. As she turned to close it, she caught my eye and I tripped over my suitcase, grazing my palms as I hit the pavement. I stood up as the door slammed shut and everything became strange: the kerb, the houses and cars looked both familiar and unusual, as if half of me had just stepped into a parallel dimension.

I knocked on Hayden's door. His lights were off and the curtains were still drawn. A pile of scrap wood lay next to a dirty mattress in the overgrown front garden.

The whole place felt empty. The whole universe felt empty.

I'd switched off my phone because I didn't want to deal with a million missed calls from Dad. I turned it on in case Hayden had left me a message. There was nothing – from anyone.

The strangeness intensified, as if the street had

disconnected from the rest of London and was gliding away over the M25 towards the English Channel.

The door opened and there he was. Unshaven and beardy, brown eyes alight, thin lips smiling. He pulled me towards him. My arms felt huge around his bony torso. He whispered in my ear, "This is best decision I've ever made." We squeezed each other so tight I thought we would be joined forever, like an amoeba reproducing itself, except in reverse.

When I stepped into his bedroom I screamed. His tiny single bed was gone, replaced with a brand-new double.

"This arrived yesterday before I knew you were coming. I'm psychic, right?" I kicked off my shoes and jumped up and down on it, giggling like a little girl. The mattress was firm, not like the lumpy painful thing he had before.

"Took me five hours to make that shit."

He showed me a long thin cut down inside of his right arm and pointed to a screw sticking out of one of the posts.

"I don't think that's supposed to be there."

"It's so new it's like I don't want to get it dirty."

"What's the point in spending the best part of a grand on a bed if you can't have sweaty sex on it straight away?"

I laughed.

He took my suitcase, squeezing himself between the bedframe and the wall, and put it into his wardrobe. His room was all bed now with barely any space to stand.

"We're gonna be living in a penthouse flat soon, I can feel it."

"You're talking like we're married."

I blushed. He snorted. Then *he* blushed – the only time I've ever seen him do so. He reached underneath the bed and produced a four-pack of Budweiser.

"Next best thing to champagne . . ."

We sat on the mattress, pillows plumped to support our backs, and drank.

"I can't believe you've got me into beer," I said.

His lips pursed and he didn't reply.

"What?"

"You reminded me of my dad. He gave me my first beer."

"He sounds pretty cool."

Hayden took a deep swig, gulping loudly.

"I dunno."

"What?"

"My dad is possibly the biggest arsehole that ever existed. And I know in the history of the world there have been a lot of arseholes, like Hitler, and Stalin, but I'm not exaggerating.

"What did he do?"

"It's not so much what he did, it's what he didn't do. Didn't speak. Didn't look at me. Unless he was angry, when his neck would go red and he would threaten to shove my head through the wall if I didn't shut up . . . He's just . . ."

"What?"

"Doesn't matter."

"Why did he give you beer?"

"Me and my friends went bowling. He took us . . . He bought us beer. He thought he was being the big man, initiating us into adult ways . . . I guess you could call it the only thing he did that was even a little bit okay."

"What happened?"

"Why are you making me talk about this?"

"I haven't made you talk about anything."

"You're doing that thing. When you look at me. Make me feel funny. Make words come out of my mouth."

"You don't have to talk about him if you don't want to."

Hayden squeezed his empty beer can and chucked it into the bin in the corner, spraying a few drops on the new bedspread.

"I hate him."

There was something about the way he said those words. A river of sadness flowed through me. I cried: big heaving sobs erupting from nowhere and all I could do was bury my face in his chest. I cried for this boy who hates his dad, who lives in this run-down house, sleeps in this double bed that's far too big, with thousands of pounds' worth of drugs in his desk drawer, living with a bunch of international misfits.

"It's okay," he said. "It is what it is."

"Sorry. I don't know what happened," I said.

"I guess tears are better for sheets than sweat."

"I hate my dad too," I said.

But he didn't reply. He just pulled me towards him and kissed me, and soon we forgot about everything.

27

My wrist is on fire. How long is this going to go on for? Why don't they use anesthetic like dentists?

Mini-bolts of lightning shoot up to my shoulders.

Maybe he's trying to hurt me as much as possible. He's a sadist tattoo artist. He only does girls, alone. The whole stencil thing was an elaborate ruse. He wants to destroy my life by tattooing *I'm a Nazi!* on me.

I remember the boy and girl outside with their dirty faces and desperate hands, and I imagine them as little babies, held and fed and cuddled. Surely, once, they were loved by a mum or dad? Now look where they are, alone, trying to smoke drugs in an alley.

Why is it everywhere I look I see pain?

Don't take yourself so seriously, Scarlett! You're on a comedown. It's day three, the worst day. You're low on energy. You're foggy-brained. You're really really *sad*.

Hayden says *when you're on a comedown, don't listen to your thoughts. When you're on a comedown, sit next to me, eat pizza and watch Netflix, drink beer. In a few days' time you'll be ready to go again.*

He told me what footballers say after every game: *We're happy we won. We're upset we lost. Next week we go again.*

And that's what we do. We drink beer. We binge-watch show after show after show after show. I put my head on his chest and listen to his heartbeat. He strokes the inside of my palm with his thumb. I look into his eyes and step into a part of life which is deeper and more real than everything else.

Comedowns are only bad if you don't know how to manage them.

He's managing them fine now I'm around. He's off doing his thing, unloading the last of the UPS. Or he's sitting in front of his Mac. He's bought a new pair of expensive headphones so he can make music without disturbing me.

But I don't think I can manage them without him.

I've only been out of the house for a few hours and it's already too much, the light is too bright, every sound hurts my brain.

Life is just *harsh*.

I need to get through the next hour.

I need to get through the rest of today.

And then, on Friday, we go again.

28

I talked about her.

I was looking at his poster of the silhouetted DJ behind the decks, arms pumping the air. Behind him multicoloured lasers shoot upwards and outwards. In front of him hundreds of dancers reach to the sky. The image made me feel like I did when I took that first UPS. I had this longing to be there – feel that feeling all over again.

I swung round to Hayden, and said, "My mum died a year ago."

I have no idea why I said those words but for some reason that DJ poster, my feelings, and my mum were connected.

Hayden lay on the bed holding a Budweiser. He eyed the slit in the can as if he was searching for something tiny inside.

"I know," he said.

"How?"

"It's our freaky mind-meld thing."

"Serious?"

"Also, you never talk about your mum but always talk about your dad. Didn't take Sherlock Holmes . . ."

He turned over on to his side to face me.

"Yeah . . . well . . . she did . . ."

"What happened?"

It was like he turned on a tap that had been rusted shut for a year. I became like a fireman's hose with no firemen to hold it, water gushing, flapping wildly, spraying everyone and anything.

I told him about Mum's brown frizzy curls, overly-small green eyes. How she liked to wear dungarees long before they came into fashion. About her small, delicate 'artist's hands' and how she was crazy good at making stuff.

Once she helped me build a model of Trafalgar Square for class. She bought me a square of wood which we painted grey to look like concrete. She showed me how to draw a cross-shaped base on card which we could cut out and fold to make plinths. When I made a Nelson statue and got the hat wrong, she took a knife and with one quick trim made it look just like the one in real life. She showed me a simple way to make mini-tourists out of plasticine and even cut out tiny cardboard cameras and threaded string through them to go around their necks. She could have got a job on Blue Peter.

Then one night when she was having a bath and I should have been in bed, I got really angry because the plinths looked wonky and I ripped up them all up. I don't know why I cared so much, but I did. It *had* to be perfect, it *had* to be amazing. Mum didn't even bat an eyelid. She just sat with me patiently as we remade them the next evening. Trouble was, it meant I missed the handing-in date. When I gave it to Mrs Anderson, the art teacher, it looked stunning. She told me that deadlines are deadlines and there was no way I was going to get an extension. She said that I needed to learn an important lesson about timekeeping. All Dad could say was, "It was a stupid thing to do." Which it was, I get that. "It was only an art project. You'll forget about it next week." But it was more than an art project. When I told Mum she just looked me in the eye and nodded, and I knew she understood exactly why I did what I did.

"I think I've only ever met two people who get me. Her and you," I said. Hayden sat there, his attention on me like a spotlight.

I told him about the day I found myself walking, alone, through the central corridor in school. Everyone else was in lessons. The headmistress spotted me and barked my name. I had no excuse to tell her. I couldn't explain why I wasn't in English or where I thought I was going. It was like waking up from a dream.

But instead of bollocking me she put her hand on my shoulder and told me that Mum had been rushed to intensive care and that I should probably go and see her. She told the secretary to call me a taxi and I waited outside the school, adrenaline pumping, weirdly excited.

When it dropped me at the hospital I knew I had to be quick. The sign said Intensive Care was on the third floor, so I took the lift and set off down the corridor. But I must have read it wrong, because I found myself outside the Maternity Ward. A cleaner with an Eastern European accent asked me if I was okay. I told her where I wanted to go and she held my hand and walked me through the corridors to the tiny waiting area. Dad was sitting there, hunched over, reading a crappy TV magazine. I ran to him and hugged him. When I turned to thank the cleaner she'd already gone.

Dad told me that Mum had called him at lunchtime complaining about chest pains. After he had checked the leaflet – *When to seek medical attention during cancer treatment* – he knew he had to take her to the hospital.

It wasn't fair! She'd only had the operation a month before and they'd only just allowed her out! Even the doctors didn't get it! They had to "run some tests". She kept twisting and writhing in her bed as if she couldn't find a comfortable position. Her skin was blue and it was like every vein in her arm had a tube sticking out of it.

Dad told me later that's what happens when the body dies: all the blood diverts away from the skin to the vital organs to keep them going, so the skin starts changing colour. He said although the cancer was in her lungs it was her heart that was giving out.

I grabbed her hand and told her I loved her. She opened her mouth but no words came out.

A nurse tugged at my sleeve and said we had to leave while they "ran more tests". We sat back in the corridor. Five minutes later the doctor came out and, looking at the floor while he was speaking, told us we'd "lost her".

I despised that guy with his wanky deep voice like a National Theatre actor. They didn't have a clue what had gone wrong and I hated them for it.

I wish, I wish I had been there the moment she died.

Hayden didn't say a word. With his free hand he put on a mix. I closed my eyes, slipped my legs between his and lay my head on his chest. For the next hour it was just us and the music. It started off sad and orchestral, then deep and ambient, finishing harder and funky as if we were back in the club. Sometimes the mixing was so seamless I couldn't tell where one track ended and another began. Other times the contrast was stark, but so *right*, sending tingles down my spine. He didn't need to reply to my story: the music said it all. My thoughts stopped and we were in bliss.

The last track was a classical violin riff juxtaposed with some tribal bongos, repeating and repeating and repeating for what felt like an age until at last an abrasive, trancey, euphoric organ kicked in. It shouldn't have worked but it did. I found myself standing on the bed, dancing clumsily on the bouncy mattress.

"Who was that?" I said when the music stopped.

"Me."

"Serious?"

"That's my new mix. That last track was my track."

"Don't lie."

"I thought of you every moment I made it."

I realised then that Hayden hears music in a way I just don't. Getting together had unleashed something. I had this realisation, that me and him are greater than the sum of our parts. We're like Power Rangers who transform into one giant Super-Ranger.

"Life is rough," said Hayden. "That's why we never stop dancing."

"Yes!" I said. "Yes!"

It wouldn't make sense to anyone – not to Dad, not to Jennifer, not to Bad Ben, Elliot, not even to Harper, Cristina or Alejandro. To anyone else we're just losers and wasters here in a shitty street in London in a run-down house on this ridiculous bed. Fuck them. We *know*. Only *we* know. And that's all that matters.

29

"Can I move my arm for a second?"

"No."

"Okay."

"Only joking, of course you can."

I gasp in relief as I bring my hand to my lap and my aching shoulder relaxes. I deliberately keep my eyes closed in case it's awful.

"What do you think?" he says.

"I'm scared to look."

"I don't think you've got anything to worry about."

I open my eyes and gasp again. The letters sit on a bed of pinkish sore flesh, exactly how they appeared on my laptop, except the navy blue makes them darker, more real, and more *permanent* than I imagined.

"I love it," I say.

He's smiling.

"Are you done?"

"It's just the *r* on the end."

He's right, it's lacking the ornate calligraphy flourish at the bottom. I hadn't noticed. I love his attention to detail.

"This is a good moment for me to go for a piss," he says.

He disappears through the back door.

I reach into my bag and check my phone. There's a message from Hayden.

Are you done yet?

Soon.

How is it?

Tell Cristina everything she said about him was right.

Great!

I miss you.

I'm not at home.

Where are you?

Tooting. There's a party. Need you here.

I thought we were having an early night.

Don't you want to celebrate?

We're supposed to go again Friday.

Okay, whatever you say. See you at home.

Hayden is supplying the party. Whatever happens, he'll be there for a while, and I'll be home alone.

Changed my mind. Can you send me the address?

30

"I'm sorry I didn't tell you about Jennifer, but you didn't have to be this dramatic," he says.

Not even a *hello*.

My throat feels like sandpaper. I shouldn't have picked up.

"And stubborn. You are the most stubborn person I've ever known."

Someone's tied ten-kilogram weights onto my legs and arms.

"I know I could have handled it better but I didn't deserve this."

"What are you talking about?"

His breathing is short and anxious.

"Are you okay?" he says.

"I was just having a nap."

The kind of nap you take when you went to bed at 11 a.m. in the morning.

"I think moving out was a bit drastic," he says.

I'm sitting in the empty landing and my voice sounds painfully loud. I wonder if Harper is in her room, listening through her door.

"What are you up to? What are you *doing*?"

You don't want to know . . .

"You've got what you wanted. I thought you'd be happy."

"No, I haven't . . ."

"Don't lie."

"I'm worried about you."

"I'm *fine*."

"I'd like to meet him. Just to see. I don't know where you're staying, even. Not for you. For me."

"No thank you."

"I can't stand not knowing about you. How are you surviving? Are you working? Where are you getting your money?"

"I'm eighteen in a week. You don't have to look out for me anymore."

I head downstairs to the living room. It's empty, musky, the coffee table is covered with empty cider cans and full-up ashtrays. I sink on to the sofa.

"I'm seriously confused, Scarlett."

"Did Jennifer give you permission to call?"

"She suggested I give you some space. I agreed with her. Though obviously we were both wrong."

"Stop pretending you care."

"Of course I care."

"DON'T LIE!"

I pray the whole house hasn't heard me.

"I think I'm going to call the police."

"You can't call the police because I'm not missing and I'm *fine*. Go away, enjoy your new life, I'm off your hands, now it's confirmed this is the first day of the rest of your life."

I hang up.

I'm shaking. He's right. Hayden can't go on paying

for me forever. I have to contribute. I open the banking app on my phone, expecting it to show me overdrawn.

There's a new deposit in my account, made this morning. Three grand.

Dad.

I laugh.

More money than I've ever had in my life!

Guilt is a powerful thing, I guess.

31

That night in Tooting was just another lesson at the University of Rave.

Hayden said I had a lot of catching up to do. He wouldn't rest until I knew the difference between classic house, deep house, soulful house, funky house, electro house, progressive house, dubstep, big room, garage, hard dance, and all the rest.

I had to become *discerning*. I had to understand *what a proper night out was*. "Summer is the best time to school yourself in the ways of the rave."

In practice, this meant going to a lot of parties and doing a lot of pills. What I love about Hayden is that he's a purist. When you're wasted you end up getting offered loads of random stuff. Alejandro and Cristina would be taking MDMA powder offered by a stranger or buying Charlie or snorting K. But Hayden always stuck to the pills. He really is *all about the love*.

He dragged me to Liverpool Street and took us on a train to Colchester, followed by a fifty-quid taxi-ride just so we could dance to trance in a wood in Suffolk. There was a circle of speaker stacks in a clearing, full of manic kids twirling round a campfire. A girl in pantaloons and a bra swung balls of fire in circular arcs, and a giant dreadlocked bloke in a tie-dye t-shirt juggled blazing torches. Some crusty old men brought me cups of tea at 7 a.m..

Hayden told me that, age fifteen, he lay down in this very muddy spot watching the sun rise between the trees, drunk on chemical love, and decided that his life would never be the same again.

"Why aren't you dancing?" I said.

"This music makes me want to puke."

"But you're wasted," I said.

"You know there's a problem when even the drugs can't make you dance."

He still had to take me here and show me how it all began. "This is where I felt how you felt that night with Mikey Miles," he said. "You never forget your first time."

Another time we're in a tiny club below a bar in Shoreditch and dancing to *Hayden's-kind-of-house*: deep and eclectic with spacey synthesisers, funky basslines, robotic mantras, yearning choruses, wild percussions, bleepy keyboards, orchestral tapestries, African chanting, sped-up hip-hop and slowed down sonatas, sometimes hard like I'm being bludgeoned over my head, sometimes uplifting like a magic carpet has whisked us away, always underscored by that *boo-pe-chi boo-pe-chi boo-or-chi* and the *boom boom boom* of the beat.

Proper house music," he said. "It's like a journey. It's like going down the rabbit hole."

There was only a couple of hundred people there, and even though most of the tracks were so obscure you couldn't buy them except on download sites designed for DJs, they roared in recognition over and over again. I met a car mechanic from Romford, a bunch of students from Kings College and the PA to the boss of British Gas, all of us exclusive members of the same private members' club, chatting nonsense for England. I bounced around like a happy bunny, slinging my arms, punching the air, everyone wanting a piece of my candy, Hayden stepping in to cock-block the guys who got too close.

"Something's happened," I said. "I'm off the leash."

He pressed his face to mine. "If I brought you here and you hated it – I dunno – that might have been it. This is my tribe, this is my home and you *get it*. I'm the luckiest guy in the universe!"

"Can we never stop doing this please?" I said.

"Never," he replied.

Then it was my birthday and I had the best birthday ever. I even broke my *no-more-than-two-pills* rule. Hayden bought me tickets for a massive festival in Hyde Park where me, Hayden, Cristina, Harper, and Alejandro danced to Mikey Miles playing aggressive, relentless tribal house music for twenty-five thousand of our closest friends. My UPS kicked in at the top of the Ferris wheel. "I can see the fields!" I screamed. "I can see the city! I can see the West country! This is better than Primrose Hill!"

Hayden didn't get it, but I didn't care.

We went on the dodgems, bought candy-floss and danced in our wellies like demented mashed-up children.

The festival wound down at 10.30 p.m., so we took an Uber to a private after-party in the back room of a pub in Croydon: barely a hundred people crammed into a tiny, sweaty black-box. Only the 'important' ones were there – Mikey Miles' agent, one of the guys who owns the festival plus a bunch of other DJs and their mates.

Hayden went off supplying while I officially mega-bonded with my new flatmates, me and Cristina curling up on a battered leather sofa while she told me about her job sorting letters into pigeon holes in a basement at Disney where she doesn't see daylight for eight hours straight. She said she reads books on astrology and pointed to the bouncer and said, "You can tell he's a Virgo because of the way he sprays his hands with alcohol cleaner every five minutes."

I told her that was fascinating and she had to teach me sometime. She said my tattoo was stunning and that now I had one I'd get addicted, and get more and more. Her next one was going to be a mandala that covered her entire stomach. I made her promise she'd let me help her choose the stencil.

In the girls' toilets she told she told me she wants a baby but Mikey Miles spends thirty weeks a year touring. How can she start a family with someone who does that? "He says he's going to retire when he's fifty. I don't believe him. He's forty-five and he dyes his hair. He never wants to be old." I gave her the tightest hug I could and said that everything would be okay.

Me and Harper danced in our own private corner of the dance floor. "You're a goddess," I told her. "You're so brave, travelling to the other side of the world, loving life in spite of your job. I'm so proud of you!"

She told me they've introduced a screen in her office that displays who brings in the most profit. "I've been top for two weeks but I couldn't care less. My boss says his sponsor status should come through any day then I can fast-track apply for my visa and he's gonna promote me to some other part of the business away from this shit. I'm gonna be the boss and start a revolution. Treat people fairly."

She pulled me close and said, "I'm proud of you too."

"Why?"

"Hayden."

"What about him?"

"He'd given up."

"Given up what?"

She put her finger to her lips and went on dancing. It was a weird feeling, being high and disturbed at the same time. I had no idea how many pills I'd taken. Four? Five? I stopped moving and did my confused face, frowning and stroking my chin.

"Screw it," she said. "I'm too off-my-tits and you should know anyway."

"Know what?"

"His dad used to beat the shit out of him. He has this inferiority complex thing. His first girlfriend dumped him. Proves that no one wants him."

"Oh. He told me. Or he almost told me."

"That's amazing he even almost told you! It's so hard for him to open up! I'm so happy for you guys!"

Then she sang *Happy Birthday to you* into my ear as I looked at Hayden, his eyes closed, arms up, wiggling his fingers to the music.

"You're not broken!" I said to him.

"What?

"You're *not* broken!"

"What are you talking about?"

I told him what Harper told me.

"I was going to tell you," he said.

"You should have!"

"It's just . . . whatever, it's true, I am broken."

"Don't say that."

"You can't deny it."

He carried on dancing, bony elbows swinging by his hips.

"So what if you are? I love your brokenness. I wouldn't have you any other way."

"You love me for me," he said.

"And you love me for me," I said.

He ran his hand down my face, sending explosions of pleasure across my cheek and into my brain.

"Never leave me," I said.

"On my parents' life. Scout's honour. My honour. On my own life."

And that was it, nothing to worry about. There never was.

You know those moments when the perfect words to the perfect song comes on?

Right then, the voice repeated.

I don't need to do anything. I don't need to be anything.

It was an American woman, talking slow and sexy.

It all just happens. All by itself.

She was right!

Life was happening, all by itself.

And I said to myself, over and over again, "Never forget this feeling, never forget this feeling."

That night Mikey Miles played for eight hours straight until midday the next morning.

I was all bliss, all love: I was walking heaven.

Best birthday ever.

We emerged, blinking, into a high street full of

anxious people scurrying around. How can they live their lives without raving? Why didn't world leaders take pills before meeting? Surely all wars everywhere would end immediately?

I felt privy to life's greatest secret.

I sat on a mahogany armchair in the window of Starbucks and typed into my phone.

There is nothing more powerful than love.

It is the solution to every problem.

This is why I had it tattooed on my wrist:

Love is the Answer.

32

I close the door gently, lock it and run across the road.

I don't think anyone saw me. My neighbours' blinds are drawn. My holiday hold-all is full up with clothes. Mission successful. No Dad-showdown. No being forced to stay in my room while he shouts at me. Now I don't have to manage with the same five pairs of underwear anymore. I no longer have to borrow a phone charger everywhere I go. He hadn't changed the locks, so I guess that's something. I walk up the hill as fast as I can.

I would have bought new ones but Ubers, club tickets, Deliveroos and rounds at the bar all add up. I even forced Hayden to take money for bills – I literally had to put it into his wallet when he wasn't looking. Anyway, these days I'm usually coming down too hard to feel like schlepping to the shops.

It's like, when I didn't have that much money, I could make it last for ages, and when I finally put a load in my bank account I burn through it like a raging fire – two grand in two months, when Hayden was fighting to pay for me. Once, he literally shoved me out the way to slap his iPhone on the reader to pay for a pint. We're not even half-way through August and I don't even feel like I spend that much. I need to start thinking about what to do when it's gone. The massive grey clocktower at the entrance to Leeds Uni flashes into my head and I quickly shove it back to where it came from.

Truth is, I didn't *really* need to come here. I just *wanted* to.

I wanted to know if my room was still there.

I wanted to see if the top floor had been converted to a yoga studio and if the fridge was full of vegan cheese.

But nothing had changed. Everything was just as I left it. The unwashed clothes on my floor. No one had even bothered to make my bed. Dad's dirty Weetabix bowl sat on the counter and there was even a Waitrose curry defrosting on top of the fridge.

Dad must be taking a principled stand against Jennifer's healthy eating.

Either that, or Jennifer never moved in.

I suppose I don't want him to know that a part of me wanted to come home, even if it was just for five minutes to collect something. He won't know I've been. Not unless he's taking a daily audit of my wardrobe. He needs to feel that I've left for good.

I have left for good.

Now I buy my toilet paper from the East Street Market down the road, from a stall in front of an Afro-Caribbean hair-care shop and a Halal butcher's. Two doors down there is an art gallery that has private views that turn into private raves. But what *is* there here? Brand new cars, endless uber-posh houses and Cenk in Food and Wine. There's no soul.

I think I'm becoming a South Londoner.

I pull out my phone. Five missed calls from Hayden. I call him back.

"Hey Babes," he says.

"I did it. The Evil One did not see. Covert operation successful."

"Can you do me a favour? Can you go to Food and Wine?"

I freeze.

Hayden has told me a thousand times that he never wants me to work with him.

"It's just that the guy I'm meeting has got delayed and he's got to get a train to Scotland. He wants a thousand for a rave in a highland castle. I need to hang around."

"Can't you just see him later?"

"He's got to catch a train."

The less I know, the less involved I am, the more protected I am. I need to be shielded, he said so. Feds are everywhere, he told me.

"But . . ."

"Just pick up for me and tell him I'll pay him tomorrow. Just get it on tick."

This isn't my scene. I just take them, I don't deal them.

"Babe, this is a one off. You know I would never even consider asking you unless I really needed it."

"I don't want to," I say.

"This guy owes me six hundred as it is. Held up my cash flow. All I need is five minutes of your time and one Tube journey. It's still festival season. People are stocking up."

"I don't think I want to," I say.

"You have to!"

Images flash through my mind. Hayden beaten up. Both of us sleeping on the street. A gravestone with Hayden's name on it.

"I'm sorry, I shouldn't have asked you," he says.

I sniff. My nose is full of snot. I feel terrible.

"I broke my promise," he says.

"Exactly!"

"But the rent is due tomorrow and I don't have it."

"I'll pay."

"What?"

"I'll pay your rent."

"It's not just the rent!" he shouts. "If I don't wait for this guy then I'm fucked!"

"What do you mean?"

Hayden's never, ever been short of cash.

"I've been a bit too generous with the credit. Now it's time for the credit crunch. It's the age of austerity for Hayden. No more deals on tick. My new job title is debt collector. I promise you. First and last time."

"Okay."

My stomach winces as I say it.

"Go to Food and Wine and tell Cenk you're here for Hayden. I'll message him."

"Okay."

"You seriously gonna do it?"

"Yeah."

"I love you! I love you so much! I'll make it up to you, I promise! This is what happens when you're your own boss. Wheeling and dealing. If you were here, I'd kiss every inch of your beautiful body."

"That's not appropriate, Hayden."

"When have I ever been appropriate?"

In spite of myself, I laugh.

"I just got really scared. When you asked me."

"I know. I'm sorry."

"It made me really frightened."

"I know."

"I think we've been out too much. I'm feeling a bit . . . comedowney. It's finally catching up with me."

"Tell me about it."

"I love you, Hayden."

"I love you, too."

It feels strange being outside Food and Wine and not going in to get vodka, or a giant bottle of Doctor Pepper, or jelly babies, or all the other crap I used to go in here for. There's the same stacks of vegetables, the giant tomatoes, dusty potatoes and bunches of parsley. Cenk serves an old man buying instant coffee. I wonder how many people know about the other stuff they sell? I almost can't believe their side-operation exists.

I step inside as the old man steps out. Cenk frowns as if he can't place me.

"Whoa," he says.

"Hi!"

"I didn't recognise you."

"Oh?"

"You got skinny."

He looks down at my thighs – which have shrunk since I started dancing for hours at a stretch. *It's the raving diet. Much better than the gym.*

"Stop there . . ." he says. "Girls should . . . you know . . . not be too skinny."

I smile to hide my irritation. Who is he to even say that?

"Is that a tattoo?"

He's wearing a vest that reveals his over-sized shoulder muscles. I present my arm.

"*Love is the Answer.* Very romantic."

"I'm here for Hayden," I say, abruptly.

"What?"

"I'm here to collect something."

"*What?*"

He looks like I've just told him I'm a four-foot elephant and I want to eat fried rats on toast.

"Hayden messaged you?"

He glances up at the CCTV monitor. Satisfied the shop is empty he reaches into his pocket and takes out a tiny flip phone. He holds it up high, squinting to read the message on the screen.

"This is wrong," he says. "No girl should do this."

"I'm not a girl," I say.

He shakes his head.

"Come."

I follow Cenk into the back room. For once his dad is there, so large he practically fills the whole space. He frowns through his glasses at a long receipt printout, his bald forehead glistening with sweat. Cenk barks something in Turkish. I don't understand any of it other than the word *Hayden*. His dad does exactly what Cenk did – looks at me as if I was a giant teddy bear in a space suit. He laughs. He thinks it's a big joke.

"Hayden said he'd pay you tomorrow."

"He what?"

"He got held up."

Cenk's dad frowns and his cheeks colour red.

"He got held up?"

"Yes."

Cenk's dad slams the receipt onto the desk.

"My darling, I think you should go home," he says.

I shake my head.

"Seriously."

I don't move.

He brings his face close to mine.

"We need the money now."

What money?

"He's doing a deal. He'll pay you tomorrow," I say.

"A deal?" Cenk's dad shouts at me in Turkish. Every syllable feels like a smack round the face.

"Bad boyfriend," says Cenk.

"Money. Now!" says Cenk's dad.

"I didn't know he owed you. He just told me to pick up."

I hate this room, with its ripped lino and boxes of ring-binders. I stand up. Cenk blocks the door.

"We've been waiting too long" says Cenk. "If you have no money, then we have to send him a message."

The totally, stupidly obvious truth – that Hayden has run out of cash – hits me square in the face.

"How much?" I say.

"Two," says Cenk's dad.

What?

"Thou . . ." says Cenk.

My chest tightens. I think I'm going to pass out. What message are they going to send? I thought Cenk fancied me?

"I'm sorry," says Cenk, taking my wrist.

"I've got money. I think I do. Let me check."

I pull my wrist away and take out my phone and open my banking app. I can barely do it, my hands shaking. They watch me, expressionless.

"A grand. I've got a grand," I splutter, tears running down my cheeks.

Cenk's dad shakes his head.

"That's all I've got!"

"You think you can get what you want by crying," says Cenk's dad. Cenk cuts in and they argue in Turkish. My head hangs, like I'm waiting for an axe to chop it off.

"A grand today, the rest tomorrow. Otherwise we collect the money ourselves," says Cenk's dad.

"Okay," I say, feebly.

Last week Hayden and I went to the Apple store when I was still high and I almost bought an iPad. THANK THE LORD I didn't.

I stand by the card machine – a different one to the normal one – as the money drains from my account. I didn't even know dealers could take card payments. Inside the top of my rucksack are five hundred pills.

"You're lucky you're my friend," says Cenk, handing me the receipt.

The moment I'm out of the shop I run across the road and into Paradise Park, take out my phone, and call Hayden.

33

"You never told me you were two grand in debt!"

"What?"

"I had to pay them a grand of my own fucking money!"

"What happened?"

"I thought they were going to kill me!"

My screaming voice is swallowed by the bigness of the park.

"Did you pick up?"

"I've got no money! I'm cleaned out! And all you can ask is *did I pick up*?"

"Did you?"

"Yes!"

Hayden exhales loudly in relief.

"They said I had to pay a grand now otherwise they'd 'send you a message'. I gave them everything. Just to get out of there."

"That's not right. They told me end of the month . . ."

"I'm shaking like a leaf."

"I'm so sorry."

"I'm *scared*, Hayden."

"I'm gonna call them now. I'm gonna get you your money back. That ain't right. What happened ain't right."

"How could you make me do that?"

"Meet me at Elephant and Castle station in one hour, okay? One hour."

He hangs up.

I stand there, alone, in the middle of the park. A bunch of primary age kids are playing football on the far side. A Romanian family cooks sausages on a barbecue ahead of me. I breathe in as far as I can, and out as slow as I can.

I have to get back to normal.

It's gonna be okay.

Everything will be okay.

But how *is* he going to pay them back?

How is he going to pay *me* back?

I'm going to go home and flush the pills down the toilet. Turn off my phone and change my number, then go to sleep. Pretend all this never happened.

But if Hayden couldn't sell those pills Cenk might *actually* kill him. I don't want to be responsible for that. And if I went home Dad would just say, "I told you so," and I'd have to live in fear of Cenk and *his* dad and I could never go to my corner shop ever again.

Oh my God.

I can never go home now.

I can never come back here for the rest of my life.

I set off towards the exit. Some older teens are gathered on the swings. They're idiots. They're too big for the park. It's a space for children. How dare they!

One of them waves and calls my name. He slips off the swing and jogs up to the railings.

"Scarlett," he beams.

It's Bad Ben.

I didn't recognise him because he's shaved his head.

Even the bum-fluff goatee is gone. He looks about fourteen, not someone who's officially an adult.

"Hey," I say, with the happiest smile I can muster.

Behind him on the other swing, sits Elliot. He too has shaved off his hair. Aya – unobtainable frigid Aya who never talks, the object of Elliot's night-time fantasies, sits on his lap, wearing a cutesy sailor suit. She's frowning like she's been teleported out of a Primrose Hill celebrity party and doesn't know what happened.

But she's *sitting* on his lap.

His *arms* are around her waist.

Bad Ben kisses me on both cheeks. The friendliness, as if nothing has happened, as if we last saw each other a couple of days ago, is disconcerting.

"You're looking well," he says.

"Your hair!" I say. I can't help running my hand over his head.

"I feel a stone lighter," he says.

"I live with Hayden now," I blurt.

"Woah."

"Yeah, it's great."

He hovers there, struggling for words.

"We're not supposed to do that kind of thing until we're thirty, right?"

"It's kind of serious," I say.

Bad Ben takes a step to the side revealing Elliot, chin resting on Aya's shoulder, looking right at me. My mind goes blank.

"We thought that as we've left school we should do something to mark the birth of a new era."

"Okay."

He leans in and lowers his voice conspiratorially.

"Plus, we thought maybe our long hair was stopping

us pulling," continues Bad Ben. "As opposed to our personalities. So we made a pact to shave our heads to test it out scientifically. Worked for Elliot but not for me."

"You mean he actually asked her out?"

"It's not really clear who asked who but they bumped into each other on the number 4 bus and got talking and . . . turns out all this time she's been gagging for a bit of Elliot action."

On cue, Elliot kisses Aya, pecking at her mouth like he's scared she's going to break.

Bad Ben grabs my shoulders.

"Save me Scarlett! I've been gooseberry all summer! I don't think I'm gonna make it to freshers' week!"

He lowers his voice again.

"She's really nice but she's not as funny as you or as outspoken as you and basically . . ." He speaks in a stage whisper, "She's not you."

"I thought Elliot forbade you to talk to me," I say sarcastically.

"Well . . . now he's getting some . . . and I saw you walking across the grass . . . I kind of feel I'm allowed to?"

"Tell him I'm really happy for him," I say, unenthusiastically.

"He's the cat who got the cream. He's insufferable, poncing around like he's the lead singer in The 1975."

He's in love with her. Then he's in love with me. Then he's in love with her.

"At least you don't have to listen to him moan about being single anymore, right?"

"This is worse! I feel so alone! This park is great and everything but I'm not into seven-year-olds."

Bad Ben gestures towards a pigtailed girl at the top climbing frame. I laugh, a little too manically.

I want to hug him.

I miss my friend.

"*Love is the Answer*. Nice!" says Bad Ben, looking at my tattoo.

Something inside me goes cold. I remember my Oyster card is dead, my phone bill is about to come out and now there's no money left in my account.

"You need to get out more," I say. "Meet people."

"Like it's that easy."

I remember the package that's in my bag. I shouldn't do it. But everything is changing. Life is going in unexpected directions. I shouldn't be rigid. I lean into Bad Ben's ear so no one else can hear me.

"Do you still want to try a pill?"

"I don't know . . . I'm kind of teetotal, remember?"

"Well, I got some if you want. Really makes it easy to meet new people!"

He looks back towards Elliot and Aya but they're absorbed in their pathetic-mini-pecking-each-others'-lips thing.

"If someone kissed me like that, I'd dump them immediately. It's like, do you want me or not?"

Bad Ben laughs.

"Okay, so thanks for the offer but I think I'll pass."

"Your choice. See you later."

I set off round the edge of the playground. Just as I turn the corner he shouts my name. I stop and wait as he jogs towards me.

"You're so annoying!"

"What?"

"You put me on the spot."

"I have to go."

"I want one, but I've got no cash. I need to go to the machine."

"Okay."

As we walk to the High Road I give him the lecture. These are a new batch, Supermen. Hayden only picked them up the other day. They are really strong. Possibly stronger than the UPS. Do not do more than one quarter for your first one. Drink plenty of water. They hit you hard. Really hard. I know, because we did a cheeky half the other night, just to test them out. We ended up staying awake until 4 a.m.

Bad Ben snatches his money from the dispenser. I lead him down the alley behind the high street and stop at the back door to a betting shop. No one is around, so I open my bag, take two pills from the batch and wrap them in a piece of tissue.

"Woah," says Bad Ben when he sees the size of the package.

"I don't normally do this. I'm just helping out. Anyway, Hayden's giving up. This is the last pick-up ever."

I don't know why I said that.

I press the tissue into his hands and he gives me the notes, already crumpled and sweaty from his hand.

"So we gonna go out clubbing then?" he says.

"Maybe . . ." I say.

He deflates, visibly.

"I'll let you know if anything comes up. Promise me you won't do something stupid like take them on your own. Do them at a party. Make sure other people know what you are doing. And *take it slowly.*"

"I will," he says.

I set off, leaving him on his own, holding the tissue. Just before I go into the Tube station I message him.

Remember, the first time is always the best.

I ripped him off something chronic. Sixty pounds for two pills. A ridiculous piss-take. I was desperate. I hope he doesn't find out the real market value. Maybe it's good if he pays over the odds because then he'll be forced to do less.

Anyway, I soon forget as I'm freaking out because Hayden is late. By the time he walks through the barriers, an hour after he said he would, I've convinced myself that Cenk had stabbed him round the back of Camden station. Before I can say anything he puts his finger on his lips and marches me back to the house. I give him the pills, explain what I've done. He opens his rucksack and presents me a with massive wad of cash.

"What?"

"Two grand."

"Serious?"

"Debt cleared. Told you I would sort it."

"That's two grand, right there?"

"A bit more, actually."

"Oh my God!" I scream at the top of my voice, before sinking back onto his bed. "I'm so relieved!"

"I told you I would sort it, I told you I was debt collecting." He takes out a chunk and hands it to me.

"For you. Plus interest."

I press the notes to my face.

"Today was the worst day of my life."

"I'm so, so, so sorry," he says.

"I thought we were going to die. I thought the last

thing I would see was Cenk's dad's sweaty face leering at me, my blood spurting over boxes of receipts."

"I'm sorry."

"I don't want you to do this any more. I want this to be your last time. I can't go through that again. I can't."

"Babes . . ."

"Please!"

He looks at the money, ruefully. He stands up and rubs his face.

"It'll take a while to sell this lot."

"I don't care."

"Scarlett . . ."

"Shit got out of hand! Way out of hand! It's a wake-up call!"

"I know! Okay! Okay! You're right! I don't know how but I will."

34

My plan came to me in bed. I was wired and couldn't sleep, listening to Hayden's comatose breathing while the orange streetlight cut in through the blinds, illuminating his smudged iMac screen and the three cups of half-finished tea he'd left around the keyboard. Despite our partying, Hayden would sit there night after night, mixing and composing, driven by God-knows-what. My idea was so mind-bendingly obvious I don't know why we hadn't thought of it before. My whole body tingled with adrenaline and it was all I could do not to grab him and shake him awake.

I got up and went down to the living room. The coffee table was covered with full-up ashtrays, dirty glasses and empty cans of Heineken. Someone had left the TV on, the volume low.

I turned it off, picked up the dirty things and took them down to the kitchen. I emptied the ashtray and beer cans into a rubbish bag and dumped them in the bin outside. Back upstairs I wiped the table, plumped the cushions and arranged the remotes neatly in a line. I even got out the hoover and plugged it in before I realised it would wake everyone up.

I wasn't going to tell Hayden. I'd had enough of him looking after me, putting me up in his house, giving me free pills and fighting me whenever I wanted to pay for something. This was my chance to pay him back for everything he'd done.

It was 4 a.m. Tidying felt good. I could visualise exactly what I needed to. I felt like I was in the Uber on the way to the club, pills already dropped, one-hundred percent ready for an incredible night.

I was on my third coffee when Cristina stomped into the kitchen in her pre-work flap, wet towel wrapped around her, cobra on her back hissing at me. She made a mug of tea and poured a bowl of cornflakes and joined me at the table. I knew I had one minute before she charged upstairs to get dressed, so I told her what I wanted and why.

She frowned, opened her mouth to say something and then changed her mind. After a long silence she said, "Yeah, sure, why not?" as casually as if I'd asked her to pass me the lighter.

She led me to her bedroom, which I'd never been in before: it was much more hippified than I imagined. A rainbow mandala-blanket covered the back wall and her bedspread was a golden sun with a smiley face set against a backdrop of stars. She'd put fairy lights everywhere possible: around the window, across the mantlepiece, over the bed, while everything else was on the floor. Dresses, knickers, socks, jeans, make-up bottles, jewellery, earrings, bracelets and piles of books were stacked against the wall. I had to be careful not to crush anything fragile as I followed her to the bed-side table where her phone was charging.

"Can you not tell Hayden?" I said, "I want it to be a surprise."

"That's nice," she replied, before picking up the phone to send me the details I wanted. Then she dropped her towel and put on her underwear. She was naked for seconds, but the whole thing made me uneasy, like a giant hand was squashing me downwards.

I got out of the house as quickly as I could.

Now I'm in a pub off Oxford Street, the old-school kind with mahogany panelling, stained glass windows and wrought iron tables. Harper and I sit on stools in the corner, our lager shandies untouched, while she puts my mascara right. I feel so much better now I'm with her.

"The trouble is," she says, "me and you – we're not girly girls."

"I think that's why we get on. We have more guy friends than girl friends."

"You're so right. Stand up, I'm done."

She looks me up and down.

"Maybe we should be more girly."

"What do you mean?"

"You scrub up well."

I blush.

"Maybe I should look ugly. Maybe looking good will complicate things."

"Scarlett, honey – you are hot. There's no two ways about it. You could wear a bin-bag and not wash for a week and he'd still fancy you."

"I don't want him to fancy me, I want him to . . ."

"You need to look like you mean business. Why do you think I do this every day?"

Harper gestures to her crisp ironed blouse, the

rouge which buries the spots on her cheek, her shiny lip-glossed lips.

"You don't scrub up badly yourself."

"I work in the pit of hell. I need armour."

I check myself in her hand-mirror while she downs her shandy.

"Not alcoholic enough," she says and walks off to the bar, returning with two tequila shots.

"I look older," I say.

"Older is good."

I picture Elliot on the swing with Aya on his lap. Maybe I hate her because I want to be like her – never-chipped nails glistening black, porcelain skin, zero spots, hair straight, teeth dazzling.

Why can't I be happy with me?

Harper holds up her tequila shot, waiting to "Cheers!" me.

"Your boss will sort it. Your visa will come. It'll be okay. I know it will," I say.

"How did you – you can see right through me, can't you?"

"I love you, Harper. I got your back."

We click our glasses and down our drinks.

"The afternoon just got easier," she says.

I haven't been on the Docklands Light Railway since my Dad took me when I was seven. I remember getting ridiculously excited because there's no driver and you can sit at the front. I see nothing much has changed and as I watch the same old red and blue carriages pull into Bank station I feel nostalgic for a time when Dad wasn't a hostile ambassador from another planet;

when he could buy us both travelcards and we could spend the day going to random destinations just for the hell of it.

The train sets off and soon the dark tunnel gives way to bright daylight. It's cool and grey, the kind of weather that disappoints people when it's supposed to be summer. I don't mind it, in fact I feel a bit like I'm seven again, soaking up the council estates with their boxy cladding and cramped balconies. I glimpse a flea market with racks of cheap sportswear and rows of fruit and veg. An ugly, misshapen tower block rises high behind it, awkward and self-conscious like the Year 8 boy who's six foot two when the rest of his class are still kid-size. To my left a young boy presses his head to the glass, watched over by his grandma. He gets it. Everyone else sits in miserable silence, reading the Metro or staring at their phones.

All of us in the same carriage, all on this journey called Life, united by the same shit, with the same worries and same fears. If I smiled at anyone they would think I'm a psycho.

My certainty has returned. For the first time ever, I know what I want to do with my life.

35

"Wait there. I'll come and get you." His voice cracks, like he's just woken up.

The sleek curved front of a Riverbus accelerates away from the pier, slicing the Thames in two. You could take a boat to work if you lived here – how cool is that?

The door buzzes. I jump.

"It's a bit loud, isn't it?" Mikey Miles stands in the doorway wearing box-fresh trainers, white Nikes with a Navy swoosh. I'm shocked to see that he's smaller than me, like a toy version of himself. No wonder he's with Cristina, the tiniest girl ever.

"Hi," I say.

"Hi Scarlett," he says, gesturing me inside.

The hallway is like an expensive hotel with no staff. It has a marble floor and posh sofas and there are pot plants everywhere. He opens the lift using the finger-print scanner and hits floor three. It's cramped and we stand a bit too close. His afro is peppered with grey and his breath smells of coffee. He yawns and stretches, revealing a strip of hair down the front of his stomach. Then we're out, down an empty corridor and into his flat.

"Your timing is good," he says. "I'm off to Paris later. You caught me listening to demos."

We step into a large open plan kitchen-cum-living room. At the far side is a glass coffee table piled with CDs, some in plastic wallets with hand-scrawled notes, others displaying expensive-looking printed artwork. A MacBook Pro sits at its edge, connected to an external CD drive. Four tall speakers stand in each corner: the really expensive kind that cost thousands. The curtains are drawn.

"People send you *CDs?*"

"A bit obsolete, right?" he says, switching the kettle on. "Tea, coffee?"

"Tea."

I'm overwhelmed as I begin to understand the competition for his time and attention. How many new tracks must he get sent every week? How many people must be desperate to be played by him, to get the blessing of being associated with him?

"You've got such a nice flat," I say.

"Wish I actually got to spend time in it."

I love this place. I love the wooden floor, the marble work-tops and the giant TV. The only thing that's wrong is that the walls are bare.

My gut pulls tight. I'm here two minutes and already I'm redesigning it. I realise I'm not just doing this for Hayden. I'm doing this for me. *I* want to be a part of this. *I* want a flat like this this. *I* want to have what Mikey Miles has.

But I'm not a DJ. I don't want to be a DJ. So what am I thinking?

He tidies the CDs into a pile and places two mugs

of hot tea and a jar of milk in the space he has made. We both sit down on the sofa.

"Why do they send you CDs?" I say.

"They send me everything. Mostly MP4s, but vinyl, too. People like CDs because they can personalise them with messages and art, make them stand out. Make me notice. I've got people who filter. This lot got through the gatekeeper. Otherwise known as my manager, my cousin Trevor."

I laugh.

"Woah."

He stands up.

"Sugar?"

I shake my head.

He sits back down, his leg touching mine.

"I've just got back from South America – Mexico, Guatemala, Argentina – I'd play a gig and find five new CDs in my bag when I finished."

I laugh.

"I gotta listen, though. Can't play the same as everybody else."

His face is older and craggier than I remember, but his bright blue eyes make up for it.

"I've been on five planes in thirteen days."

"You must have a lot of air miles."

He smiles.

"Get off plane. Drive to club. Superstar for three hours. All alone in an empty hotel room. Repeat."

"Wow."

I'm not sure what else to say and I can feel my cheeks getting hot.

"I guess you don't sleep much?" It comes out sounding pathetic.

"Back in the day I didn't sleep at all. But it's much better now I don't partake. You get to be an expert at grabbing forty winks." He rubs his mouth like he's realised he's said a bit too much.

"I'm not complaining. I'm the luckiest guy in the world. Really, I am."

He stands up and opens the curtains. The dark grey muddy Thames fills the window, the far bank lined with warehouse flats. In the distance the three sharp points of the Shard taper towards each other.

"Must be all worth it when you're playing."

"Yeah. It is. I guess."

He sits back down and extends his arm behind me.

"You said you had something to ask me."

"Yeah . . ."

This is it. This is the moment.

"You know Hayden? Cristina's flatmate?"

"I know Hayden."

"Hayden you might *not* know is a DJ."

Mikey Miles exhales.

"I've got a track – a track and a mix – it will beat anything on that table. It's like this – mash-up – I can't explain it, but I know if you played his music, or he played out with you *one* night, you'd see how good he is. All he needs is a chance."

"I didn't realise you were here to pitch me."

My heart sinks.

"You could have just emailed."

"Or sent a CD."

"Or sent a CD."

"But this is really important."

"And it's also important to everyone who makes every single demo sent to me ever!" he snaps.

This isn't going how I expected.

"Hayden's your boyfriend, right?"

"Yeah."

I had been convinced that coming here was the right thing to do.

Mikey Miles shakes his head.

"What's that supposed to mean?"

"It's just. . . ."

"Fine," I say. I take out my phone and pull up Hayden's mix. Cristina gave me Mikey Miles' email as well as his number. I send him the track.

"Done. See you later."

I get up and walk into the hall. He follows me.

"I'm sorry, I'm tired . . ."

"It's fine . . ."

"Why are *you* asking me? Why not Hayden?"

"Because . . . I don't know . . . I wanted to help him."

"He's a wimp."

Half of me wants to punch him. The other half knows he has a point.

"Every time I play, I'm scared out of my skin. And then I do it and knock it out the park."

I fold my arms.

"It was nice to see you, anyway," he says.

"You, too. I like your flat."

"You said that already."

"I think you need some pictures."

He smiles and opens a door, revealing his bedroom. At the head of his bed is a spray-painted canvas of an old cassette tape painted bright green, electric blue and hot pink. Along the tape head is written CASSETTE LORD.

"I have one picture," he says.

"Who's the artist?"

"Cassette Lord."

I laugh.

"Obviously."

"Sorry again. I just get a bit sick of people wanting stuff all the time."

"Yeah, I know, I just thought – sorry too – because of the personal connection we could . . ."

"I've noticed you, Scarlett. I've always noticed you. I remember the first time I met you – you were off your tits – you got us shouting absolute bollocks. Something about a visa."

"Oh my God, how embarrassing."

"There was something about you."

My body is tingling. His bed. His hair. His eyes.

"I guess I got the wrong end of the stick when you messaged me."

He takes my hand.

Mikey Miles. *The* Mikey Miles. Said there's something about *me*.

He kisses me. I let him. It's nice. He grips my waist, my hands rest on his chest.

"No!"

I pull myself away.

"This is wrong."

I step back into the hall and open the front door.

"What's the problem?"

"Your girlfriend?"

"I don't have one."

"Yes you do."

He shakes his head.

"Yes you do!"

He takes a step towards me.

"Scarlett . . ."

I slam the door behind me. Thankfully, the lift has an exit button. I don't need his fingerprint to get out.

36

I stand by the water's edge as the Thames gently laps the quay. There's no one around, just block after block of new-build flats with empty balconies. It's like everyone who lives here is Mikey Miles, rich enough to own a flat, successful enough to never actually use it.

How could I be so naive? How could he be so arrogant as to assume that the only reason any girl would want to talk to him would be for one thing? Why did I spend so much time tarting myself up? Or was it me, was I leading him on without realising it?

What was all that stuff about *noticing me?*

I didn't do anything. Okay, I did do *something* but I pulled out super-quick, so it doesn't count, right?

I could be in his bed right now, watching him pack for Paris.

But I'm not. So I don't have to tell Hayden. He doesn't even know I'm here. As far as he's concerned it never happened.

I turn, half-expecting to see Mikey Miles watching me from his balcony window. But I don't have a clue which one it is and they all look dead, not a single light on, not one sign of movement.

Mikey Miles is small. He's *old*. He's got a belly. But he has that, *thing,* that famous people have, this *aura,* that makes you just *want* him without knowing why.

I picture Hayden, his boy-smell, his bony ribs, his giant bed, his kooky smile, his relentless jokes, his brown eyes with gold flecks, sitting in the back seat of an Uber, whispering *I love you* into my ear. I take out my phone and bring up his picture. He's brooding, looking at his iMac screen, creating a tune. I press it to my heart and walk along the quay, tears running down my cheeks, not a clue where I'm going.

What will I say to Harper and Cristina? Mikey Miles said no. End of story. He's out of the picture, he doesn't have a girlfriend, he's got no reason to tell them the truth.

But why did Cristina give me his number if they'd split up? She didn't look like someone who had just ended a relationship. And why didn't anyone tell me?

I climb a long flight of stairs, up on to a small green, past a couple of women eating sandwiches, their suit-jackets folded on the grass, blouse sleeves rolled up so their arms can catch the sun. The skyscrapers of Canary Wharf loom before me, all shiny marble and glistening glass. I head down an escalator, along the polished walkway of an underground shopping mall, past clothes boutiques, jewellery stores and overpriced restaurants, and up the escalator into the DLR station.

I want to call Hayden and tell him I've found the perfect place for a rave. The glass and steel arched ceiling, the bulbous, fluorescent streetlamps. I want to switch off the electricity, put a stage across the tracks, turn the WH Smith into a bar, get a massive disco ball hanging over the platform. Everyone here thinks they're so sharp, with their well-pressed suits and polished shoes, their post-salon hair and tanned skin. I want them to rip their shirts off, grab a stranger and hug them, stick their fingers into their mouths and whistle to the heavens.

I want to feel like that right now.

As we pull out of the Wharf my phone vibrates.

It's Elliot.

My head says cancel but my thumb presses answer.

"Hey," he says.

Chocka-chocka-chocka.

He's in his room, typing.

"Long time no see," I say.

"I know."

We stop at Poplar. A man in sportswear with a pug-faced dog gets on and stands in the corridor. I shift away from him, up a seat next to the window.

"Scarlett, you there?"

"I'm gonna go into a tunnel in a minute, just so you know."

"Okay."

Chocka-chocka-chocka-chocka.

"Elliot. You and Aya? What the hell?" I say.

The dog barks, making me jump.

"What do you mean, what the hell?"

I sigh. I didn't mean to sound so aggressive.

"I mean . . . I'm really happy for you, but . . . how . . . *how?*"

"I'm really happy for me too."

"Sorry to sound surprised, but . . . I am surprised."

The dog's tongue lolls out of his mouth, saliva dripping on to the gangway.

"So how's *your* summer going?" he says.

"Good."

Chocka-chocka-chocka. It's strangely comforting. A bit of me wishes that he's organising a surprise, like he was when he got the Comic Con tickets.

"I miss you," I say.

"Me too."

"I miss our platonic hanging out."

"Me too," he says, before adding. "You're the sister I never had, Scarlett."

"And you're the brother I never had."

I'm going to draw a line under everything that happened before and pretend I never had that conversation with Bad Ben on top of the Heath. Siblings is good. Siblings works.

"I'm sorry for being a dick about Hayden. I think I got scared that something bad would happen."

"I'm fine."

"I know you are. I should have trusted you. I mean, you're happy, right?"

"Totally."

I lift my knees on to the seat and curl up against the window. I've got a feeling that Bad Ben never told him that I know his true intentions for Comic Con.

"We both got what we wanted. We spent years obsessing about it, and now we have it."

"Exactly."

The guy with the dog sits next to me. I turn my back to him. The dog licks my thighs. I look at the man to get him to stop but he's too busy playing Candy Crush.

"So, about what you sold Bad Ben," says Elliot.

"Errr. . . . Yeah?"

"Got any more?"

"More?"

"All finished. Need some more."

"Umm . . . I thought you didn't . . . I mean, really?"

"Yeah . . . er . . . so can you help us out or not?"

"Why isn't Bad Ben asking me this?"

"He was going to, but I said I'd call cause . . . we needed to talk, didn't we?"

Elliot is doing drugs. Elliot, Bad Ben and Aya are doing drugs. Together. This should be a good thing. So why do I feel disappointed?

The carriage falls dark as we enter the tunnel.

"So, can you?" he says.

The call cuts out before I can reply.

37

My eyes open. The house is silent. Hayden lies sleeping, his back to me. I hug him from behind, dig my nose into his skin and inhale. He makes a noise which is half accusation, half laugh. I roll back the other way and listen to his heavy breathing. But I still feel like I'm in trouble and I'm not sure what to do.

I get out of bed, put on my dressing gown, slip on a pair of his tracksuit bottoms and one of his grey t-shirts, grab my phone and step into the hallway. There's six missed calls. Two are from Mikey Miles and four from my Dad. Two new voicemails. Adrenaline pumping, I press my phone to my ear.

Hi Scarlett. Listen. Sorry about earlier . . . It's just . . . I think we got our wires crossed . . . I'm not. . . . I'm not a Grade A dick, I promise . . . I was thinking about you on the plane . . . so I gave the mix a listen. I liked it. I mean, it's got some rough edges, but there's promise. Real promise.

There's a long pause. I think he might have hung up. Or maybe a dropped call . . . But then his voice cuts in.

The crowd went nuts. I'll be honest, I was surprised. Totally kicked off. The walls were shaking. You were right, Scarlett. You were right.

So listen . . . I wondered if Hayden wanted to open at a night I'm doing – All Night Long – at Community in Shoreditch – the first Saturday of September. It'll be billed as the opening but he'll get three hours. But you have to understand, this is a paid gig. I'm sticking my neck on the line. I'm pulling in favours with promoters. Hayden has to step up. If he wants to do it, get him to call me by the end of the day.

"Yes!" I scream. "Yes, Yes, Yes!" The automated voice says, "You have three more voicemails." I can't, I'm too excited. I end the call, burst back into the bedroom and rock Hayden to wake him up.

Hayden stands bare-chested, sipping coffee. We're both wearing pairs of his tracksuit bottoms, like some incestuous grungy twins.

"Isn't it the best news? This is your chance! This is your break!"

"You played him *my* tracks?"

"All Night Long! In Shoreditch! Paid! A-ma-zing!"

Hayden puts down his coffee and shakes his head.

"He played your track in Paris. He said the crowd went nuts."

"You went behind my back?"

"Well – technically . . ."

Hayden frowns.

"It wasn't ready."

"It was ready enough to send the crowd nuts!"

"It wasn't ready! It doesn't even have a name!"

"Hayden, who cares!"

"You went and took *my* music, before it was ready, and showed it to Mikey Miles? Before. It. Was. Ready. Without telling me."

He sits down at the kitchen table and puts his head in his hands.

"You have to tell him yes. You have to call him now."

"I do things by myself, for myself. Tell him I say no."

The circuits in my brain are scrambled. Is this really the boy I've been living with?

"How can you be so ungrateful?" I hiss.

"How can you be so disrespectful?" he shouts. His eyes are deranged, one bigger than the other. I feel Mikey Miles' lips on mine. My gut twists inside out.

"I took a massive risk to make your dream come true and now you're shoving it back in my face!"

"You betrayed me."

Does he know? He can't know. He *can't*. I put my hand on his shoulder and he pushes me away.

"I love you," I say.

He shakes his head and looks at the floor.

"I love you!" I say again, and he pushes me hard back against the oven. Pain shoots through my lower back. Something snaps. I pick up an empty beer can from the sideboard and throw it at him. He ducks and it hits the wall. He grabs my shoulders and I push him backwards, pick up a dirty plate and hurl it his head. He deflects it with his arm and it smashes on the floor, pieces of china everywhere.

"I was trying to help," I say.

"Fuck you," he says.

I step forward, place my hands on the underside of the kitchen table, and flip it upside down, splitting it the down the middle with a loud crack.

We both stand there, breathing heavily.

"You crazy bitch. Get out of my house," he says.

I run upstairs, grab my bag and still wearing his clothes open the front door and run.

38

Dad stands in the doorway, wearing a t-shirt with *English is important but accounting is importanter* written on the front. I balance my weight evenly on both of my feet and try to look together.

"So, you finally got my voicemail," he says. His voice is croaky.

"No."

"You were expecting some results?"

Truthfully, I'd forgotten about exams. Right now, A Levels feel part of some long-gone era, like primary school, or nursery. Even stepping into my hallway feels like stepping back in time, even though I was here a few days ago. My old purple hoody hangs on the coat stand and my Hello Kitty umbrella still leans against the wall. In the kitchen the same pieces of paper are pinned on the fridge: one advertising the Paradise Park Summer Fete, a letter from the college containing the summer term dates, a flyer from the same old pizza delivery firm that we've never used.

"The college called me at work to say you hadn't turned up. So they posted the results here. They also scheduled you a meeting with your head of year – yesterday, actually. So that's two no-shows."

"I . . . forgot." I say.

I thought he wouldn't be here. That I could just spend some time in my room and feel crap. I didn't know where else to go. I was going to call Harper. I just . . . he shouldn't be here.

"I take it you still like English breakfast tea?"

I open the fridge. It's almost empty: just a couple of bottles of beer, a half-full carton of milk, a pack of butter and some jam. Still no Jennification. No curly kale, no almond milk, no soya mince. Where's the yoga studio timetable?

"Why aren't you at work?" I say.

Dad shakes his head. He takes out a packet of Lemsip from the cupboard and waves it in my direction.

"I've been working through it but today I had to give in."

He makes my tea, carefully squeezing the teabag with a spoon.

"We need to talk."

The letters are written in indelible black, on official paper. *E. Sociology. D. English Literature. E. History.*

"Your worst nightmare has come true," I say.

I thought he'd be shouting, raving and waving his hands around.

Instead, he's solemn and serious and weirdly calm.

"I thought it *could* happen, but I didn't actually think it *would* happen," he says.

"I did my best."

"You *think* you did your best. Actually, you did your worst. I mean – it takes a lot of effort to mess up this much."

He's not accusing me anymore. He says it like a statement of fact. I don't feel the need to argue.

"So I called Damian," he says.

Damian is my head of year. We call our teachers by their first name.

"He has a name for it. Kamikaze exams."

"I worked my butt off! I promise!"

"For the whole year you've been a B student with a real shot at an A, even A* if you went for it. Simple as that. This was pure self-sabotage. I could see it coming a mile off."

"You sound like I did it on purpose, like I woke up and said, 'I'm going to screw up my exams!'"

He sighs in a way that says *that's exactly what I feel.*

"They wanted to talk about retakes. Actually, they just want to talk to you. I filled them in on the situation. It's the oldest story. Boys come through the door, exams go out the window."

I resist the urge to fling my tea over his face. The thought of Damian knowing about Hayden is just . . .

"They think you should stay on a year and take them all again in May."

The cold hard facts of my life come crashing into my consciousness.

But I've changed. It wasn't kamikaze. Maybe I realised that what I was doing isn't what I wanted to be doing after all. Maybe I screwed my exams because those exams are not the right exams for me.

My right direction – my guiding light – Hayden – has just been snuffed out. I feel so sad I've turned to stone.

"What do *you* think happened?" he says.

"Maybe I'm just dumb."

"You know what Damian thought? He thought

that Mum's death hit you much harder than we all realised."

He waits for my reply but opening my lips feels like lifting a thousand tonnes.

"I said to him that if that was true, then why now? Why not show this struggle earlier in the year, why the sudden last-minute meltdown? I told him you were a strong, resilient young woman . . ."

His voice cracks. I look up, but he's stuffed away the feeling.

"I told him that you'd fallen in love, travelled to la la land and moved in with some mystery boyfriend and now you'd decided that school doesn't matter any more and I stupidly let it happen with my stupid blessing and funded you."

He's right. I did meet a boy and decide all that other stuff doesn't matter. But cooking for Dad, the same old boring, soulless emptiness, that wasn't living, it was zombie life. But he's talking like what I've been doing doesn't *mean* anything. It means *everything*.

"In many ways you're a complete mystery to me," he says.

I bite my lip.

"I think when you're a bit older you'll really regret what you've done."

He's staring at my tattoo. I slap my hand across it.

There's a gaping Hayden-shaped wound right where my heart should be.

"What happened with Jennifer?"

"Don't change the subject."

"Why isn't she here?"

"We're not talking about Jennifer, we're talking about you."

"I don't think I want to do retakes."

He blinks.

"Yes, you do."

"Maybe I'm not cut out to be academic."

"It's only A Levels, they're hardly academic."

I see Mum's face. She's smiling at me like she did that day in the hospital when I asked her about boyfriends. With the eyes that don't judge me, whatever I'm feeling.

"If you leave college you have to leave the house. I'm not making that mistake again."

"I knew it! You never wanted to be my parent. You never wanted to look after me. You just wanted me to do well at school so I'd disappear to university, and now that's not going to happen you just want out, out of sight, out of mind, so you can carry on with your shitty job which is the only thing you care about. I'm just another column in one of your spreadsheets that you want to delete."

"No . . ."

"Try and bend your tiny numbers-obsessed brain and realise your daughter is not the person you want her to be."

Everything has shattered into five thousand tiny pieces. Dad thinks I'm scum. Hayden thinks I'm a traitor. I've finally crossed over one hundred percent into the other universe. The place where I'm the only person in it. Where every soul, every person, every plant, every animal is an alien – and I'm never coming back.

The doorbell rings. Dad hesitates, disorientated, and stands up straight as if switching back to normal mode. He opens the door, greeting whoever is there. I half-listen to the chatter. Whoever he's speaking to is laughing and cracking jokes.

I freeze. I know that laugh.

He's at the door.

I watch from the kitchen entrance.

If he sees me, he doesn't let on, he's talking to my dad like a salesman whose life depends on making the sale.

"Sorry I'm late. Scarlett and I were saying it was about time we all met. Bury the hatchet. Not that there's a hatchet to bury. But I've heard so much about you, Scarlett thinks the world of you."

I can see he's running his mouth but Dad can't tell, he's confused, I can see the back of his head, the wispy grey hairs, I know his brain is computing a thousand things a second, and I know there's no way he can reconcile the boyfriend he imagined in his head with this assured, assertive guy in front of him.

Who I love.

"So, what do you actually do?" says Dad. He sounds like the Queen. I stifle a snigger.

So here we are in Archway, in a new posh canteen with bare brick walls and bright open kitchen. I'm having poached eggs and avocado while Hayden and Dad chose giant fry ups with posh organic sausages and crispy fried bacon. The vicious Dad who cornered me in the kitchen has disappeared. I want to warn Hayden that he's a wolf in sheep's clothing.

"I'm a DJ."

Hayden catches my eye. He's wearing jeans and a casual shirt. I didn't even know he owned a shirt. It suits him. He's left the top button undone and he's wearing the dress shoes which previously lived in the corner of his wardrobe underneath a pile of socks. I think he's polished them.

The fact he dressed up makes me giddy.

"And what does that *involve*?" says Dad.

The best Hayden showed up. The superstar-DJ Hayden. Who can be better than Mikey Miles. Who can change people's lives.

"The essence of DJing *is* . . ." says Hayden, eyes twinkling, ". . . playing one track after another."

Dad frowns.

"But it's not just that. It's playing the *right* tracks in the *right* order at the *right* time. Boom!" Hayden claps his hands together. Dad and I nod in agreement.

"Sounds simple, but it ain't."

"There was me thinking it was just a bunch of young kids off their face." When he says *off their face* a part of me dies. His voice is so stuffy and posh, like a Radio Four presenter.

"It is," says Hayden. "I'm not gonna lie. Drugs are an integral part of club culture. But *proper* DJing, *proper* clubbing, the drugs are just by-the-by. It's all about the music."

Dad cuts open a sausage. Hayden's like the naughty boy who can get out of trouble by smiling and cracking a joke.

"For me, when I play it's all about getting *out* of the way. It's my personal taste in music. It's about the feeling. The energy in the room. Tuning into where everyone is at. There's a point in the evening – if it's working – where something happens – something takes over. It's like I can do anything, play anything –

the music just flows – me and the room – there's no difference – we've merged into one. But it's not *me* doing it. It's something else."

Dad carefully pierces his egg yolk, orange goo spilling on to the plate.

"I suppose that's how I remember it. Except in my day we were in fields and it was all illegal."

My jaw hits the table.

If Hayden is surprised he doesn't miss a beat.

"You used to go raving?"

"Not much. But I did go, yes," says Dad. "When it was all rumours and whispers and everyone bundling in a car to some field in Sussex."

Dad's avoiding my eye.

"Of course it's all changed. It's big business now. It's a machine. My mate's a DJ – Mikey Miles, you know him?"

Dad shakes his head.

"He just tours, relentlessly. Finish at 5 a.m. Saturday morning in Italy, start again 8 p.m. in Germany. He has to be on it, new tracks, new mixes, filming the peak moments when the crowd kick off, posting them to social media. He's knackered but his manager is like, "'If you stop playing, if you stop moving, in this game, you're dead.'"

"Trevor," I say, sniggering again at the name.

"Yeah, Trevor," says Hayden.

"And that's what you want, is it?"

"That's what I want," says Hayden, looking me in the eye. "Because it's the best job in the world."

"Do you get much work?" says Dad.

"I'm just getting started. Scarlett's been helping me. Next month in Shoreditch. She got me the gig. It's a big break for me. She's . . . she's amazing . . ."

"Scarlett's got a lot of thinking to do at the moment."

"Your daughter is talented. So so talented. She will succeed at anything she puts her hands to."

Dad drags his fork through the remains of his egg yolk.

"I'd like to hear your music," says Dad.

"Sure."

"I'm not sure you'd like it, Dad."

"I'd still like to hear it," he says. "In fact, I'd like to go. To your big break. I'd like to see you in action."

"What?" I say.

"Yeah."

Dad concentrates on chopping up the tomato he clearly doesn't like and that he's left till last.

"You've sold it to me."

"Sure thing. Give me your name and I'll put you on the guest list."

I kick Hayden hard under the table. Amazingly, he doesn't flinch.

"That would be good."

"I'm going to be part of it too!" I blurt out.

It's another blindsiding revelation, coming from nowhere, and I mean it with every cell in my body. "I don't know how, but I'm going to work in the industry. With Hayden. I just know I am."

Dad looks at his plate, forks the tomato into his mouth and says nothing.

39

It's like kissing him for the first time, rough, groping, gasping, eyes closed, pulling his hair, squeezing his ass. A bus comes and goes before he presses me against the bus shelter bench, my back squashed against the glass. We could do it right here, in broad daylight, early afternoon, on the pavement in front of everyone. I tug his waistband and let my fingers slip inside.

"Get a room, guys!"

Hayden jumps up and away, revealing . . . Elliot . . . and holding his hand . . . Aya.

They've barely been together for a month and she's turned them into a perfectly coordinated androgynous couple, him in skinny jeans and a striped tight t-shirt, her in a spotless Nike hoodie, hair tied up in a ponytail and hidden under a baseball cap. I should have known better than to do this five minutes from my house.

"Hi," I say, wishing I wasn't so flustered, had washed my hair, wasn't wearing sweatpants and my trainers weren't scuffed. I hide my fingernails so they won't see the dirt.

"Hi!" says Elliot, a little sarcastically.

I go through the painful routine of kissing and fake-hugging, as if this is a happy surprise.

"Elliot – Hayden – Hayden – Elliot."

Elliot holds out his hand and I watch Hayden crush it. I never liked Elliot's weak handshake.

"You guys look like you were having fun," says Aya. Her eyes are eager, like she wants to please us.

"You perving?" says Hayden.

"Ew, no thanks."

I want to stab her.

"You guys look dressed up," I say. "Where are you going?"

"Shopping," says Elliot.

"Seriously?"

I put my arm round Hayden while he pulls out his phone and opens the Uber app.

"So . . ." says Elliot, "About what we were talking about."

"I know," I say. "Hayden's DJing first weekend of September. We should all go. Shoreditch."

"Shoreditch, I love Shoreditch!" says Aya.

"At a club called Community."

"I know that club!" says Aya.

You're not supposed to know it. It's my world, not yours.

"Let's all go together. Hayden will sort the other stuff."

"You're a DJ?" says Aya. "Sick."

I cringe.

"That would be good," says Elliot. "We can finally all hang out."

Why did I do this? Why did I just arrange a night out that I totally don't want? Why did I just arrange to sell drugs to my friend who hates drugs?

"Our driver's here," says Hayden.

"How were your results?" I say to Elliot.

"One A, one A star and one B," he says, looking at the pavement.

"No!"

"What about you?"

A red Volvo pulls up ahead of the bus stop and beeps its horn. Hayden walks towards it.

"Not quite what was expected, let's put it that way," I say.

"But you got your offer, right?" says Elliot, alarmed.

"I'll call you!" I say, running to joining Hayden.

As we drive off I see Elliot still waiting at the bus stop, watching us drive away.

"Sorry, sorry, sorry, sorry, sorry, sorry."

Hayden speaks right into my ears, his forehead pressed against my temple.

"I love you."

"I love you too. I thought I'd lost you."

"Me too!"

Waves of relief wash over me and I feel weightless, like a helium balloon rising up into the sky.

"I'm sorry I smashed your table."

"That's something you don't hear every day. Casual remorse for casual violence."

I laugh.

"I'm sorry I burnt your house down."

"I'm sorry I chopped off your foot."

"I'm sorry I axe-murdered your family."

We're laughing. Whatever happens, we always laugh.

But then he pulls away and looks out of the window as our Uber crawls through the Euston Road traffic. A homeless guy shouts and raves, gesticulating wildly at another homeless guy who's lying in a zipped-up sleeping bag.

"Maybe I didn't want to believe that something good had actually happened to me," he says.

I grab his hand and squeeze it. I glance up at the rear-view mirror and catch the driver watching me. His brown eyes are familiar.

"I have to admit. You scared me for a moment," says Hayden.

"Why?"

"You had a . . . this look."

"What do you mean?"

"The only way I can describe it is that you actually became the Incredible Hulk. For a second. I thought, that's why she likes the comics. They're based on her life!"

I blush.

"I've never done anything like that before."

"Seriously?"

My balloon is popped. I'm hurtling back to the pavement.

"You have a temper."

"You can talk. Your eyes went all weird, I thought you were going to stab me."

"Yeah, well, it's in the past now."

I laugh again. I rest my head on his shoulder and we ride on in silence.

"How did you know to come to my house?"

"I put myself in your shoes . . . I thought, where would I go if I was Scarlett and I'd just done what I'd done?"

"Yeah but *I* didn't even know where I was going until I got there."

I sit up with a start.

"I reckon we're going to find out that we had the same parents and were separated at birth."

"That would be incest. And it would mean we're adopted."

"Yeah, I know . . . I still think it's going to happen, though."

The indicator tick-tocks as the driver turns a corner and my stomach churns as he accelerates forward.

"I think I know why I lost it," I say.

"Why?"

I whisper in his ear, so the driver doesn't hear.

"We need a break. Too many comedowns. We've been caning it. I thought I was okay, but maybe my synapses are fried, maybe my neural pathways are destroyed."

"Maybe," he says.

"It'll be good for your gig."

"Maybe."

"Mikey Miles is sober."

The moment I say the name Hayden frowns, the same cute frown I saw from my window all that time ago, and I know his shutters are down and I don't want to open them in case a bomb goes off.

"You're right," he says. "Enough pills. Enough booze. Enough."

The driver's eyes are soft and creased. He's smiling at me. I remember them now! It's the same driver from that night I snuck out of my house and went to Elephant and Castle. His long black beard greying at the edges, the pristine white skullcap on his head. I like the way he looks it me. It's kind. I remember that phrase – *I have always relied on the kindness of strangers* – I think I know what it means.

I shiver as Hayden kisses the inside of my neck.

"You've got one week to design me a logo."

"What?"

"You got me to basecamp. I'm making sure you come up the rest of the mountain."

2 weeks later

40

Hayden didn't come home.

He sent me a message at eight thirty-one last night.

Guess what? I've officially given up! Can I get a badge saying Officially Given Up? There's no longer a suspicious bulge in my underpants. I'm walking down the street and I'm not worrying about the feds. I mean, I'm still worrying about the feds, but if they stopped me I've got nothing on me! If they searched my room all they'd find is a suspiciously hot girl! They can't arrest me for that, can they?

It was the kind of message that leaves you so buzzing that you smile so wide that it hurts your cheeks and you feel like talking to strangers on the bus. Which is where I was, on the way back from Sainsbury's. Maybe I'd underrated natural highs. I mean, we'd both decided that organic happiness was the way forward, right?

So now he's disappeared.

He went right off the radar.

It made no sense.

Everything had sorted itself out. We were *sober.* All week.

No drinking, no smoking, no cheeky halves at dinnertime, nothing apart from cups of tea, chocolate biscuits and jelly babies. A lot of jelly babies.

We were up so early we even had breakfast with the rest of the house.

"So nice to see you guys around," said Harper. "Normally you're all locked up in Hayden's room being antisocial and having drugged-up sex and making us feel lame and single."

It shocked me, this *reality*. It was like, up until now, every breath, every thought, every action was blazing with our togetherness. Our love was like a white hot, all-consuming fire. Did we burn the people who came too close? Did we suffocate them with our toxic fumes?

Now that I wasn't buzzing off my face or totally bone-knackered I had the space to think about this stuff. A little too much. I had the space to *notice* stuff.

Like Harper's Sainsbury's Basics muesli she eats out of the box. Alejandro's chocolate pastries from Lidl that he dips in jars of dodgy fake Nutella. Cristina's cornflakes that she never finishes and never washes up the bowl afterwards. Breakfast: it's so lonely – they're all so lonely. The house is so full of loneliness and I'd never even realised.

So I did what I always do when I want things to get better. I washed up everyone's dirty dishes. I mopped the kitchen floor before bed. I folded other people's washing without them asking me to. I wanted them to know I cared. I wanted it to feel like home.

I was just so happy and relieved that me and Hayden had found each other, two broken people who were putting their lives back together again.

Ten days ago, at breakfast, Hayden stood up and tapped his mug with a teaspoon as if he was about to make a toast.

"I'd like to take this opportunity to make an announcement,' he said, pausing for effect. "I am hanging up my raving shoes. I've had my fun. More than my fair share. But it turns out that if you win the competition for most-amount-of-drugs-consumed-in-one-night, you lose the competition for functioning-as-a-normal-human-being. What's the point of dealing drugs if your brain's so battered it can't even count? I have the self-control of a three-year old. If there's a hundred pills in my pocket I will chomp every single one. One day there will be a blue plaque on the front of this house saying *Hayden raved here*. That's good enough for me. But now I want to be the person *in* the DJ booth, not just clinging to the DJ booth because I can't stand up. So, I'm very happy to tell you all that these Supermen are my last batch. Once it's gone it's gone. No more dealing. No more pills. No more booze, no more spliff. Ever. I'm going one hundred percent clean."

He smiled, as if waiting for the applause.

"Screw you, Hayden," said Harper.

Hayden frowned his cute little frown.

"What do you expect *us* to do?"

"Now we have to go to some dodgy bloke in the club who sells us baking soda laced with rat poison," said Alejandro, putting his head in hands.

"You're supposed to be happy for me," said Hayden.

"Because giving up drugs is supposed to be the happy ending for all of us? What if we think that drugs improve our life? What if *our* happy ending means *not* stopping?" said Harper.

"Guys. I know this is a shock. I know you've got it in you to find someone else. Someone even better than

me, who sells the purest MDMA out there. I believe in
you guys."

"Life is so much easier when you live with your
dealer," said Harper.

"I think this is a good idea," said Cristina, unsmiling.

"Thank you!" said Hayden.

For a while the only sound was Harper crunching
her muesli. Eventually, Alejandro stood up.

"You're a brave man."

He shook Hayden's hand.

Harper sniffed. A tear ran down her cheek and
dropped into her muesli.

We all laughed.

"If it's the right thing for you then it's the right
thing for you," she said. "But it's the end of an era."
She put her face in her hands and sobbed. I tried to
hug her but she pushed me away, holding up her palm
as if to say "*end of*".

"It is the right thing for me," said Hayden. "And I
could never have done it without Scarlett. She's joining
me on this adventure into healthiness. She might be
younger than all of us but she's wiser than all of us. I
mean it."

Alejandro applauded, and stopped when no one
joined in. I hated that half-hearted attempt at congratulations. Or was it just that I'm incapable of receiv-
ing a compliment? I blushed hard and prayed for the
moment to pass.

Then Alejandro asked Hayden how many pills were
left and they all put in their last orders. I think Hayden
felt guilty because he gave them a massive discount
and sold them all pills for two pounds each, which

made everyone really happy and lifted the mood. Back in his room he couldn't stop kissing me and my worries disappeared into thin air.

Sober Hayden was like a man possessed. He was on his iMac at 9.30 a.m., searching Beatport for new tunes, mixing, rehearsing, and composing. At 5 p.m. he'd head out to sell the last batch.

He even delivered to Elliot's house, sitting on his sofa, asking him to explain the difference between the Amazing Spider-Man and the Superior Spider-Man while counting out pills on his table. He didn't have enough and offered to come back later. Elliot offered to lend him some rare sixties comics as a guarantee. Kind of cringey but that's how charming Hayden can be.

He went into Food and Wine and told Cenk's dad that he had retired. After all that drama they begged him to reconsider and offered him a cut-price deal to keep him going, to keep him in it, but he said no. He told me that Cenk had given him a man-hug and wished him well.

He told me that he thought the whole reason he'd got into dealing in the first place was so the universe could bring him to Food and Wine and let him meet me in Paradise Park. Everything happens for a reason, he said.

And yesterday he'd come home in a brand-new navy-blue t-shirt, a large, fluorescent yellow *H* emblazoned on the front, both its arms blurring to the left as if the letter was speeding into the future.

It's Hayden's logo.

I designed it.

While he worked on his tunes I sat on his bed and did my bit. I spent hours researching DJ websites and club flyers. I downloaded Photoshop and watched every YouTube tutorial I could, deciphering toolbar buttons, scouring the web for free images and fonts, trying something new, pressing Undo, trying something new, pressing Undo.

My old battered laptop creaked under the strain, but I didn't care. I loved it. I loved every second of it.

We both agreed there should be no cheesy name, like *DJ Hell* or *DJ Mayhem*, or *DJ Drop-the-Beat* or some shit like that.

He was always going to be Hayden.

Before I left school to come to college the headmistress gave us a speech about taking risks. She showed us a slide of Steve Jobs and Steve Wozniak, the founders of Apple, working out of a garage, building a computer. She was trying to teach us that to dream big, you have to start small.

That's how we felt in his bedroom, like this was the beginning of something.

And when I saw the t-shirt I had to rip it right back off him. Everything was coming together.

And now he's disappeared.

I'm here on his bed. He's not next to me. It's nine in the morning and there's no message on my phone. I've had three hours' sleep and in fourteen hours he's supposed to be on stage.

41

I've had enough of freaking out, so I head downstairs. No sign of Harper or Alejandro – they must be still asleep. Cristina stands with her back to me in a black nightie, its white lace appliqué barely covering her arse. She hovers over the boiling kettle, her sexuality radiating out like a ray-gun blast, and I almost head straight back out.

But I can't. Not today.

"Is there enough in there for me?"

She spins round, startled.

"Sure."

"I didn't know you liked coffee," I say, noticing the granules in her mug.

"Sometimes. When I don't sleep well."

I take a cup out of the cupboard. I can't do small talk this morning.

"Hayden didn't come back last night."

"Oh no," she says. The boiling water rumbles and roars like thunder. "Why?"

"I don't know. He's disappeared."

"Serious?"

"Serious."

"That's not good."

It isn't. I wait for her to ask me if I am okay, to offer to help, to offer a solution, but nothing comes.

"He's DJing tonight."

"I know. We're all going, remember?"

I take the Nescafe from the cupboard, but my hands are shaking and I drop it, scattering dark brown grains across the chequered lino. I go down on my knees and grab the manky dustpan and brush from underneath the sink.

"He just sold the last of his stash. He messaged me to say he was coming home. He was so happy he didn't have to worry about the feds anymore. What if they stung him? What if he actually sold his last batch of pills to a police officer? How cruel would that be? He gets arrested the day he actually gives up!"

"You are being paranoid."

"But why isn't he back? Why didn't he text me?"

"Have you called him?"

"Like, a thousand times."

She stands over me, watching my pathetic attempts at sweeping. I seem to be spreading the granules outwards rather than into a neat pile. With a tut she bends down and snatches the brush.

"I'll do it. You need to relax. Go for a walk. Hayden will come back. I promise."

How long does a person have to be missing before you can go to the police?

I Google it.

Twenty-four hours.

Shit.

I call Harper.

She doesn't work Saturdays, she should be here. I leave a message explaining what happened.

But I don't want to go to the police because then

I'd have to talk about who he is and where he was and pretend he wasn't a dealer, and I'm crap at lying. Well, I assume I'm crap at lying, because I've never lied to the police before. There's no way I can cover up the fact that all Hayden's been doing for the last three years is non-stop breaking the law.

But what if going to the police is the right thing to do?

I head upstairs to Harper's room, knock, and open the door. She's not there. A plate of leftover pizza crusts lies on her unmade bed. Jumpers, blouses, dresses and coat hangers are scattered across the floor. Her backpack – normally next to the bed – isn't there.

Maybe she went out after work and stayed with a friend.

Maybe she met a guy.

Maybe she's with Hayden.

I picture them making out on some dingy club sofa, crooked and spread-eagled, like when Harper snogged Alejandro the first time I came here. I shove it out of my mind. I am paranoid. Cristina is right.

There *will* be a reason. A good reason.

I call Harper three more times and each one it goes to voicemail.

What about Alejandro? I don't have his number. I walk to the top of the stairs and knock. After some scuffling and the sound of footsteps the door swings open.

"What?"

Her starry-sun bedspread is all scrunched up, her coffee rests on the middle of the bed by an open book. Probably a psychology one. I'm struck by how unfair it is that the smallest person in the house gets one of the biggest rooms.

"Do you have Alejandro's number?"

She sighs.

"Sure."

She turns round to look for her phone.

"Harper's disappeared, too."

"Scarlett!"

"I don't know what to do."

"I'll send you his number."

"Thank you," I say.

"And stop worrying!"

Alejandro and I have come a long way since he blocked my path in Hayden's hall and called me beautiful. Now I see him as this kind of cute raving little brother, like a lucky mascot – there's something wrong if we're out and loved up and he's not there. Thank God I think he twigged pretty fast he's so not my type which is just as well as him and Harper have their thing. We don't talk much – but he's part of the family, we don't need to – until now. I just pray his fried brain is functioning enough to help me.

He answers his phone within seconds. I tell him I need to speak to him and he sends me the address of the sandwich bar where he works.

I get off the bus by the Shard. It's just as impressive up close, massive, shiny, pointy, a proper landmark. I decide that when I find Hayden we'll go on a date at the top. It's Saturday morning and it feels busier than rush hour, hundreds of tourists and families, many of them heading to Borough Market where Mum once bought me a burger for twelve pounds. I make my way to the High Street and soon I see him, in white shirt and tan apron, raised up in a booth barely big enough to be labelled a shop, rows of ugly baguettes laid out in front of him. Chicken and bacon. Egg and mayonnaise.

Chicken salad. The food capital of London is down the road and he's round the corner selling manky sandwiches. But then he smiles when he sees me – and it takes me aback, because he's genuinely pleased.

A stream of customers buys coffee and baguettes, and he painfully, ponderously serves them, as if it's his first day and he's trying to remember how the coffee machine works. His friendly looks and smiles continue, making people turn and look. I feel icky them thinking I'm his girlfriend. I just want to get this over with.

Finally, there's a gap in the flow and he jumps out on to the pavement.

"Hayden's disappeared!" I say.

"Seriously?"

"Yes!"

"Where is he?"

"If I knew that I wouldn't be here!"

Alejandro winces.

"Sorry," I say.

"Have you called him?"

"Of course I've called him!"

A woman arrives and in a stereotypically loud American voice demands to know if the chicken and mayonnaise baguette has normal or low-fat mayonnaise. Alejandro stands like a rabbit in a headlight, torn between the both of us. We're saved by the arrival of his colleague, just in the nick of time.

"It's my break," he says. "Let's talk."

We find ourselves walking into London Bridge station. We drift around the massive concourse that's like a giant aircraft hangar, roof miles high, lined with alternating strips of wood and rows of harsh spotlights.

At its centre pairs of long escalators lead up to the platforms. Rows of wooden seats are dotted around, but they're all occupied, so we perch on this weird metal fence thing that runs around the edge. It isn't big enough to be a bench, hurts our asses and has no discernible point to its existence. I fill Alejandro in on every last detail.

"I'm scared. He *always* calls. He's never *not* called. That's why it has to be serious. This is his big break. It's so unfair!"

Alejandro goes silent, before finally mumbling, "Hayden disappears."

"What?"

"Hayden disappears."

"Hayden disappears. What do you mean?"

"He always does it, he always comes back. I live with him for over a year. He always disappears."

"I don't get it."

The tannoy blares an announcement which echoes round the concourse and hurts my head.

"What happens when he disappears?"

Alejandro's eyes roll up inside his head. I thought he only did that when on drugs.

"After the party where I met you. He told me he didn't leave his house for days . . ."

"Well, he disappeared to me cause none of us saw him. I think he gets depressed or something."

"He's disappeared because he's depressed?"

Alejandro shrugs. I fold my arms and scratch my elbows.

"I saw him last night."

"You what?"

"I saw him last night. I picked up."

"I thought you already did that."

Alejandro shrugs.

"I needed extra. Some friends from Spain are coming next week. I had to cover my ass."

"Where?"

"In Camden. With Mikey Miles."

"You what?"

"In the pub. With Mikey Miles."

"Shit."

"You didn't know?"

"No!"

"I thought he would have told you."

"He didn't."

"It didn't look like they were getting on."

"What do you mean?"

"I dunno. I just turned up and paid him, I didn't want to get involved. But Mikey Miles didn't look happy. When he saw me he stormed out. Hayden pretended it didn't happen. Just sold me the pills and walked away."

"What pub?"

"The Good Mixer."

"Where?"

"Camden."

42

Why didn't he tell me that he'd met Mikey Miles?

I mean, he had good reason, right? He's playing for him. So it must have been business. A chat about the set times, how the night's gonna work, going over the music policy, just in case Hayden wants to drop some Acid House for a laugh. It must have been a networking social, a chance to bond before the big night.

But then why did they argue?

Did Hayden ask to play for longer?

Did he say the money was crap and demand to get more?

Did Hayden freak out?

Did he tell Mikey that he couldn't do it and wasn't ready?

Was he thinking that nothing good ever happens to him, like that night in the kitchen?

Mikey Miles wouldn't tell him that we kissed . . . would he?

He wouldn't organise a meeting the night before his club night and say, "By the way, I tried to shag your girlfriend the other week, she kissed me back, I think she liked it."

I mean, why would he do that?

I call Mikey Miles, but it goes straight to voicemail.

I call Hayden, but it too goes straight to voicemail.

That's bad. Before, at least his phone actually rang, which suggests his phone was on, which suggests he had it with him. But going straight to voicemail suggests his phone is now off. And an off phone feels worse than an on one.

I jump on the Northern line and take a jam-packed Tube to Camden. It's market day and practically the whole train gets off at the station. On the escalator I get stuck behind a group of girls, barely older than Year 10s, hair straightened, full make-up, a catwalk parade of denim shorts, summer dresses, patterned camisoles and chunky sunglasses. They lean on the handrails, soft-skinned, baby-faced, casual and aloof and I almost cry. I feel so old. I've had more life happen to me than they have combined. More than my fair share.

Outside, they disappear into a warren of market stalls while I try to orientate myself. Trance music blares from a leather jacket shop. A pram knocks into my shin and a drunk in a winter coat swears loudly at himself. I ask a topless guy who's handing out flyers where The Good Mixer is and he winks and asks if I want to go for a drink. My cheeks burn and he puts his hand on my shoulder, tells me he's "only joking" and points to a side street.

"Down there on the right."

I wind my way across the road, past a goth shop displaying every variety of black boot you could imagine, in between two markets stalls selling tourist tat, tea towels printed with St Paul's Cathedral, model red-phone boxes and Union Jack t-shirts, past a cocktail bar, its happy hour starting now (midday) and a

Chinese restaurant, and there it is, printed white capitals on a navy-blue sign, The Good Mixer.

A guy with a mop-top indie-boy haircut and grey round his temples sits at the bar drinking a Guinness, his guitar case propped up next to him. I avoid his eyes, order a beer and sit down.

Why am I here? Did I think I could catch Hayden's scent like I'm some kind of sniffer dog? I get out my phone and Google drug arrests in Camden. I scan the news on the Metropolitan police website. Someone got convicted for armed robbery. A couple got assaulted in Swiss Cottage. But no drug dealers in Camden.

I fire up Twitter and check every London police account that I can find. I search for all tweets mentioning 'police' and 'arrest' in London last night.

Nothing.

There's no way I can go into a police station and give Hayden's name and ask if he's been arrested.

Hayden was here in this pub less than twenty-four hours ago.

And now he's gone.

I drink fast – at least the alcohol calms my nerves – as my phone vibrates: it's my dad. I'm meant to be having lunch with him, now we're on this weird reconciliation-but-not-reconciliation thing. I buy some chewing gum from a newsagent and jump back on the Tube, thinking about what I'm going to tell him.

43

"What is it?" says Dad, as he chews on a spring roll. "Not hungry?"

I reluctantly spoon some egg fried rice and toxic-shiny beef on to my plate.

"Hayden. He's . . . not very well."

"Oh no," says Dad, insincerely. "Is he going to have to cancel?"

"No! I hope not."

"I've been looking forward to it."

A shiver runs down my spine. Somehow Hayden turning up at my house and mounting a charm offensive, our elation at our reunion and Dad's big reveal about going to a rave thirty years ago created a bizarre atmosphere where inviting him to listen to Hayden DJ seemed like a cool thing to do.

I shove some rice into my mouth and force myself to chew it. I feel like ants are crawling up and down my thighs.

It was an *idiotic* thing to do.

That's when I realise that drinking a beer broke mine and Hayden's sobriety rule.

But if Hayden was in the pub with Mikey Miles he must have broken it last night.

Does that mean our great commitment to giving up

dealing and drugs was just a stupid delusion? If we can break it without even thinking after less than two weeks?

How much other stuff am I deluded about? Can I ever trust anything? What's Hayden's secret? What's he hiding from me?

I swallow some rice and it scrapes uncomfortably against my oesophagus on its way down.

"What time should I get there?" says Dad.

I hate his expressionless face, his small mouth, his tired eyes, rimless glasses, his bald patch, I hate the mole on the top of his head. I hate the way he sits stooped over the table. He's inevitably going to become one of those old people who walk around at right-angles.

"What happened with Jennifer?" I say.

"Hmm?"

"What happened with Jennifer?"

I want him to tell me how messed up it got, how horribly wrong things went.

He chews his food irritatingly slowly.

"It didn't work out."

"Yeah, I know that, I'm asking you why."

"She changed her mind."

"Yeah, obviously she changed her mind. I'm asking you why."

Jennifer was the one who calmed him down and stopped him calling the police when I went out all night. She was trying to stop me having to cook for him. She could see what was wrong and what needed to happen.

Weirdly, I kind of wish she was here now.

"I think the thought of being part of another family was too much for her."

What he's saying is that she didn't want *me*. She didn't like *me*. He's saying it's *my* fault.

"I don't believe you. I think she was well up for making a nice new cosy-cosy family."

"Do you?"

He stands up and opens the door to the garden, letting in a cool gust of wind. The lawn is overgrown. New weeds tower above the bushes.

"You're just like her, you know," he says.

"Like who?"

"Mum. You see right through me. I could never hide anything from her."

My tear ducts well up.

"She was good at gardening, too."

The left corner of his mouth twitches in an attempt to smile.

"The real reason Jennifer is not here is . . . is I don't understand why she's not here. We just started fighting. After that night you stayed out. We had these massive rows over . . . nothing. Over which supermarket to go to. I'd stand up and she'd scream at me for being in her way. I don't know why. It was like before we loved each other and now we couldn't stand each other."

He walks into the garden, distracted by something. He bends over one of the flower beds – if you can even call it a flower bed – and pokes at some foliage with his foot and then scrapes his sole on the lawn. He walks back to the door, slips off his shoes and comes inside.

"Neighbour's cat's been shitting in our garden."

I laugh. Why am I laughing?

"Jennifer said that I hadn't finished grieving."

He says it with a smile, in his cheery voice. Our eyes lock together. His smile falters. A tear rolls down his cheek and I shoot out of my chair and hug him. He lets out three big sobs into my shoulder. We stay there, close, my face pressed into his chest, before he pulls himself away and walks upstairs to the bathroom. A minute later he returns with dry eyes and an expression that tells me the moment is over. I clear the plates – my appetite is gone – put on the kettle and make us some instant coffee.

I just blurt it out.

"Hayden has disappeared."

"What?"

"He's disappeared."

"What do you mean?"

"He went out last night and hasn't come home."

Dad stands up with a start and clenches his fists. Again, I laugh.

"You can't punch him, he's not here."

"He disappears the day of his gig?"

"Yes."

Dad sighs in a way that says *what a pathetic idiot*.

"I actually think something genuinely bad has happened."

Dad shakes his head. I can see the thoughts ricocheting around his brain. He mutters under his breath.

"What?"

"I just want to protect you! That's all I ever wanted to do!"

I've never heard him shout before, I think he's going to take his coffee cup and smash it over my face. My hands grip the underside of the table and my biceps flex.

I can't smash another one. I'll get a reputation.

I watch the steam rise from the top of his cup, the tiny bubbles of froth around the rim.

"You've always had something vulnerable about you, Scarlett. Really vulnerable."

He says it like I'm a burden.

"No," I say. "That is the most patronising thing ever. Why do you need to feel so powerful? Why do you need to control me? What are you so scared of?"

I *know* Hayden is a good person. I *know* he is. Wherever he is, I will never stop caring about him.

"Look at what's happened," he says, as if that explains everything.

"All I want is for you to let me be who I am!" I scream.

He blinks, like I've just chucked water over him.

"See you later," I say, grabbing my bag.

I have the strongest urge to go to the bench where we met. I want to sit there and . . . I don't know what. Maybe that fateful, magic meeting place will help. If I sit there I might understand why everything's gone wrong. I might be hit by an insight that will change my perspective and make everything right again. Or maybe it's the only thing I can do to make me feel close to him.

I march up the road to Paradise Park. We're a week into September and the sky is already grey and full of bruised clouds. There's a bunch of blokes in green and yellow bibs playing a football match. The playground is crowded with buggies, babies and screaming children. And the bench is . . . someone's sitting on it!

Back to me, hoodie up, hunched over, as if they are about to puke.

I shiver. That's my bench! I'm even getting goose bumps like the first time I met him! I need to sit there!

He sways from the hips. Please don't vomit. I can't sit somewhere filled with fresh sick.

Maybe if I concentrate hard enough he'll get up and move away.

I should march up to him, tell him it's my bench and he needs to leave.

If I don't sit there I'm not sure what will happen.

No, wait! Those scuffed Nikes. Those tracksuit bottoms.

Surely not . . .

Shaking, I sit down next to him.

Slowly, clumsily, the person heaves himself upright. It's Hayden.

He struggles to speak, lips shaking, mouth distorting. He makes a honking growl, like a wasted Chewbacca.

His pupils are huge.

He's off his nut.

He buries his face in my shoulder. I wrap my arms around his back. He feels fragile, as if I could crush him, and he doesn't hug me back.

He knows about Mikey Miles. I'm sure of it.

"Hayden," I say. "I'm sorry."

"No!" It comes out like a grunt and is muffled into my coat but it's definitely a *no*.

He pulls his head away and his eyes roll up into his skull. His tongue rolls around. I steady his face with my hands, one on each cheek.

"I'mmmmm sorrrry," he says.

He follows me like a docile animal. At the park gates a young boy cycles towards us on a tiny bike with squeaking stabilisers. For some reason Hayden finds this funny and gives him two big uncoordinated thumbs up. The boy frowns and cycles off quickly. What has he been taking? He's always held it together before. Pills? Acid? Smack?

We head towards the Broadway. As we pass Food and Wine Hayden pulls his hood up and bends double like an old man, as if he doesn't want to be recognised. He lopes along like the Hunchback of Notre Dame, before toppling forward and hitting his head on the pavement. When he stands up a trickle of blood runs down his cheek.

"Just stay on your feet and follow me," I say.

I need to get him home. I need to get him sober so I can find out where the hell he's been and why he's in this state.

I don't take my eyes off him for the entire Tube journey. His head lolls like a newborn baby's and I steady it with my hand. I watch the other passengers reflected in his inky-black pupils.

At Bank station he places his hand on my knee, grips it hard and closes his eyes, his forehead covered in sweat. I can *feel* his chemical rush. Maybe he double-dropped. Or triple-dropped. Or quadruple-dropped.

Opposite us are three girls clutching H&M bags. They yak into each other's ears and giggle. Hayden could be dying in front of their eyes and no one would lift a finger.

It takes double the time to walk home but we make it. I grab his keys from his pocket and open the front door, shouting some loud *hellos*. No one's in. I lead Hayden to his bed and tell him to get some rest but he ignores me and shuffles over to his iMac. He spends an age logging in, finger hovering over the keyboard, searching for the right letter, clumsily typing the pass-word. The password box shudders, indicating the wrong entry. I picture him in an institution, needing help to go to the toilet. Has he permanently destroyed his brain? Will he ever be the same again?

The blue t-shirt with the yellow *H*, the one I designed and got printed at the print shop, lies crumpled at his feet, his dirty trainers rocking over the neck-line.

"Pick it up," I say. "You're making it disgusting."

Hayden stands up and manoeuvres round the bed, one hand steadying himself against the wall. When he reaches me he brushes my cheek with his fingers, an attempt at being affectionate. But he pushes too hard and his nails dig in.

"Ow!"

Frowning, he grabs my head and pulls it to his chest and mumbles something.

"What?"

"I'm sorry."

"What happened?"

"I'm sorry."

"You've already said that a million times."

A chill runs down my spine. This isn't a sorry-I-messed-up kind of sorry. It's a harder sorry, a much-worse-terrible kind of sorry.

"What happened, Hayden?"

He loses balance and we fall backwards on to the bed. He lands on top of me, laughs and looks at me as if he expects me to do the same. It's like he has no idea what he's doing *and* he's more in control than he lets on.

I disentangle myself and sit up.

"Cristina's . . . pills," he says.

I remember what he told me at the party that night at his house. Cristina's always asking for loads of pills on tick. For her friends.

"You don't have to give her stuff for free. Does she owe you money? Are you having money problems?"

Hayden nods.

I knew it. He's always been a dickhead with money, too interested in making the other person laugh, being the big man dealer. When he said he was sorting it out I believed him.

"How much?"

"Mikey . . . Miles."

"What about him?"

"He . . . he . . . he . . ."

"Nothing happened! Only for a few seconds!"

Hayden frowns.

"He tried to kiss me, he's a dick! I kissed him for literally three seconds!"

I didn't *plan* on saying it, I didn't *want* to say it, it just flew out. He must know, right?

Hayden holds out his hand, I take it and pull him up so we're sat side by side.

"Cristina."

"What about her?"

He does the running-his-hand-down-my-face-thing again. He really needs to cut his fingernails.

"What did Cristina do?"

Did she make him take pills? Did she refuse to pay him back? Does she owe him the money that he owes Cenk? Did he ask Mikey Miles for a loan? Is this why he tried to hide himself when he walked past Food and Wine?

He looks at me for a very long time.

"Later," he says. "I have to go to work."

He hauls himself back to his iMac.

Okay, okay.

He's right.

There are more pressing things.

We can deal with the money later.

Tonight has to go well. It has to be a success.

I pull out my phone. There are six messages from Elliot, all wondering where the rest of his pills are. Hayden was meant to deliver them last night. He must have forgotten. But Elliot's the least of our worries. It's 2.30 p.m. Hayden has to be at the club in six hours. I look up. He's managed to log in. He turns round and gives me the thumbs up.

"Tonight could change our lives forever."

I don't know why I say it. Actually, I do. I still believe it.

44

Watching Hayden ham-fistedly use a computer at zero miles an hour gets boring fast, so I head outside and walk up to the Elephant and Castle roundabout and call Elliot.

"We're getting ready," he says, as soon as he picks up the phone.

"Me too," I say.

"Aya's going to do my make-up."

I sigh.

"You got a problem with that?"

"No."

"Why did you make that huffy noise?"

"Sorry."

"Hayden was supposed to call me."

"I know."

"What's going on?"

"Nothing."

There's a heavy, angry silence.

"He got busy. Meet me outside the club at ten."

"Ten!"

"Just do it."

"We don't have enough . . ."

"I know!"

I'm not schlepping across London to sell drugs to Elliot. Besides, I don't have any drugs to sell.

I buy a six-pack of Budweiser on the way home, and when I step into the hall I can hear the thud-thud-thud of his music upstairs. I stand in his bedroom doorway and watch him. He sits, hood up, staring at his screen, music on. He's so still I think he may have passed out but then he lifts up a hand, hits the space bar, the music cuts out, and he turns and gives me a gormless, loved-up grin. I chuck the beers on to the bed. He watches them intently before turning away.

He does have stamina. At Harper's party he carried on for days. I swear he was already off his face when he woke me up and convinced me to sneak out. I have to have faith that he can turn up and deliver.

Even so I can no longer bear to be in the room, so I walk up the stairs to the top floor. There's no window here and it's carpetless. I sit on the dusty, worn wood, and hug my knees to my chest.

Cristina's door opens and I jump out of my skin.

"Told you he would appear," she says.

"I thought you were out."

"No."

"I shouted hello."

She shrugs.

"Maybe I didn't hear you."

She wears jeans and a t-shirt and clutches her phone, which is playing tinny music, some awful guitar-playing male singer wailing on about kissing a girl in the rain. The sound clashes with Hayden's music and hurts my brain.

"Did he tell you where he went?"

I should confront her. I should say this is all her

fault. I should tell her she has to make it right, but my courage drains and I wish I could fall through the floor all the way to the kitchen.

"No," I say.

"Hmmm," she says.

She hugs me insincerely, bony arms barely touching me.

"You will have a great life," she says.

It's a weird thing to say. Before I can respond she closes her door. I need to speak to Harper. *"Don't you ever leave her on her own out there ever again,"* she said. Well, he's left me on my own. I need her to burst in and tell him to get his act together.

I call her again.

Voicemail again.

I go back to his room and put on my outfit, an oversized black dress with large Looney-Tunes cartoon characters printed on – Daffy Duck, Bugs Bunny, and Wiley E. Coyote. I carefully apply my make-up, lime green eyeshadow with glitter around my temples. Hayden mixes a thumping tribal house tune into a jazzy, piano-driven one and the beats are in time. There's an open beer by his keyboard. He must be sobering up.

It's dark when we arrive at the club, a massive old red-brick warehouse with tall dirty windows and chipped maroon window frames. Probably a hundred years ago people slaved away in this place: children and adults packing boxes, sewing clothes, manning machines, working sixteen-hour days for twelve pence pay. Tonight a thousand ravers will pack the place out, a thought which sends a tingle down my spine and makes me forget my growing dread.

Hayden wears a New York Yankees baseball cap and a tie-dye t-shirt with an old CND ban-the-bomb logo, No Bad Vibes written underneath. I never knew he had this and am puzzling to work out when he bought it. His USB stick, attached to his keyring, hangs down from his trousers, loaded with his music and decorated with mini yellow smiley-face stickers. The MDMA-fuelled smiles have disappeared, replaced by pursed lips and the frown I fell in love with. It's annoying the heck out of me now. He hasn't looked at me once since we left the house. He let me hold his hand while we were walking, but his fingers stayed limp.

We reach the backstage entrance, a battered maroon metal door. He presses the buzzer.

"You can go now," he says.

The door swings open, revealing Bearded Guy who did the guest list from that night in Paradise. I wait while they small-talk rubbish – his boiler is broken – he's found a new hairdresser – his beard is getting bigger. Finally, he disappears inside.

"I haven't got a ticket," I say.

"You're on the guest list."

He steps into the atrium and turns to face me.

"It's probably better you don't come."

"What?"

His left eye is bigger than the right.

"Things have changed."

"What do you mean?"

"Things have changed."

I know what he means. My stupid Mikey Miles confession.

"It meant nothing. It was totally stupid . . ."

"There's someone else."

"Excuse me?"

"There's someone else. I thought it was over, but it's not, I thought I was over her, but I'm not. I thought they let me down. But they told me they made a mistake. It's kind of changed everything."

"Excuse me?"

"There's someone else."

"Excuse me?"

My whole body shakes. My skin feels like it will burst and my insides splatter on the wall.

"But . . . I love you," I say.

"This is really bad timing . . ."

"This makes no sense."

"It makes no sense to me, either."

My cheeks are crimson. Blood red. You could fry an egg on them.

"Sometimes life goes in unexpected directions."

"This makes no sense."

"It was only a few months . . ."

"It was only a few months!"

I'm dizzy. My insides are twisting in knots and then those knots are turning into knots and then those knots are turning into knots and I think I'm going to . . .

"Who is it?"

He shakes his head.

"Who is it?"

"I'm sorry . . ."

"Who is it!?"

45

That anorexic bitch! Manipulative muesli-eating mind-fucker bitch! How I could I be *so stupid*? How could I be so utterly fucking, insanely naively, one-hundred-percent played-for-a-fucking-idiot stupid!?

The very first time I met him I knew something was up.

He said to me that someone had let him down.

I asked him who.

He changed the subject.

Somewhere, a very long way away, an alarm bell rang.

Now I know why.

I ignored it.

Because he listened to me.

He was the only person in my life who *listened* to me.

And he was the hottest guy who'd ever even *looked* at me.

And when I looked him in the eyes . . .

You know what, I bet his shitty box-bedroom used to be the spare room. He only moved in there a couple of weeks before I sat on his bed, watching him undercharge moronic idiots for their pills because he wanted to look like their best mate, and I thought he was special for it.

Led down the garden path.

Every single person in that house knew that Hayden used to go out with her.

"I'm getting back with Cristina."

"Getting *back*?"

He nodded.

"What?"

"We were childhood sweethearts."

He actually said *childhood sweethearts* and his voice went all weak and sentimental, as if they were some fluffy romantic couple who held hands and ran through cornfields. As if it's a no-brainer to dump me, I mean who wouldn't, it's his *childhood sweetheart*!

"You said you loved me. You said I was coming up the mountain with you."

"I meant it when I said it. It's hard to explain."

Every. Single. Person. In. That. House. Knew. This.

And no-one said anything.

Why?

"When you told me that you went round to Mikey Miles' flat. . . . something changed."

"You said that I was a wise person who was helping you turn around your life."

"But I got second thoughts. I tried to ignore them. I tried to convince myself . . ."

"So all that praise was bollocks, just you trying to convince yourself?"

He ran his hand through his hair, sheepishly.

"What happened last night?"

"She called me. She wanted to meet up in Camden, she'd been drinking with work mates. She told me what she told me and I was like, *What the fuck?* So I called Mikey, turns out he was round the corner in a studio,

I couldn't believe they'd actually ended, I had to hear it from him. He was like, 'Take her, I don't want her.' It wasn't the nicest conversation I've ever had. I . . . thought I'd moved on . . . But it all came flooding back. Boom!"

"And you went out with her and took a load of drugs?"

"I was confused . . . I didn't want to hurt you . . . I found a baggy in the bottom of my pocket. . . . I thought I'd sold them all, my head was doing me in so I thought, why not?"

"So a quick conversation in a pub and you decided to dump me."

"Listen. She dumped *me* for Mikey Miles, then I met *you*, I was doing too many drugs – *we* were doing too many drugs – I just felt so bad that she had dumped me for this superstar. I got with you. I thought I was over her. But I wasn't."

And for a second I almost felt sorry for him, and I'm like, why am I feeling sorry for you when you're behaving like a Grade A arsehole?

Then Bearded Guy appeared and asked us if everything was okay. And Hayden said yes, went in, and closed the door.

He slammed the door on me.

And now I sit on the pavement.

It's like someone's just ripped off a layer of skin, as casual as you peel off that bit of plastic that comes on your new phone.

I want to talk to Harper.

Why didn't Harper tell me this?

Where *is* Harper?

"You're so good for Hayden."

"Hayden got dumped by his childhood sweetheart. I'm so happy to see you two together."

She used those words, *childhood sweetheart.*

What you meant to say is that you haven't seen him this happy since he was with Cristina, you neglected to tell me that little bit of important information.

I lived there, *with his ex,* for three whole months!

While she was going out with Mikey Miles!

When Harper knocked on the door after she caught me in her room, *Cristina* was in there.

Another distant alarm bell.

After the party he wasn't just depressed from the comedown, it was because he was dumped! He didn't call me. We only got together because I bumped into him.

Another alarm bell.

They rang so far away that it's taken over quarter of a year for the sound to reach me.

Why couldn't I hear them? Why couldn't I see them for what they were?

It doesn't make any sense!

How can all those words, all those I-love-yous, how can all that tingling, that knowing, our psychic connection, how can that feeling be worth nothing?

I knew he was my soul mate! I *knew* it!

Was it just like taking a pill you think it actually means something and then it wears off and . . .

Was I just some pawn in some long-drawn-out game between Hayden and Cristina?

Love is the Answer.

I hate my tattoo.

I scratch it.

Maybe if I scratch hard enough I can rip off my skin and the doctors will have to give me a skin transplant.

I press my fingernail as deep as I can.
Why won't I bleed?
Someone calls my name.
I want to bleed. I need to bleed.
Someone is shouting my name.

"Scarlett, are you okay?"

There's Elliot, Aya and Bad Ben waving. They wait for a chain of cyclists to pass and cross the road.

"You look like it's the end of the night, but it's actually the beginning," says Aya, laughing at her own joke. I get to my feet and give the biggest I smile I can.

"Hey guys!"

Elliot hugs me weakly, Aya air-kisses me on both cheeks and Bad Ben does this enthusiastic greeting I've never seen before which involves using our thumbs like a thumb-of-war and of course I don't understand how to do it, so we both look stupid and I'm too aware of my red face and the non-bleeding scratch marks on my skin.

"How's it going?" says Aya.

She's too hot. She's insanely hot. Elliot's only gone and got the hottest girl in our college. She's wearing a beige mac – like my Dad's – but of course it's smoking sexy on her and not middle-aged and stuffy like it is on him.

Underneath, she wears a super-tight mini-dress covered in glittering stars. On her feet are big black shiny boots. Elliot looks so much more confident now. He's like a grown-up version of Elliot. He's the Elliot that Elliot always wanted to be, he's finally left his top-floor fortress of comic books, room service and masturbation. Life has given him what he's always wanted, while I've just. . . . I've just . . .

"I'm fine," I say.

"Scarlett," says Elliot, eyes expectant.

He wants drugs. They all want drugs. They don't care I'm a gibbering wreck.

"Follow me," I say and march off down the road.

"Wait here guys," says Elliot, and follows me.

"Where are we going?' he says, but I'm ahead of him, I ignore him, I pretend I don't hear and I've no idea where I am so I can't answer him anyway. I lead him down a narrow alley with a brick wall on one side and a council estate on the other.

"Scarlett," he says – urgently, a little pathetically, and I know what he means. *This is dodgy. What the hell is wrong with you?*

But he doesn't say it.

The alley opens out into a tiny park. A small patch of green to our left, and a concrete playground to our right. Some East African kids play with a semi-deflated football while their hijab-wearing mum sits watching.

We sit on a bench next to some bushes.

"I never imagined we'd be doing *this* a couple of months ago," he says.

"Shhh," I say. "I haven't got anything."

"What? Where's Hayden?"

"He's given up, hasn't he? But I know someone who might be able to help."

His face flushes. I can feel his nerves.

"Hold on," I say.

I take out my phone and call Alejandro.

Success.

He's at home, he's showered, he's changed and he's down the road. He's loaded with pills and he can help us out.

"He's coming. We have to wait here."

Neither of us says anything for a very long time. Is this really the same boy that I'm supposedly best mates with? Is it the new t-shirt? The shorter hair? The getting sex? Has Magus, the old-school super-villain who created doppelgängers of all the superheroes, made one of Elliot? How can it be so easy one day and so difficult the next?

"Life moves fast," I say.

He visibly flinches. His eyes flick around as if looking for the feds.

"What do you mean?"

"Think back to the Forbidden Planet when we first met, when we were in single sex schools and sexually frustrated. We were babies."

"I guess.

"We're both pretty experienced now!" I say, a little too enthusiastically.

"I'm not going to tell you what I get up to in bed, if that's what you're angling for."

"No! God, no! I'm just saying . . . I dunno . . . the only thing that's for certain in life . . . is change . . . I guess . . ."

"Yeah. That. And death. And taxes. And Marvel rebooting super-heroes in movies that are lamer than the ones before."

I laugh. Too loud and too shrill. We watch the boys play football. One of them is Arsenal, the other Tottenham. They do their own commentary and celebrate wildly when they score. Five-four. Five-all. Six-five. Seven-five.

"Are you angry with me?" says Elliot.

"No."

"Are you sure?"

Well, I mean you totally judged me for taking drugs and going out with Hayden and now here you are buying drugs off me, so you were a complete dick but I'm not going to say that.

I put my hand on his arm. He jumps, like I electrocuted him.

"Are you angry with *me*?" I say.

"No, of course not."

"Good."

"Scarlett, I think that . . ."

Alejandro strides into the park, waving and smiling. Elliot doesn't finish and stands up nervously, his hands in his pockets.

46

It's come to this. Me and Alejandro, in a bar, drinking pints with chasers. I chose vodka because the label illustration was a sixties-style Russian rocket piercing the earth's atmosphere, smoke and fire billowing from the base. Seemed an appropriate drink to begin the night with.

"Did you find Hayden?" he says.

"Yeah, I did."

"That's good," he says, as if finding Hayden is the same as finding lost keys, and we can all move on and forget about it now.

I drink half a pint in one go.

"You're grumpy," he says.

"Am I?" I say. "I don't mean to be."

They've set aside the corner for the DJ, two small tables pushed together and a pair of CDJs on top. He's the old-guy-who-looks-after himself type, with close-cropped grey hair and a tight white top hugging pecks like plates. He's playing jazzy, funky, gospel-style house music. All the singing about epiphanies and conversions and a love that conquers all isn't having the required effect.

"So . . . you and Harper," I say.

"What?" he says, looking down and to the left. I

once read that if you look down and to the left it means you have something to hide. Or was it the right?

"Are you going out or what?"

Down and to the left.

"Every time you get mashed you get off with each other. It's about time we talked about it."

His face flushes red. I enjoy his discomfort. I want to hear about someone else's crappy relationship.

He mumbles something, inaudible against the music. I lean my ear towards him.

"I want to . . . but she doesn't want to," he shouts.

"Where is she?"

"Gone. Forever."

I frown. He produces a cheap Android phone, opens his messaging app, finds one from Harper and hands it to me.

They got me. They came to my work, shoved me in a van and grilled the hell out of me. I woke up in South London and now I'm going to bed in the outback. My mum's lost the plot. Everything sucks.

"Immigration police," he says, as if I couldn't work it out myself.

She didn't get her visa.

I thought she had it in hand.

And then, when she was down and out and in need of a friend, she called him and not me.

Maybe she cares about him more than she lets on?

"She's right," I say. "Everything does suck!"

He laughs. It irritates me.

"Do you love her?" I say.

His smile disappears. He rubs the condensation on his pint glass with his forefinger and thumb.

"This is kind of personal," he says.

Coward.

And yet she still messages him first.

Why are the people who are supposed to have my back disappearing in a puff of smoke?

Why isn't Alejandro on the phone, shouting, "Enough! We are meant to be together! I'm buying a one-way ticket to Australia right now!"

Screw it.

I wanna buy tickets for a real rocket. Isn't Richard Branson selling them? Isn't there an app for that? When's the next one leaving?

But Dad is coming. Elliot is coming. It's like they've both mind-controlled me. I want to go home but my body won't let me. They have to see tonight as a triumph. For me.

In World War Hulk Professor X and Emma Frost try to mind-control Hulk but they can't do it. He's out of control, he's too angry, the white-hot furnace of his rage protects him.

And what does the white-hot furnace of my rage do for me? Nothing. It rips open my heart, twists my intestines, and punches my pancreas. Soon my insides will be rubble and ruins. I'm like a malfunctioning Hulk.

I watch Alejandro's face – his goofy teeth, his shifty eyes, his nervous smile. I hate his weakness. The girl you love has just been deported and here you are, getting wasted as always.

He's a sad, lost boy.

Even more lost than me. If that's possible.

I'm suddenly flooded with so much compassion it almost knocks me to the floor. Hate and compassion is not a good mix so I down the second half of my pint and neck my vodka shot.

We WILL have a good time, Alejandro.

There is NO CHOICE but to have a good time.

Tonight, a GOOD TIME will be had.

We duck into the front yard of a car mechanics' shop.

"Let's drop."

"Okay."

"Actually, let's double drop."

"Serious?"

"I'm in the mood."

He hesitates.

"These are Supermen."

"I know."

"They're strong."

"I know." I roll my eyes. "Everything Hayden gets is strong."

"You always take it slow."

"It's really sweet that the biggest druggie I know is telling me to pace myself."

He frowns and shakes his head.

"Okay! I'll do one. But give me a few. For later."

"One is still a lot."

"Thanks, Dad."

We stand there, hunched over his plastic baggy. He places three little pills into my hands. Superman. Man of Steel. The Metropolis Marvel. Can fly through space faster than the speed of light. At least someone's on my team tonight.

Alejandro reaches into his jacket pocket and produces a can of Coke. I place a pill on my tongue. He opens the can.

"On three," I say.

We both take a swig and hold the liquid in our mouths. I count down with my fingers and we swallow.

He shuffles back to the pavement. I find an old Tesco Metro receipt in my pocket. I'll wrap the other pills in there.

Screw it. I chuck another in my mouth and swallow it with no liquid. I shudder at the bitterness. It feels stuck, lodged half-way down my food-pipe.

Alejandro's on the pavement, waving me forward. I stuff the remaining pill in my pants and join him.

47

Bearded Guy checks his iPad. Yes, we are on the guest list. I spot Elliot on tip-toes at the back of the queue, straining to see us over someone's shoulder. It feels good to be a VIP. Bearded Guy unhooks the rope and we head straight to the main room.

It's stunning. The entire ceiling is glass. The half-full gas-holder next door looms over us, brutal and industrial, the night sky visible through its skeletal top frame. A giant disco ball hangs in the middle, myriad spots of spinning light cascading across the ceiling.

It's already crowded.

It *is* going to be a good night.

Alejandro mimes drinking a drink. I tell him to buy me a vodka-tonic. The DJ stands on a small stage, nothing more than a blurry silhouette against a bright projector screen. Even this far away, there's something about the way the hair around his crown sticks up, the slope of his shoulders, the way he bobs to the music . . .

Alejandro reappears with a vodka and tonic in a plastic glass. I grab it and down it. Alejandro laughs. I shove the empty cup back into his hand.

"Another one."

Now he looks uncertain.

He wants to say no.

He walks back to the bar. Thank you.

I turn back to the screen and my heart stops.

H.

My *H* – the *H* that I designed and made with all my love. One second it stands strong, as tall as the ceiling, the next it shrinks down to a dot before spinning out, bigger and bigger, wider and wider until the whole screen is black. Then multiple *H*s, all in a row, like a little army bouncing up and down, perfectly in time.

How did they make it do that?

It looks *good*.

Oh my God, that's my *H*!

I head towards the decks, pushing through the crowd.

I recognise the classical violin, the bongos. It's disorientating – hearing them on an industrial-size sound system, and not a pair of iMac speakers – and there it is, the organ, heavy, rough, making even more sense than it did in his bedroom.

They're cheering, whistling, clapping. I punch the air. I whoop in delight.

Maybe it's the right tune for the right moment.

Maybe he read the crowd, maybe he felt the mood.

Somehow, he's not screwing it up.

Someone taps my shoulder. Alejandro. He's been looking for me everywhere.

I snatch the vodka tonic, down it and ask him for another one. He shakes his head. How dare he!

Anyway, I'm not going to look at the DJ. I'm going to pretend he's someone else. But there's Cristina in a boob tube, arms aloft, all bony ribs and knobbly shoulders, bottle of water swaying above her head.

I want to celebrate. I have to celebrate. I made this happen. This is my moment too.

I'm by the decks.

How did I get here?

Okay I will look, just once.

He's actually up there, industrious, nervous, fingers jerking away from the buttons like they're giving him electric shocks. He smiles, a real smile, and for a split second he looks up and our eyes lock. Then he hooks an earphone over his ear and nudges the jog dial.

I. Will. Not. Let. Anyone. Ruin. Tonight.

I pull Alejandro close to me, his knee slides between my legs and we dance up close. I put my arms around his shoulders and he holds me by the waist. At least we're on the same page. We both want to have a good time. It's not rocket science. He presses so close I topple back. I pull away and raise his hand, he twirls underneath and then I twirl back. It's nice to hold a hand.

It's nice to feel a body.

"You're really special," he shouts into my ear.

"I know," I say.

Even he deserves a chance, right?

I pull him away and push him up against the speaker stack. Then I flip one-eighty so I'm doing the same. "Can you feel it?" I scream, but of course he can't hear me. I can't hear me. The vibrations power through, coursing through my body, destroying the badness, the gunk, the poison. It's a carpet-bomb wall of sound.

This is the only way to heal our hearts.

I take his hands and pull him close.

Other bodies are nice, I decide.

Closeness is nice, I decide.

Then his tongue is in my mouth and there's warmth

and there's niceness and there's closeness and if my brain could bleed it would.

This is it, this is where I want to be, a tongue in my mouth, a body pressed close, bludgeoned to death by the beat.

My foot skids, my leg swings up, my hand reaches for the railing and misses, I'm in freefall, my head cracks on hard concrete. Two strong arms lift me up.

"Easy now."

"You saved my life," I say.

"Can you hear me?"

"Why are you so stressed? We're supposed to be enjoying ourselves."

A rush of pleasure so strong my eyelids fuse shut. My mouth clamps tight. I cannot move a muscle. I'm a lichen-covered rock, poking out of a stormy sea of delight.

This is why they call it ecstasy, right?

I can't open my eyes.

A brown-skinned man with a nose-ring laughs. I like it. I step up to him, take his hand and lean in to kiss him, but I miss his lips and kiss the wall, then I laugh because it's so funny.

Someone yanks my arm and leads me away.

"Sorry nurse," I say. "Guess it's time for my meds."

I think I've got a great sense of humour. I should be a stand-up comedienne.

Where are they taking me?

"Wait here!"

At least I think that's what they said. A thousand fire alarms ring in my ears. I don't mind. Hearing is overrated. I could stay here forever. I could die right now. It would have all been worth it.

A cool evening breeze. People chatter and somewhere the roar of a road. It's all muffled like it's two rooms away. My head nods. My pupils are so dilated there's no white left. Just pools of black, like a pond at midnight. I'm a creature of the dark hours. The owls and the cats and the bats are my friends. An orange hue pulsates, breathing, living. It's life-giving, life-sustaining energy. I extend my hands to warm them up.

"The lighting here is fabulous."

"That's the streetlight, love."

"Am I in the street?"

"No, you're in the club."

"Clubs are cool."

Someone hands me a bottle of water.

Alejandro!

Is it Alejandro?

I hold out my arms, but no one hugs me.

I'm so high.

My mouth is parched.

"Kiss me!" I say. "Someone kiss me!"

But no one does.

"What's wrong with you? Look at me! You might never get this opportunity again!"

"Scarlett?"

It's Mikey Miles!

Mikey Miles is here to save the day!

His Afro has grown. It's as big as a jungle. I need a machete to hack my way through. Does he realise that he might not be able to DJ? Does he know that his Afro won't fit in the main room? He's going to have to play Wembley stadium. It's the only place with enough space.

"Hey, Mikey, I'm a rock. Did you know that? I'm a rock and the thing about rocks that we don't realise is, basically, they actually like being rocks. They're happy being rocks. Rocks are having a really good time, being a rock is like being at a permanent rave."

"She's bleeding. Anyone got a towel?"

Who said that?

I'm going to need the Incredible Hulk to open my mouth. I remember the Incredible Hulk. I used to really like him.

"Hey, Mikey. Can we rewind to the other day, please? Can we go back to the bit before I slammed the door? Because I didn't tell you it was really nice and I think we should do it again. Has anyone told you you're *really* good at kissing . . ."

Did I say those words, or did I just think them?

"That's all well and good but I'm your father."

Mikey Miles is my dad?

No, wait!

What was I thinking?

A hooded cobra. It coils around my legs, rising up, eye to eye, its wispy tongue tickling my nose.

"Excuse me. You're supposed to be on Cristina's back."

Its scales are shiny like polished onyx.

"You can't poison me because I'm a rock and you're scissors. Rock beats scissors."

She's hugging me. She's not allowed to hug me because she's stolen my boyfriend.

My tummy hurts.

It's telling me something.

It wants to leave.

Thank you, it's been great digesting food for you all these years but now it's time for me make my own way in the world.

I'm going to give birth to my tummy.

I heave and retch and heave and retch.

The Hulk is here. He understands. He's here to help. His fist is as big as my head. It punches a hole in my chest, reaches into my belly and squeezes and squeezes and squeezes.

48

My mouth is red raw. My nose is blocked. My muscles are lead. It's a sauna under this duvet.

A throat clears.

I know that throat.

"Scarlett?"

His voice cracks, just like when I went to the club and didn't come home. His cold fingers touch my cheek, making me yelp.

"Sorry," he says.

The wrinkly forehead. The wonky smile. The rimless glasses that could do with a clean.

"Would you like some water?"

I grunt. He rises and the chair scrapes against the wooden floor, sending an earthquake through my brain. I sit up, blinking at the daylight, my wardrobe, desk, my old dressing gown hanging on the back of the door. I'm relieved.

And then I remember:

Dad lunges for the door.

Bearded Guy steps across to block him. Dad shunts into Bearded Guy with his shoulder. Bearded Guy grabs Dad's wrist. Dad drops his iPhone, smashing the screen.

Me, slumped on a bench in the dirty office next to

an open safe full of cash. Smiling and clapping like I'm watching a performance.

Dad turns to me and shouts, "Are you out of your mind? She's going to die!"

Can I make it out the door before he comes back?

I swing my legs on to floor and haul myself to my feet. My knees buckle and I collapse back on the bed.

My body won't listen to my mind right now.

I slide underneath the duvet and pull it over my head.

He places the water on my bedside table

Maybe he'll think I've fallen back to sleep.

One deep breath, two deep breaths, ten deep breaths, fifty deep breaths.

I lower the duvet and peek over the edge.

He's looking right at me.

"You can go now," I say.

He doesn't reply.

"I'm still alive, thank you for getting me home, I'd appreciate it if you leave."

He doesn't reply.

Bearded Guy hands me a bottle of water.

"Say sorry to each other," I say. I grab Dad and Bearded Guy's hands and try to make them shake. I dance in the office even though there's no music.

"Look at her skin! Look at her eyes! My daughter is poisoned!"

"She's overdone it, she just needs some space."

"How can you be so blasé?"

"Take your hands off me! I'll call the police!"

"Be my guest! They'll shut you down!"

Sitting in the taxi. Talking and talking and talking all the way home.

What did I say to him?

"Okay. Say it. I can't feel any more ashamed than I already do so a bollocking from you won't make a difference."

He shakes his head.

"I'm going to help you, Scarlett. I'm going to make it right. I'm learning the hard way and I'll make some more mistakes – but I will make it right."

He leaves the room.

I don't know what he's on about.

Nothing can make it right.

That ship has sailed.

There's a delicious moment every morning, in the no man's land between sleep and consciousness, when I extend my legs and stretch my arms to wrap myself around him like a boa-constrictor.

And every morning my hand swishes through the air, grips rough cotton instead of soft skin and I roll over onto an empty Hayden-shaped space.

And even then, spread-eagled on my empty bed, I still feel him here.

I look in the mirror and I see his face.

His decks and iMac sit on my desk.

When I look out of the window he kneels on the pavement, beckoning me to come to a party.

Any second now he'll open my bedroom door so hard it'll slam against the wall. He'll empty his pockets of notes and pills and jump into bed with me.

A 4/4 beat blares out of a van, all muffled vocals and distorted bass and I'm right back on the dance floor, his fingers pressing into my hips and shockwaves shooting up my spine.

It's like having a toothache. Searing pain from your gum to your toes. Even the tiniest tap from a fork is enough. All you have to do is leave it, not eat on that side, hang an out-of-order sign on one half of your mouth. And yet you can't help yourself, you chew, you press it with your tongue over and over, you cry out again and again, and you still keep doing it, because some stupid part of you believes that maybe this time it won't hurt.

For a few months of my life I was the Scarlett I'm supposed to be.

Life was how it's supposed to be.

All those times he pressed his forehead to mine and said, "I love you."

Those three small words embedded in my body grew roots into my bones, injected their happiness into my blood.

And he dropped it all in a heartbeat.

It's all nothing.

It was all bollocks.

How can something be everything and nothing at the same time?

Love is the Answer.

Love was the answer.

Love is the biggest sham in the history of the universe.

He loved me. He loves me.

I'm so confused.

It doesn't make sense.

None of this makes sense.

The one person who I cannot live without has betrayed me, yet all I want is for him to come back.

49

We almost had an argument about it. I said that I didn't need to go in. I didn't want to go anywhere. He said he wanted me to do it as a precaution, a sensible thing to do. His face went red, his finger jabbed towards me and he was about to go into full-on *I-am-the-boss* mode. But then he stopped himself, took a deep breath, rubbed his forehead. Because he held back it touched me and I said I'd go.

We sat there in the doctor's tiny room and I made my big confession. *This summer I've had more pills than hot dinners. I don't think I have any serotonin left. My A Levels are in tatters. My university place destroyed.* The doctor prescribed me a selective serotonin re-uptake inhibitor. It got a bit tense, I refused to take more drugs, that's the last thing I need. The doctor eventually agreed to diagnose nervous exhaustion and he recommended five weeks of rest. If nothing had changed by then we would start the citalopram or paroxetine or some other ugly chemical I don't want to take. Diagnosis: *depressed*. My whole life reduced to an ugly, meaningless word.

And now every day is the same. Dad draws the curtains and places tea by my bed. I pretend to be asleep. He chatters about the roadworks at the bottom of the hill, or the Tube strike, or some other bollocks, before wishing me a breezy, *Have a nice day!* and heading back down the stairs. He's even started cooking. Kind of. Posh ready-meals. Home-made, organic ingredients and definitely-not-frozen. He leaves them by my bed, or if I'm pretending to be asleep, outside my room.

He never mentions "what happened," though he did leave a brochure for a college that specialises in A Level retakes by my bed. My old laptop is still at Hayden's so once he's gone to work I wrap myself in my duvet and go downstairs into his study. I fire up his desktop and go to a pirate movie website and I continue my project to watch every single super-hero movie that has ever been released.

I start with the Hulk, of course. *The Incredible Hulk. The Trial of The Incredible Hulk. Hulk Returns. Planet Hulk. The Death of The Incredible Hulk. Hulk Vs.*

Locked in an endless battle, misunderstood by a government that wants to destroy him. All he wants is to save himself from the monster inside him, but it's hard to do when they keep firing missiles into your chest.

Spiderman, Spiderman 2, Spiderman 3, The Amazing Spiderman, The Amazing Spiderman 2, Spiderman: Homecoming. Venom. X-Men. X-Men United. X-Men: The Last Stand, X-Men Origins: Wolverine, X-Men: First Class. The Wolverine, X-Men: Days of Future Past, X-Men Apocalypse.

The war is never over. Any victory is just a temporary rest before the forces of evil gather and begin again, rebooted, renewed, refreshed.

The war is never over.

Because that's how life is, right?

Milk. I need milk.

For my cornflakes.

For my tea.

Why didn't he buy it?

Why is shopping so hard for him?

Why is he so pathetic he can't even check the fridge before he goes out?

There's twenty quid on the kitchen table.

He still thinks I should do it.

After everything that's happened it's still my responsibility.

I pick up my mug and lift it high, poised to hurl it, smash it, destroy that piece of shit!

My large, oversized, tannin-stained mug, with *Sports* in red, *Direct* in blue, in large, bold, capitalised, italicised, butt-ugly type.

An awful promotional mug from an awful sports chain which I never actually shop at but they were giving them away free when I was walking past so I took it.

This mug, full of over-brewed, tawny lukewarm, left-for-too-long tea, always by my side, more loyal than a dog.

If I break this mug I will die.

I put on my dressing gown and Converses, grab the twenty-pound note and leave.

It's kind of liberating, walking down the street in dirty night-clothes, greasy hair piled high over my head.

But then there's Food and Wine, boring and normal and not a little terrifying. Big new boxes of fruit piled by the door. Apples, plums, pears. Since when did they stock plums? Apples, plums, and a murder contract out on Scarlett.

If I walk in there and they take me out the back and shoot me, who cares? There's no way I can walk to Archway or Highbury looking like this. Poor Scarlett. She met her death because she couldn't be bothered to walk an extra twenty minutes.

Actually, forget milk, I'll call the police and dob Cenk and his dad in.

Cenk and his dad in prison.

That would make me feel better.

That would make me feel alive again.

Revenge on Cenk and his ridiculous dad.

But what have they ever done to me?

Cenk likes me!

He fancies me!

To Cenk, I'm just a good girl who's made some bad choices.

He's right, isn't he?

And there he is, with a brand-new goatee, selling a lottery ticket to a greasy guy in a high-vis boiler suit who looks like he's just come off the night-shift fixing Tube lines. His thick arms and heavy hands work the machine, he's like a gorilla stuffed into a hamster cage.

I place the carton on the desk and keep my eyes on the counter. He tells me the price and I hand him the note.

I should have listened to him. Maybe working twelve-hour days behind a shop desk and running drugs on the side teaches you wisdom.

"I need to talk to Hayden," he says.

Every nerve end tingles.

"I'm not with him anymore."

"But you know where he is. He's changed his number. I can't call him."

"That's probably because he's given up."

"Ha!"

Cenk laughs.

Why did he laugh?

Why is Hayden hiding from him?

Can I get a badge saying Officially Given Up? There's no longer a suspicious bulge in my underpants.

When we passed Food and Wine he pulled his hood up and bent double.

Like he was avoiding them . . .

What new lies has he told me?

"We know all about him giving up. We just want to give him a leaving present. We owe him."

What, for years of loyal service?

I pick up the milk. My hand shakes.

"If he's changed his number I can't help you."

"You know his address?"

I nod and then regret it.

Cenk tears a strip of blank receipt paper from the card machine, grabs a pen and hands both to me.

"He's not my business any more. I'd appreciate it if you never spoke to me about it ever again."

"It's urgent," he says.

Why should I cover for someone who's been so mean to me? Why should I care when I've been so royally screwed? Hayden has wrecked his life and I'm still standing here feeling like I should protect him from the consequences?

Why should I save him from himself?

"What kind of leaving present?"

"A nice one."

I pick up the pen.

"Like, an *actual* present?"

"Yes."

"Nothing bad?"

"We love Hayden."

"Okay. For a minute I thought you were going to do something bad."

"You know me, I'm a nice guy."

Cenk smiles. The first time I've seen it. A little, half-moon smile.

"Phew. That's okay then."

I pick up the pen and write.

9 days later

50

"There's someone here to see you."

Dad opens the door without knocking and places a hot fish pie with peas on my bedside table.

"I'm busy," I say.

"They won't take no for an answer."

A floorboard creaks. They're outside my room.

It's Hayden. He's come to apologise. He wants to get back together with me. He's here to tell me it's a big mistake.

What about my greasy hair, my skin full of black-heads, my pyjama bottoms and my old Hulk t-shirt, the same one I wore when I first met him, now with a tea stain that won't come off. What about the fact I'm in bed even though it's only 7 p.m.?

"I'll tell them to leave," says Dad.

He opens the door.

'Wait!" I say.

What would I do if it was?

What if I blew my one chance and didn't see him?

He *should* see me like this. See what he's done to me.

"Okay," I say. Under the duvet my hands are shaking.

The door opens.

It's just Elliot, clutching a blue plastic bag, the kind you get in Food and Wine.

"Don't look so disappointed."

I force myself to smile.

I watch him note the chaotic state of my room, my unwashed clothes, the dirty dishes. He sits down awkwardly on the side of my bed, wrinkling his nose. Maybe I stink. I pull my duvet up to my neck like it's a shield.

"I left you, like, a hundred voicemails," he says. He picks up my phone. "When was the last time you charged this thing?"

He's in chinos and a polo shirt. His hair is growing back out and it's combed in a side parting. He looks like a preppy American. He's eyeing the fish pie.

"I'm having a digital detox," I say.

"How's that working out?"

I don't answer.

"Well, at least David picked up the phone. He told me you're ill so I said I was gonna come round."

I frown.

"I called your house phone? You still have one of those, remember? He said you were asleep."

"Bastard."

"No, he's actually being quite nice."

Suddenly I can't speak.

Elliot sighs and rubs his face.

I dig and dig and the longer the silence continues the more I want to scream. It's like there's a thick concrete wall grown up between us, with anti-grip paint and barbed wire across the top. Eventually I blurt out, "So I won't be joining you in Leeds. I didn't get the grades. I wish you all the best," and my voice sounds like nails down a blackboard. It's so harsh that Elliot hands me the greasy glass of water by my bed.

"We went out on Saturday. Like a reunion-slash-pre-uni drink. Everyone was asking after you."

"When you say everyone, you mean Bad Ben."

"Also Brownyn, Kamali and Zoya. Ricky and Anthony. Even the Somali gang."

"The Somali gang went to the pub?"

"Yeah, I know. I just said, like, I have no idea. I know she's ill and that's all I know."

"None of them cared when we were still in college."

I drink the water and picture their concern.

"I'm sure you also told them I'm a drug addict. Who got dumped."

"Scarlett. What? I had no idea . . . I just saw you at the club . . . and then you disappeared."

"Bad Ben told them then."

"No."

"Aya?"

"I don't think so."

"You *don't think so*, you're her boyfriend."

"No one knows what's going on with you!"

I'm not sure I believe him. Why should I care what a bunch of people I'm never going to see again think?

"It's a bit late in the day – but it's like we all realised that we're not all that bad. Even Bad Ben. He hangs out with Khadija now. He's finally found someone who shares his passion for Photoshop. They geek out about filters and custom brushes. Well, until two weeks' time, when he buggers off to Glasgow."

"What?" I'm sitting up. I'm awake. "What?"

"I know, right? I think he's in love with her."

He walks over to my Hulk poster. The corners are frayed and there's a rip at the top. But it's still striking, the silhouetted Hulk, shoulder muscles like mountains, biceps as thick as his thighs.

"Would you like me to do some tidying up?" he says.

My back tenses and my fingers grip the duvet.

"Stop locking me out," he says.

"I'm not locking anything!"

"I just wanna help . . ."

"No-one can help, that's the whole point!"

He gives me wounded, doe-like eyes.

"It's all right. You have my permission to tell everyone that my boyfriend, the only person in the world who understands me, has one hundred percent dumped me for someone else. Add it to your Snapchat story."

"Oh, Scarlett."

He reaches up to the corner of the poster and attempts to stick it back to the wall.

"I didn't have a clue what I'd find here. I thought there might be a morphine drip and you'd be emaciated, and all your hair fallen out. You could have been dying for all we knew."

"Like mother, like daughter?"

"Yeah! Sorry . . . I don't know. You make stuff up to fill in the gaps."

"I might as well be . . ."

"Don't say that."

He steps towards me.

"Where's the key, Scarlett?" He sticks an imaginary key into my chest and turns. "I know there's a way in."

"I can't be happy-la-la-go-to-Comic-Con-dress-up-in-costumes, okay? That time is over."

He sighs, picks up a stray t-shirt, folds it neatly and places it by the door. Soon my t-shirts, jeans and sweatpants are in a nice neat square pile. He's so good at clothes-folding he could get a job at GAP. When he's done he turns to me and says, "Do you want me to go home and kill my mum?"

"No."

He sits back down on the edge of the bed.

"I'm sick of you telling me I don't understand. What am I supposed to do?"

"It's just . . . when things are going well, something always comes and messes it up . . . *always.*"

He takes my hand. I pull it to my cheek. He falls on to the mattress next to me, swings his legs on to the bed and we lie, hugging, him on the duvet, me underneath.

"You're not the only person who's split up," he says.

"What?"

"Yeah . . ."

"*What?*"

"She got a bit pill-obsessed . . . Can I tell you something? I . . . didn't even take them. The first time they did them they just sat at home . . . I went to bed early . . . It was just her and Bad Ben staying up till 6 a.m. doing God-knows-what. I dunno. I think Bad Ben was doing drugged-up drawings."

"What about All Night Long?"

"I think they had a good time. I left early. We didn't even have that much to talk about."

"That night should have been a life-changing event! You're telling me that they came to All Night Long, took Supermen and you only *think* they had a good time? What about the music?"

"We're not all druggies," he sighs.

"You're such a moralistic arsehole."

I can feel his breath on my cheek.

"Maybe they got off with each other?"

"Aya and Bad Ben?"

"All alone while you're asleep."

"I highly doubt it."

"Stranger things have happened. You got off with her."

"You can be a bitch too, you know that?"

He cranes his neck up. Our eyes lock. We're both so raw, so vulnerable, so angry, so close. It would be the easiest thing in the world to kiss him.

"I've always loved you Scarlett. I messed it up but I always loved you."

"I . . . love you too."

A hot tear rolls down my cheek. His lips touch mine.

"No," I say. "Not now. Not now."

He sits back up. The spell is broken. He picks up the blue plastic bag.

"This is for you."

I don't open it.

"So what the hell are you doing with your life? What is actually wrong with you?"

"I don't know. I'm working it out."

"Wanna come round tonight?"

"No thank you."

"Okay."

"I'm sorry, Elliot. I'm really, really sorry."

He sighs and walks to the door.

"Bye Scarlett."

"Bye Elliot."

When I hear front door shut I open the bag and take out an envelope. Inside is a card, a picture of a giant teddy-bear, holding a heart, on which is written *Get well soon*, signed by Elliot and Bad Ben. For a second I think about tearing it up. But I don't. I get up and open my desk drawer. Lying there, on its own, is the cartoon Bad Ben drew of the three of us. I take it out, leave the card and the drawing on my desk, pick up my cold fish pie and go back to bed.

12 days later

51

The creak of the stairs warns me that it's time to turn over in bed and pretend to be asleep. Dad catches his breath and opens my door.

"The floor guys are here."

"What?"

"New pile for the upstairs."

"You never told me."

"You didn't ask."

"Why?"

We both glance down. My carpet doesn't look too bad, especially considering it's beige. It's thinner than it used to be. There's the odd smudge. It's not exactly at the disgusting-needs-to-be-replaced stage.

"And while they're doing it, I thought you and me could go out."

A car-door slams. I get out of bed and look out the window. Two stubbly guys, one tubby, one skinny, like Laurel and Hardy, root about in the back of a van.

"You can hang out with them if you like."

"You planned this, didn't you."

His eyes are blank and he doesn't respond. I sigh.

"Where do you want to go?"

"Surprise."

Outside, the casual jokes and loud, alien voices of the carpet guys make me shudder.

"You're such a bastard!" I say.

I do stink. I hope it wasn't this bad when Elliot was here. The hot water, the soapy suds, my perfumed shampoo – they're supposed to feel nice, I think they *used* to feel nice, once. I put on the first clothes I can find – a pair of pre-ripped jeans, an old Colgate toothpaste t-shirt which I once thought was cool and my blue puffa jacket. Now I'm standing in the hall, my legs shake. The front door opens and the chubby one brushes past me while Dad chats to the tall one about the Arsenal striker getting a broken leg. Every word hurts my brain.

"I can't go out."

They stop their conversation and look at me.

"I can't."

Dad steps toward me and does something he hasn't done for a very long time: he takes my hand.

"C'mon."

I shake my head.

"I've got you, I promise."

I'm stupidly slow, gripping his arm and taking one feeble, shaky step at a time. My cheeks are hot, my body burns. I feel like a hospital patient being taken for her daily walk.

"Here's our ride," says Dad, and points to a blue saloon car across the street. "Bet you didn't think your old Dad knew how to call an Uber?"

It can't be. Only Hayden does Ubers. If there is an Uber, then Hayden will be inside it. Dad will open the passenger door, I'll slip inside and as we drive down the Broadway Hayden will clasp his hands together and beg to have me back. Or maybe he'll take one look at me, realise I'm beyond repair and throw me out of the moving car. Maybe Hayden and Cristina are inside and they've just printed the wedding invitations and they can't wait to show them off.

I trip and fall sideways. Dad grips my arm and hauls me up, before we both stumble backwards and crash to the pavement, him landing on his bottom with me on top of him.

"It's okay," he says. "Everything is okay."

We cut through Hampstead Heath, circle round Regent's Park and past Sherlock Holmes's house and somewhere on the Westway, the long road that leads west out of London, I fall asleep. I'm woken by Dad squeezing my hand. I groggily exit the car, stretch my arms up as high as I can and let out a half-roar-half-groan.

"Oh my God," I say. "I've turned into an old person."

"What do you mean?"

"I fall asleep and make noises when I stretch."

He chuckles. The houses here look similar to the ones on our street, red-bricked with pointy roofs, well-kept, shiny grey BMWs and Audis in the drives; but we're obviously somewhere different so the whole effect is uncanny, like I'm in an alternative universe. Unexpectedly, I'm excited at discovering our mystery destination, my legs feel sturdier and I surprise myself again when I slip my arm through Dad's. We turn right at the T-junction at the end of road and follow a yellow brick wall, stopping at some ornate iron gates topped by a gilded royal coat of arms.

"Kew Gardens," I say.

"Yup."

"Why?"

"Why not?"

Dad pays for our tickets and we're in, walking down a wide central path past perfectly-mown lawns and flower beds full of leafy plants. Mini-explosions of amber, orange and russet have broken out on some of the trees and a large domed greenhouse sits on the horizon like a fairy palace. Dad stops and takes out a letter from his pocket. I glimpse the heading – the same royal coat of arms – but as I lean forward to read what it says he folds the paper in half and stuffs it back in his pocket. He leads me off the beaten track through a secluded rock-garden and around a small pond to a bench by a willow tree.

"What do you think?"

"What."

"It's a bench."

"Yes."

"Why are you showing me a bench?"

"Look closer."

It's varnished orange-red, and looks new. In the centre is a small brass plaque on which is written:

Sarah Anderton, 1966-2017. *Mother, daughter, wife. Gone but remembered and loved forever by husband David and daughter Scarlett.*

"I'm not very good with dedications . . ."

"You did this?"

Dad nods.

"Surprised?"

Beneath his big wonky smile lies apprehension. He takes half a step back as if he thinks I'm going to hit him. Why would he think that? And then, suddenly, my barriers drop. There never was an elaborate plan to kick me out of the house. Right now, he is doing everything he can, his absolute best, to love me. Obsessing over my grades, grounding me, controlling me, even when he ignored me and we carried on in our zombie routine, it was all his messed-up way of showing love. He's just rubbish at feelings. He does real-world solid stuff like money and benches and pieces of paper, which prove you're supposed to know something. That's what makes sense to him. But he's trying, despite his rubbishness, he's trying so, so hard. A tenderness floods out of my heart and fills my body.

"I'm sorry I've been so nasty," I say.

"You . . ."

He's about to say *you haven't* but he stops himself, because it isn't true.

"It's okay," he says. "I haven't exactly played a blinder myself."

A loud sob emerges from the pit of my stomach. I cover my mouth with my hands but then there's another and another and I can't stop, they're coming from a place that's so deep and hidden I didn't know it existed. There's Mum's head, just a few wispy patches of hair remaining. There she is, buttering my toast in the kitchen, walking down the stairs in her dressing gown or gluing a piece of cardboard, her tongue poking out of the side of her mouth. She always did that when she concentrated.

And then I'm screaming, "Why did you give me hope? Why did you say that I 'would know'?! Why did you say getting high would make things better? Why did you make me think that falling in love would solve everything? Why did you give me that shit advice!? Why aren't you here so I can have a proper go at you!"

I laugh at the stupidness of it all, shouting at a bench in Kew Gardens. Dad puts his arm across my shoulders and I bury my face in his chest and when I finally stop crying his coat is soaked, my eyes are bloodshot and my cheeks bright red.

We sit there for a while. There's nothing more to say. He kisses my head.

"I'm seeing Jennifer again."

"What?"

Fireworks go off in my brain. Why is he saying this when we're remembering Mum?

"I can't not tell you."

"Since when?"

"Since the night . . . when I helped you home from the club. I needed some advice and she was the only person I could talk to."

I wait for the anger, the urge to storm away, the desire to tell him he's screwed up. But it doesn't come.

"Is that why you've been acting as if everything is hunky-dory, even though I don't leave the house and have dropped out at school and wash less than I should?"

He laughs.

"Have you got a secret bat-phone hidden in your room, a hot-line to Jennifer for every time you need advice?"

He laughs louder this time, then purses his lips and frowns.

"That night you looked so . . . vulnerable . . . I just realised that I didn't have a clue about the right thing to do . . . yes, Jennifer said, maybe you need some time to figure things out and maybe I shouldn't pressure you. I thought you were okay and so strong and doing great, but . . . it wasn't true and deep down I knew it and couldn't admit it."

Some heavy weight drops away.

"Just because I'm seeing her doesn't mean that I've stopped loving Mum. I know that sounds weird . . ."

We watch the clouds roll by, some of them bruise-coloured, some puffy and light. A patch of sunlight emerges on the grass ahead of us and disappears again. Typical weird English weather.

"That night . . . at the club . . . in the taxi back. . . . you kept telling me how much you loved me . . . how you wished we could be friends . . . that there was no reason why we shouldn't get on . . ."

"Did I?"

"I felt awful that the only way you could tell me the truth was by taking so many drugs you might die. When you were six you used to run up to me and tell me everything: what you loved, what you hated, who you cared about at school, who drove you crazy. And now . . . you look at me . . . like I'm an idiot. Whom you don't tell anything."

"You're not an idiot! You're my dad." I'm a blubbering mess again. Snot drips over my lip and into my mouth and tears block my vision. Dad holds up his sleeve and I wipe my nose on it. We both laugh.

A robin lands in front of us. It hops about, this way and that, forward, back, side to side, chirruping, cocking its head.

"I think it's trying to tell us something," I say.

"You always did have a poetic imagination," he says.

"That's a polite way of saying *Robins don't talk, you idiot.*"

He laughs.

"What do you think Mum would say, if she was watching us now?"

"I don't know."

"I think she would be proud of us."

"I think you're right."

52

The next morning, after Dad has gone to work, I tidy my room and change my bedclothes. I shower again and before I dress I empty my entire wardrobe and examine each item, one by one, and place it into a 'keep' or 'destroy' pile. A plain yellow t-shirt – keep! A vintage patterned Christmassy jumper – destroy! There's no logic, I just flow with the feeling that runs up from my gut. A pair of distressed jeans – keep! An Avengers baseball cap – destroy!

The clothes that make the cut I sort into piles – jeans, sweats, t-shirts, tops, dresses, underwear. I put on a stripy camisole I forgot I had and some baggy charcoal sweats and my Converses (the more scuffed they get the more I love them). I chuck all the 'destroy' clothes into a black bin bag. I walk up to the Broadway and drop them at the Cancer Research charity shop. I practically skip back down the road, but as soon as I get home I remember all the clothes I left at Hayden's. My shiny dress shoes and pleated skirts. My favourite onesie. My other Hulk t-shirt – the one that isn't completely disgusting – burgundy with an old-school toxic-waste-green coloured Hulk on the front. My laptop is there, too. Not that anyone would want to steal it, it's so ancient. But it's mine. I love it.

But if Hayden and me is over – and Hayden and me *is* over, it couldn't be *more* over – then I need to get that stuff back. Why should I lose a bunch of my favourite gear? The longer I leave it, the greater the chance he's chucked it in the trash.

But I don't think I can ever look him in the eye again. If I saw him face to face, I don't think I could take the pain. My blood would get poisoned, my chest would split open, and I would die, right there on the floor in front of him, a pile of stinking blood and guts.

But I need to do *something*. I need to move on *somehow*.

I take the Tube to Leicester Square and ducking into the doorway of a Bureau de Change, I enter my destination into my map app. The thick blue line pops up – five minutes' walk – and I follow it, past some clothes boutiques, across the Seven Dials roundabout, round the back of a theatre, taking a quick zig-zag down a couple of backstreets and I'm there. I push open the door and run up to the desk, pay five pounds for a day membership to a smiley man with an absurd handlebar moustache and climb the stairs, two at a time.

I'm five minutes late and the class has begun, booming RnB filling the room. It's packed, so I sneak along the back wall, dump my bag, slip off my trainers and find an empty spot in the corner.

Jennifer is standing at the top of the room, wearing baggy black dancing trousers and a lacey camisole that exposes her slender shoulders. The front wall is ceiling-to-floor mirror and she is watching the class in the reflection as she demonstrates stretches while confidently calling out instructions. It's supposed to be a beginners' class, but I am barely able to follow it. When she tells me to turn my hips outwards weird muscles in my inner thighs that I didn't know I had throb and ache. One moment I'm stretching to the ceiling, the next I'm touching my toes, craning my neck to copy Jennifer or anyone near who looks like they know what they're doing.

We take a quick break, during which we pay her – luckily I've got just enough cash – and she greets me warmly but without familiarity. I discover that what we've just done was only a warm-up session. Now the proper routine starts. She puts on a Rihanna ballad and begins to demonstrate the movements herself: kicks, then a turn, and even though I guess this is very simple stuff she's so graceful it's worth the payment just to see her dance. She's careful to include everyone, stopping now to correct the way one girl is pointing her toes, again to tell another girl to tense her abdominal muscles. She comes over to straighten my neck as I clunk through the routine like an elephant.

At the end I'm red in the face, sweaty and elated. I sink down on to a bench outside the classroom while Jennifer laughs and chats with some of the regulars. I'm about to leave when I see her coming towards me, beaming.

"You did really well!"

"No, I didn't."

"Have you ever danced before?"

"No."

"You did really well!"

Her eyes glance from side to side.

"I didn't expect to see you here," she says, quietly.
"I thought maybe we could go for a coffee," I say.

Ten minutes later I am sitting at a window table in a busy Cafe Nero. Jennifer turns from the counter and walks towards me, carrying two hot chocolates on a tray. She looks elegant, a knee-length coat slipped over her dancing clothes. She is wearing gleaming white trainers. She places our mugs on the table, returns the tray to the bar and sits down opposite me.

"For the record, I don't normally recommend one of these after class," she says.

Her brilliant white smile is warm and hard at the same time. Her dancing had the same qualities: soft and strong. My shoulders tighten. The mini marshmallows in my mug look like the drowning passengers in a shipwreck, about to be swallowed by a sea monster.

"You can go out with Dad."

"Pardon?"

"You can go out with Dad."

"I didn't realise I needed your permission."

My cheeks go hot.

"Sorry to be prickly," she says. "I didn't expect you to get to the point so quickly."

My face is burning.

"You're reaching out, I appreciate that."

"You can come and live us with if you want," I say.

"This is very brave and kind of you, Scarlett, but you don't sound like you mean it."

I take a sip. The milk is only warm, not piping hot like I like it. If I don't drink the chocolate now it's gonna get cold, but if I drink it quickly I'll look like a slob. And I hate it if anyone calls me a slob, like Elliot did, because I know they're right. I am a slob. I realise it's not just Aya makes me feel this way. Anyone who looks polished: Jennifer, pretty much the rest of the world, has the same effect.

"Okay. I'm. . . . sorry for wading in and trying to be Mrs Fixit," she says. Her tone is also forced. She sounds like a kid at primary school who has been made to apologise.

"Who's Mrs Fixit?"

"In the movie Wreck-it Ralph there's two characters in this computer game: Wreck-it Ralph, who climbs around smashing up an apartment building and Fix-It Felix, who uses a magical hammer to fix everything."

I remember Elliot and Bad Ben went to that movie. I missed it because I had 'flu.

"My friends have seen it but I haven't. I can't believe you know more about the movies than me."

She smiles.

"I thought I could waltz right in with my magic hammer! I never had any children."

Why did she say that? Why doesn't she have children? Was it a choice? Did she spend too much time with the wrong man? Did she try to have kids and fail? What happened, what went wrong?

She sighs.

I have to close my eyes, because I can't handle both our sadnesses at the same time.

"And you made it very clear I wasn't welcome."

"I didn't say you weren't welcome."

"Your negative energy made it clear. The way you sat. The way you sighed. The way you spoke. Practically knocked me off my chair."

I need to swallow marshmallows. I need a sugar-rush. I bring my cup to my lips and take a sip, forcing myself to make it small.

"I'm not criticising you. I'd make *me* not welcome if I was you."

Her eyes become soft. She doesn't think I'm a *complete* monster. Her hand is half-way across the table, inviting mine to touch it.

"I can relate to Mrs Fixit," I say.

"Really?"

Her tone suggests she knows all about me. I picture her and Dad sitting in this café, Dad unloading all his fears and opinions.

"I tried to do a Mrs Fixit thing and it totally screwed up," I say.

"Uh-huh."

"I made someone's dream come true and they got really furious with me."

"People have to want to be helped, I guess."

I'm disorientated by the unexpected direction the conversation is taking. The chocolatey milk floods my tongue thick and fast, and in three large gulps it's all gone. Jennifer's eyes widen in surprise.

"I had to finish it before it got cold."

We both laugh.

"I really enjoyed your class. Even though I was rubbish I feel really good now. You're so confident. I can't believe how you move like that."

"Thank you. It's not magic. It's years and years of hard practice."

"I could never . . ."

"You're a sensual, sensuous woman – don't beat yourself up so much. I saw the way you danced – you might not have nailed all the steps, but you *felt* the music. Not everyone can do that."

Tingles shoot from my feet to my head. I want to do another class. Shit. She must be a good teacher. I wonder how she and Dad got back together? Was Dad as broken as me? Did he turn up and make a big dramatic gesture? What did they say to each other? How did they mend it?

"I had this relationship. It's gone so wrong it's not even funny."

"Uh-huh."

"He dumped me for his ex. I think he only ever got together with me so he could make her jealous and get her back."

Jennifer's hand extends searchingly towards me. I move mine to meet hers and our fingers interlock.

"What he did was unforgivable and I keep telling myself to move on, but I still want him. How wrong is that? He just cut it off for no reason. It doesn't really feel like it's over. He's the only person I feel alive with. And I know he feels the same. I thought he felt the same. It's so confusing."

Jennifer sighs deeply.

"You love him."

I nod.

I am not going to blub with Jennifer. I have been doing too much blubbing. I am over losing it with my blubbing.

Now Jennifer grips my wrist, turns it over and runs her finger over my tattoo.

"Love is the Answer."

I nod.

"They say you never forget your first love," she says.

"Mine was completely shit."

"Listen. Once a year I go to India for a yoga retreat. And I learnt something there last year. In Sanskrit, the ancient Indian language, there are ninety words for love."

"Okay."

"In English there is only one."

"I don't get it."

"What I am saying is that I think that's a great tattoo. But what you are going through – maybe there're other types of love."

"I can't imagine any other love than the love I feel. And it feels like poison."

"I don't doubt that. Maybe you can find love with a guy . . . that isn't like this . . ."

"Right now, I don't think I could be ever be with anyone else."

My head hurts. This is too heavy. I need to change the subject.

"Are you going to move in, then?" I say.

"No. Well, not in the short term, and if I did we'd all have to agree it was the right thing. And none of us should consider it for a long time.

I nod.

"My new motto is 'Take things slowly'." Her eyes sparkle as she says it. I laugh.

"Are you not a taking-things-slowly person either?" she says.

"Not exactly."

We laugh again. She's nothing like Mum. She's hippy and healthy and a bit woo-woo . . . but weirdly,

I feel she gets it . . . and if she's a bit like me . . . and she and my dad are happy . . . then maybe there is hope . . . somewhere down the line . . . one day . . . in the distant future . . .

"But I would like to come round and hang out?" she says.

"That would be great."

"Scarlett?"

"Yeah?"

"If your hot chocolate is too cold, you can ask them to make it again."

"Yeah. Good point. I'll remember that next time."

53

The Elephant and Castle platform is crowded and when the lift doors close my personal space shrinks down to nothing. A tightly-packed Sainsbury's bag sits on my right toe. A guy with slicked-back hair plays Candy Crush at full volume. A woman in a suit shifts from foot to foot. Panicked and claustrophobic, I close my eyes and hold my breath as we ascend to street level. The lift opens out into the ticket hall and I'm stuck in a traffic jam as people make their way through the barriers. I shuffle along behind Slicked-Back-Hair-Guy until the reader rejects his Oyster card and I crash into his back. I think I might pass out. The guard beckons him over, I tap my card on the reader, the twin halves of the barrier spring apart and I step, disorientated, on to the pavement.

Randomly, I decide to check my email. There's a message from Harper.

Scarlett. Sweetheart. I'm so sorry I didn't get to see you before I left. Immigration police turned up at my work and told me I had to leave RIGHT NOW. My boss didn't get his sponsorship status in time so my visa expired. He was supposed to offer me a new job and never did. He strung me along. Arsehole. It was pandemonium. I couldn't even pack my clothes. I had these fat-arsed officers surrounding me. Why are all the feds always fat? They interviewed me, scared the living hell out of me, threatened me with deportation, so I just booked a ticket home, there and then. Imagine me, turning up at my parents', aged twenty-three, stinking, in dirty clothes, with nothing apart from my phone and my wallet. "Hi Mum, I've just been basically deported!" That was fun.

Didn't really think it through, though. I've been trying to get hold of people in the house to see if they could get some of my stuff sent over. I'd pay for it. I mean, my mum would pay for it. But no one has replied to my emails. Is everything okay? Can you check with them for me?

I miss taking-the-piss-in-London. There's no clubs here. Just a "pub" that closes at 10 p.m. The only drug available seems to be badly-cut smack, and I'm not so desperate to try that . . . yet. What a load of horse-shit.

Basically, I miss your beautiful face and hot arse. I miss your perfect romance. When you two got together it gave me hope. It showed me that true love is possible.

Please write me back,

Harper

Why now? Why do I get this email now, when I'm about to go to his house? Thirty minutes ago I was feeling strong and optimistic and now I'm back to being a wreck.

As I cross the main road I feel as if I'm stepping back in time. My head is on his shoulder as our Uber circles the roundabout. I pass the Italian café with the bitter coffee and overpriced paninis and I want to message him to ask him what he wants from the Tesco

Metro. Entering the road where he lives, I see her: the angry woman in the burkha. Today she is sitting on her doorstep, playing catch with her son. She smiles at me as I pass. I smile back. And there's his old mattress, still dumped in the front garden, black and mouldy from the rain. The curtains are still drawn just as they used to be, hanging in the same dusty creases and rumples that have been there for years. My summer memories force themselves into the present like wild ghosts intent on making me mad.

I knock.

Nothing.

I knock again.

Silence.

I should go. Get the hell out of here. Kiss goodbye to my stuff. Never come back.

Feet on the floorboards, someone exhaling. A bang. The door opens.

His front lip is swollen to twice its normal size. Someone has blacked his right eye. His baggy vest hangs loose to reveal bandages strapped across his chest. He's even skinnier than before, shoulders bony, cheekbones sharper, face white. He looks like a vampire who's been mugged.

"Hi!" he says. He smiles. It looks painful.

"Are you okay?" I say.

"Never been better!"

I follow him down the stairs to the kitchen, to the same scuffed and scratched table and torn, worn lino. But the breakfast cereals that used to line the work-top are gone and no dirty crockery is piled in the sink.

"How's it going?" I say.

"Really good," he says, switching on the kettle.

"I've come to pick up my stuff."

"Oh, yeah. I was wondering when you were going to do that."

"Shall I go upstairs?"

"Sure."

I'm prepared for him to have moved his stuff upstairs to Cristina's big couple-room, the room that was really his. But when I open the door the stench of boy-sweat knocks me back. The duvet is bunched up at the end of the bed. The iMac is switched off. An empty Budweiser can sits next to the keyboard. I squeeze myself round the bed and open the wardrobe. All my clothes are heaped in the corner, my laptop propped up at the back. I can see nothing of hers. No make-up bag or clothes, not even a stray hair-clip. I fill my rucksack as quickly as I can.

Downstairs, he is sitting at the table alone, hands cupped round a mug of black tea.

Every fibre of my being wants to ask him what happened.

I tell myself that it is none of my business.

It is not for me to care about it.

He has to sort himself out on his own.

Now is the moment to leave.

There's another mug of black tea in the empty space across from him. He looks at it, then looks at me.

"Sorry, I'm out of milk," he says.

I feel some invisible force pull me towards the seat, another pulling me towards the door, and I think I might split in two.

He gestures for me to sit down.

I take one step forward and hesitate.

"C'mon," he says. "You've got time for a brew."

"Okay," I say.

The brown and gold flecks in his eyes are at once familiar and terrifying. I see everything he's thinking or experiencing in those eyes. He's like a crab without a shell. I don't need to ask the question.

"I'd gone out to buy washing up liquid. Yeah, me, buying cleaning materials. I know, right? I'm whistling a tune, in my own world, nothing out of the ordinary. Sunny day, blue skies. I open my door and this hand comes from behind me and slams it shut. None other than that hairy Food and Wine wanker. 'Hi Hayden, we've got a present for you.'"

He captures Cenk's cockney-Turkish accent perfectly. I laugh. Hayden smiles, then winces.

"What was the present?" I say.

"What do you think? A Grade A beating! From Cenk! Look at me! Two broken ribs! I'm the winner in the Getting Battered Top Trumps!"

I laugh again. I sip the tea. It's rank, but I don't care. It's always been like that with me and him: we could be hanging out in the sewer and the putrid smell would intoxicate us and for us the collective crap of a million people would glow with meaning.

"I thought you were done with him."

"I may have miscalculated what I owed them. By a grand. Good job I never became an accountant, eh?"

I stand up and open the fridge. There really is no milk. It's empty apart from a beer, a Pot Noodle and an onion.

"Where is everyone?"

"I'm the last one left," he says. "Last man standing. I made it to the end. I should get a prize."

"Where have they gone?"

"Harper got deported. After that, Alejandro disappeared. Just didn't come home one day. Won't answer his phone. And Cristina's at work. We can't pay the rent for all of them. Expecting the bailiffs any day."

He says it all so casually.

"Can't you get new flatmates?"

"Yeah. I guess. Good thinking, Batman."

I curse myself for being helpful. For displaying an interest. And then I'm angry with him. Why is he so resigned to everything going wrong?

"Look," he says, "I didn't tell you about Cristina because at the time it was over and I wanted the past to be the past and draw a line under things and . . ."

"Just don't," I say.

"I have to tell you . . ."

My whole body stiffens.

"Hayden . . ."

"I never told you properly, I have to!" He shrieks the last sentence and the shock of it shuts me up. He takes a moment to compose himself.

"We met Mikey Miles at a club. Well, obviously, where else are you going to meet him? We got invited to the afterparty at his flat. Got chatting to everyone – promoters, other DJs. I was telling him how I was a DJ and he was like, *send me a mix*. I was like, *this is it*. I went nuts for this mix, spent like a month on it, had to be perfect, the flow had to be just right, and right before I send it to him Cristina comes up to me and tells me that she doesn't want to go out with me anymore and Mikey Miles was her new boyfriend. Five years. We'd moved to London together. She was my first proper girlfriend. I knew things weren't great – but it was a kick in the teeth, know what I mean? And then she's like *I've made a mistake* and *I'm confused;* five years with her, I felt obliged, like we'd had this contract together and it had never been properly . . ."

"You wanted to draw a line but actually you were under contract to her . . ."

"Let me finish! Yeah, so it did creep me out a bit that you got off with him. And you got him to listen to my music . . . like history repeating itself. . . . it's freaky . . . it messed me up . . . but Cristina was like, *Going out with a famous DJ is shit, he's never around, it gets boring when everyone worships him all the time and he's never in the country for more than two days. I want it to go back to the old days* . . ."

He looks me directly in the eyes.

"It was like I couldn't help it; like I owed her. Five years. I owed her. She started telling me all this stuff. *Scarlett is a baby. Scarlett is only just eighteen, she's going to want to experiment with guys, she's flighty, it won't last.* It messed with my head. And you did kiss him . . ."

"For half a second . . ."

He squeezes his eyes together and a tear runs down his swollen cheek.

"And now it's like we're on hold and I don't know what's going on. I've messed up so bad. My head got confused and I made the wrong decision."

This is not what I wanted to hear.

"Every day I regret it. Every single day."

This is the opposite of what I need.

"I miss you," he says.

"I miss you too," I say.

I love him. I love him so much. I would do anything to be back in that place – our secret raving hideout –

our sacred space in the middle of the club that no-one knows about apart from me and him. Lost in the mix, where everything is whole, everything is love. All anyone else would see is someone damaged beyond repair, but I see beyond that . . . I see underneath it. I see his beautiful, fragile soul. That's always been the trouble.

"What do you mean, you're on hold?"

"I don't know if we're together or split up. Everything's really weird. But it's different with you . . . me and you . . . it's once in a lifetime . . ."

"Cristina split up with you the day you met me, didn't she?" I say.

"Yes."

He blurts it out, like a confession.

"You said someone let you down that day. I had been let down by my dad. You never told me who let you down."

"Yeah."

"I should have made you . . ."

He sighs and shakes his head.

"Did you and Cristina share that room?!"

"Yeah."

"The day I met you I was so angry I could have killed someone. And so were you. We were both so *angry* . . ."

"Exactly," he says, "You're the only person who gets it."

I close the fridge door. I want to move across to my chair but I walk towards him instead. He takes my hands.

"I love you," he says. "I love you, I love you, I love you."

I'm falling again, hard and fast. Dad and Jennifer and Elliot flash through my mind and I'm rehearsing what I will say to them, how I will explain this. I'll be like, *it's all a misunderstanding,* and *we've put it behind us* and I'd be back here and somehow we'd find new flatmates, I'd get a job, he'd be DJing and . . .

Hayden pulls me towards him. His lips open and my head dips down. I can feel it coming on, that hit, that high, that blazing fire. Time slows right down, a second becomes an eon, and the big bruise under his eye fills my vision, that deep purple like a heavy, ugly storm cloud where Cenk's hard fist smashed into the bone, and I realise, *I did that.* That is my fault. I made it happen, and somewhere deep down, I *wanted* it to happen. I wanted Cenk to do it and I commanded Cenk to do it when I gave him Hayden's address. Nice Scarlett, caring Scarlett, innocent Scarlett, couldn't admit to herself that she ordered her revenge, but there it is, centimetres away. And then I know that it can never feel like it did that first day in the park, that underneath all our love, all of the time, was an icy river of hate, the kind of hatred that seeps into the soil and poisons the grass and the flowers and if I kiss him now that's where we'd end up, in some barren, toxic wasteland. We were two people running away from the darkness, destined to fail. How long would it take before he changed his mind again? How long would it be before one of us hurt the other? Stabbed the other? Our love was born savage and always will be.

"No!" I say. "We're not good. We're not good for each other."

"Scarlett . . ."

"No. I can't."

His bottom lip quivers. He knows I mean it. I walk out of the kitchen.

"This is your fault," he cries and follows me up the stairs. "You gave him my address!"

"I thought he was getting you a birthday present."

"I don't believe you!"

"Can you blame me? Can you blame me for telling him after what you did to me?"

"I'm going to go to the feds. I'm going to have you done for GBH. You owe me. It's my darkest hour and you owe me. You have to stay! He took my money! We're going to be homeless because of you!"

I open the door and he grips my arm, digging his nails into it, pulling me towards him, gripping my neck, squeezing, cutting off the air. I'm letting him do it, why am I letting him do it? He squeezes tighter and blobs of colour fill my vision. I pull my arm free and shove my fist into his chest, he howls in pain and lets go of me and I run down the road, eyes dead ahead, not looking back, not slowing down until I'm through the ticket barrier and back on the platform.

54

I schedule the meeting for 10:30 a.m. on purpose, so everyone will be in lessons. I don't want to see any students, it's too embarrassing. I'm wearing my new navy hoody with the hood up, hiding my new neon pink ombre highlights. A radical haircut seemed like a great idea at the time, but the moment I stepped through the college gates and realised that people were actually going to see me I got a bit shy. My security card is long expired, so I have to go in the front entrance, like a visitor. I'm half-expecting a sympathetic welcome from the admin lady, but she's frosty as hell and why wouldn't she be? She's never met me. She directs me to a touchscreen with a webcam mounted beyond it. I type in my name and email address and pose for the picture. A minute later she hands me my visitor photo ID. I pin it to my hoodie and I'm in, a stranger in my own college.

The Head's door is open and he beckons me in, hopping up from his desk and gripping my hand tight. He's a tall guy whose red-veined cheeks and bloated face make him seem like he's just stepped out of the pub for a cigarette.

"Nice to see you!" he says. "How's it all going?" His tone is disconcertingly intimate. This is the first time I've spoken to him, but he makes me feel like he's known me for years.

"Good!" I say, my hood sliding down. "Well, better than I was."

"Tough time?"

For a second I feel I'm about to unload everything that's happened in one massive emotional dump but I catch myself just in time. He smiles: sympathetically, but also impatiently.

"My mum died. As you know. And a lot of other messed-up stuff happened . . . I kind of went through a few peaks and troughs . . . I think I made the wrong A Level choices as well. I mean, that's probably not why I messed them up . . ."

He looks down at a piece of paper on his desk. It is a printout of the very long email I sent him.

"What I don't get is why you think you'll prefer an e-college over a real one . . ."

"I like the idea of not starting over somewhere. I can have a Skype call once a week with the tutors. Just until next year. Maybe then I can come back here."

"Skype once a week?' he says, witheringly.

"If I hit the accelerator, just Art and Design GCSE, no others, and do it in a year – then I can take the A Level."

"Listen . . . we let people retake the whole year if they need to. But we've never really allowed people to retake . . . from two years behind."

He lets his last sentence sink in.

"I know of a college in Kensington. It was set up for people in your situation, who have taken a year or two out . . ."

"I like it here," I say, a little wounded.

Making that H for Hayden. Like making that model with my mum. Why did I lose sight of what I love? How could I let that happen?

"Scarlett. Can I ask you a question? When your mum . . . passed. You spoke to Sadie, didn't you?"

"Yes."

"Is there anything she or we could have done better in supporting you?"

'Um . . . I dunno."

"If it wasn't working out with her we could have found someone else if we'd known . . . or recommended a CBT course . . . it's my job to make sure what we offer is effective . . . we spend a lot of money on our pastoral services, we want them to work."

I smile. It's a good skill, I decide, being the boss of hundreds of students and making them feel like you care for each one.

"To be honest . . . all the counsellors in the world wouldn't have helped, the place I was in."

I don't think he believes me. And he's right about starting again. If I redo my A Levels I'm going to be at least twenty before I graduate. That's pretty messed up. I haven't thought this through.

"Can you give me the details? Of this Kensington place?"

"Sure. January thirty-first is the deadline for applications, both here and everywhere else."

"Okay."

"Are you sure there's not more we can do? It's not too late to retake your final year here. If you got the grades, you could go to university when you're nineteen. You could keep on with Art as a hobby, and focus on it more after you leave."

"No. Thank you."

I feel sad that four months with a boy could carpet-bomb my life like this.

But deep down I know I'm doing the right thing.

I'm stepping through the gates when someone calls my name. It's Aya, looking stupid glamorous as usual in a glistening black puffa jacket with a silver fur lining.

"How are you?" she says.

What does she know about me? How much crap did Elliot tell her before they split up?

"Er . . . okay."

"Are you coming back to college?" she says.

"Um . . . yes and no."

She frowns. So I explain what I want to do.

"You want my number?" she says.

"Why?" I say a little aggressively.

"I'll be at uni in London! So . . . I'm around. Okay, maybe no."

She turns and walks away and I feel painfully guilty. She's lonely, I realise, as lonely as me. Asking me for my number was a big deal for her. How much time have I wasted hating her when I had no idea what she was really like? I think of what Elliot said about everyone starting to like each other.

"Aya!"

I run up to her.

"I can't pick up for you anymore. Right now, I'm not even sure I'll ever go raving again."

"I don't want to do that anyway. I want to focus on my studies."

I think Elliot was being harsh on her.

"I get it," she says, "You don't want to hang out because of Elliot."

"No. I'm being an idiot. Let's do coffee sometime."

"That would be nice."

She smiles, showing brilliant shining perfect white teeth. I'm still jealous but I want to hug her. It's weird.

"Give me your number," I say. She reels it off and I missed-call her.

"You're looking insanely hot today," I say.

She smiles from ear to ear. I'm glad I said it. She reaches up to my hood and pulls it down, taking me in.

"So are you."

I can't help smiling too.

Elliot and Bad Ben sit behind a table with piles of Bad Ben's comics laid out in front of them. Elliot reads one while Bad Ben sits back with his arms folded, anxiously watching him, his right leg jangling up and down. I perch on the edge of the table, soaking up the atmosphere. Table after table of comic book writers, all with their own books, some of them professionally published with glossy covers, some, like Bad Ben, with DIY-style photocopies. I clutch the schedule: talks and workshops and signing sessions. *How to pitch your work to editors. How to create a story that publishers will want to franchise.* This isn't like Comic Con, where we can all pretend to be sexy superheroes and meet our jaded idols. This is for the artists – the creators – the cutting-edge guys. The doors only opened twenty minutes ago and already the place is buzzing.

I slip off the table and wander through the hall. It's like I'm sailing across the ocean while the tectonic plates are shifting and whole new continents, complete with mountains and rivers and trees, emerge from the depths around me. Comics about beasts from other dimensions. Comics about losing your virginity. Comics about lizards who go to secondary schools. I feel like there's a lizard in my stomach, clawing and biting its way out. I want to be here, I realise, with *my* project, with *my* thing, I want people to queue up for *me*. The trouble is, I have no idea what that thing is.

"Love is the Answer."

A guy behind a table smiles. His thick glasses are partly obscured by an overhang of brown curls.

"That's a tattoo you'll never regret."

His wonky smile and lumberjack shirt gives him a geeky-sexy, alpha-male-nerd vibe.

"Oh, I regret it," I say. "Big time."

He raises an eyebrow.

"Kind of. Maybe I don't. The jury's out," I say. "Or maybe love isn't the answer I thought it was. But maybe it still is in a different kind of way."

"Deep," he says, nodding. "Card?"

He hands me a business card. The front of it is an anime-style cartoon of himself sitting at his desk with paper, pens and MacBook Pro.

"Maybe you can explain what you mean over a drink one day."

"I'm . . . not dating right now," I say.

His facade falters. He seems disappointed.

"Fair enough."

"But thanks anyway . . ."

I slip the card into my pocket and head back to Bad Ben's table.

"You've certainly developed the concept," says Elliot, putting down the comic.

"That's . . . all you can say?" says Bad Ben.

"Yeah." Elliot shrugs.

"Scarlett, can you have a look?"

I pick up the comic. On the cover is the same ultra-sexual cartoon girl that he showed us in the common room. She still has huge breasts and wears the same pink lace knickers that peek out above the waist of her jeans. But now she carries a pistol and she's firing it at two policemen in a coffee shop while the customers duck for cover.

"She's empowered, right?" says Bad Ben, looking at me.

I open the first page and notice her name.

"Woah! That's totally creepy!"

"At first I was thinking who's a famous female warrior from history? And I then realised you're a warrior and I'd rather name her after you."

"Thanks, but I'm so not a warrior. If there was a war, I would hide under my bed."

"You're tougher than me, tougher than Elliot, although that's not saying very much."

Elliot punches Bad Ben on the arm.

I flick through the pages. It seems this Scarlett character's family were killed by a bomb planted by the goons of the President of Russia, so she's gone under-cover so she can assassinate him.

"I am so not as tough as this."

"To me you are."

Bad Ben is like this weird mixture of completely intuitive and painfully naive. And he really, really loves me. And I see that now.

"I'm super-proud of you. I think it looks amazing and I hope you sell every single one of these copies. I'm gonna buy this off you, and the cartoon you did of me, and frame them on my wall."

I slide behind the desk, hug him from behind.

"You're turning him on," says Elliot.

"Come here, you bastards," I say. "Group hug."

With Bad Ben to my left and Elliot to my right, I put my arms round both their shoulders and squeeze them so tight they cry out in pain.

"You better promise me that you'll still be coming and visiting throughout your whole course. No moving up north!" I say.

"Never!" says Bad Ben.

"Never!" says Elliot. "But you can let go now."

I have no idea what the hell is going on between me and Elliot. Just the thought of being close to a boy makes me shudder. But that card is in my pocket and I know I'm not going to throw it away. It's like there's a thick fog around me and I can only see one metre to the left and one metre to the right and I can only be sure of the step I'm taking right at this moment.

And then, in the centre of my chest, I feel a gooey warmth, spreading outwards, filling my torso, flooding my limbs and tingling the tips of my fingers and toes. I'm in the right place, with the right people and I'm excited to find out.

Acknowledgements

To the sixteen or so people who listened to terrified me read the earliest draft of the very first chapter, when all I had was 1000 words – thank you – you know who you are. Thanks to Laura Hestley for continuing to be my first reader and writing buddy all these years later and for the feedback, criticism and encouragement. Thanks to Tom Harris, Joan Hoggan and Imogen Miller Porter for beta-reading, feedback, and support. Thanks to Malcolm Stern seeing my potential and helping me unlock it. Thanks to my agent Caroline Montgomery believing in the book and the excellent notes which took it to another level. Thanks to Linda and Charlie at QuoScript for their enthusiasm, care and imagination in bringing Love is the Answer to the world. And thanks to my partner, Tara Richards and my mum, who walk by my side with ever-present love and belief.